Romantic Lady

Fawcett Crest Books
by Sylvia Thorpe:

THE SWORD AND THE SHADOW
THE SCANDALOUS LADY ROBIN
BEGGAR ON HORSEBACK
THE GOLDEN PANTHER
ROGUES' COVENANT
SWORD OF VENGEANCE
CAPTAIN GALLANT
ROMANTIC LADY
THE RELUCTANT ADVENTURESS
FAIR SHINE THE DAY
SPRING WILL COME AGAIN
TARRINGTON CHASE
THE SCARLET DOMINO
THE SCAPEGRACE
THE SILVER NIGHTINGALE

Romantic Lady

Sylvia Thorpe

A FAWCETT CREST BOOK

Fawcett Publications, Inc., Greenwich, Connecticut

ROMANTIC LADY

THIS BOOK CONTAINS THE COMPLETE TEXT
OF THE ORIGINAL HARDCOVER EDITION.

A Fawcett Crest Book reprinted by arrangement with
Hurst and Blackett, Ltd.

Printed in the United States of America

Contents

1

"A Marriage Has Been Arranged—"

"THERE is no doubt about it," Miss Cresswell declared in a tone of strong resolution. "It will have to be Gretna Green!"

This recommendation appeared to find no favour with the two other occupants of the elegantly appointed drawing-room in Brook Street. The lady seated beside her on the sofa uttered a scandalized denial, and the young gentleman who had been staring moodily into the fire raised his head to say impatiently:

"Out of the question, my dear Caro! Setting aside the impropriety of such a course, we should have not the smallest hope of reaching the Border."

"Faint-heart!" Caroline retorted mockingly. "Is one of Wellington's officers to admit defeat without even striking a blow?"

Captain Wilde's only response to this was a frown, and

a return to his contemplation of the fire, but his sister leapt at once to his defense.

"That is as unkind, Caroline, as it is unjust! I am sure no one could deny that Roland has done everything in his power to win Lady Linley's consent to the marriage, and it is the outside of enough to be making jests at his expense when he is in such despondency."

"But despondency can accomplish nothing, Letty," her friend replied emphatically. "As for being unkind, surely we have all known each other too long and too well for either of you to suppose that I would ever deliberately do anything to hurt you. I was not jesting! Roland's only hope of marrying Jennifer Linley is to find some means of carrying her off and getting the knot safely tied before her mother, or anyone else, can prevent it."

Mrs. Fenton, a fashionably dressed young matron with a pleasant but somewhat insipid countenance, allowed herself to be mollified by these words, but gave it as her opinion that anything as reprehensible as an elopement should be put firmly out of her brother's head. The Captain shrugged this aside.

"As to that, if Jenny were willing and the thing could be arranged, the proprieties could go to the devil for all I care," he said recklessly. "There would be a deal of scandal, I know, but we could stay in Hertfordshire until the time comes for me to go back to Spain."

"That is another thing," Letitia said quickly. "It is all very well to talk glibly of taking Jenny with you when you rejoin your regiment, but it cannot be thought right to drag an innocent, gently bred young girl to a foreign land in the tail of an army. Every sensibility must be outraged by such a thing!"

"Nonsense!" Miss Cresswell retorted bracingly. "Any number of soldiers' wives follow the drum, and Jenny would not cavil at the discomfort as long as she could be with Roland. It has always been so, even when she was scarcely out of the nursery. The only thing that broke her spirit was that false report of his death, and now that she knows he is safe she is quite her old self again. You have not seen her recently, Letty. I have."

"Perhaps you are right," Mrs. Fenton conceded reluctantly. "It is true that as a child she knew no fear whatsoever as long as Roland was by. Everyone was used to remark upon the degree of affection between them."

"Oh, they were made for each other, no doubt about it," Caroline agreed emphatically, "and it is downright wicked of Lady Linley to force the poor child into marriage with another man merely to satisfy her own ambition. If I thought it would do the least good I would tell her so, too!"

Neither Captain Wilde nor his sister found the least difficulty in believing this, for lifelong acquaintance with Caroline Cresswell had taught them that her outspokenness was equalled only by her optimism in the face of misfortune. This latter quality they had seen tested to the uttermost. The only child of a happy-go-lucky, spendthrift gentleman who was prevented as much by his natural disinclination for work as by his ancient lineage from turning to trade for a living, Caroline had grown up in the shadow of debts and duns, her only respite from them being the five years during which her father, prevailed upon by Mrs. Wilde, to whom he was distantly related, had left her in that lady's care to acquire an education. Caroline was deeply attached to Mrs. Wilde and her family, but this had not prevented her, when she reached the age of seventeen, from leaving their home to keep house for the father whom she adored in spite of all his faults. For four years she struggled to make a home for them both, but when her graceless parent succumbed to a chill she found herself without resources of any kind.

She could have returned to Mrs. Wilde at Brightstone Park, but this would have savoured of accepting charity, and Caroline was independent to a fault, and instead made her home with her father's only brother, where she filled the post of unpaid governess to his numerous offspring. Henry Cresswell, as indolent as his brother but lacking his pride, had prudently provided for himself by marrying the daughter of a rich tradesman, preferring ostracism by the class into which he had been born to going without all those comforts which he regarded as necessary to his existence. He had been willing enough to offer his orphaned niece a home, but having done so paid her no further attention, and as his wife, who ruled the household with a rod of iron, disliked the girl and spared no opportunity of showing it, anyone of a less resilient temperament than Caroline would long since have found the situation intolerable.

Roland was the first to break the silence. He had apparently been considering the prospects of a flight to Scotland with his lady-love, and finding them discouraging.

"It would be quite impossible," he said gloomily at length. "Lady Linley watches Jenny so closely that she cannot even leave the house without being observed—her abigail told us that when she brought the letter this morning—and now there is this plan afoot to send her into the country."

"Perhaps," Caroline suggested hopefully, "Jenny may find it easier there to slip away then she would do in London."

Roland shook his head.

"She might slip away, Caro, but both she and I are too well known in that neighbourhood for our flight to pass unobserved. It is not the actual departure which worries me, for I dare say that could be contrived somehow, but the fact that we would inevitably be pursued. To be overtaken on the road would be disastrous."

"Disastrous indeed!" Caroline agreed promptly. "And there is not the least use in supposing that you would *not* be pursued, for even if Reginald were not at hand to go after his sister, there is Jenny's Uncle John, while if he could not go, I do not think it is beyond her ladyship to come posting after you herself."

Captain Wilde nodded morosely.

"That is the most daunting prospect of all. Reginald or his uncle I could face if need be, but not her ladyship."

"There is another possibility which you have both overlooked," Letitia put in. "Mr. Ravenshaw might learn of it, and take matters into his own hands."

"Perhaps," Caroline remarked thoughtfully, "for him to learn the truth would be the best thing that could happen.

No one could then blame him for crying off from the engagement, and no man, surely, would wish to marry a female whose affections are so irrevocably fixed upon some-one else.'"

"Guy Ravenshaw might," Letty replied pessimistically, "from sheer arrogance, if nothing else. It is well known that he cannot bear to be crossed in any way."

Miss Cresswell frowned.

"What a disagreeable creature he must be," she said reflectively, "but I dare say you are right, Letty. For him to have reached the age of—six-and-thirty, is it not?—without ever showing the least inclination towards marriage, and then to offer for a girl who has only been out for a matter of weeks, argues a very strong degree of attraction indeed. Especially since, from all accounts, he could take his choice of any marriageable girl in England."

"Well, I am sure it is no wonder if he has fallen in love with Jenny, pretty and good-natured as she is," Mrs. Fenton agreed, "but I cannot think he is capable of making her, or indeed any woman, happy. An impatient, harsh-natured man, and quite tyrannical, I believe, in his disposition. One has only to consider how he has treated that poor young cousin of his, bullying and threatening him, and behaving in the most unhandsome way. To be sure, Pelham Ravenshaw is a trifle wild, but he has such engaging manners that one cannot but like him."

"It grows increasingly clear," Caroline said severely, "that we cannot allow Jenny to be sacrificed to such a monster. It is equally clear, however, that her elopement with Roland must be kept from him at all costs, for he would certainly set out in pursuit. I dare say he is a first-rate swordsman and a crack shot."

"Lord, Caro! I'm not afraid of Ravenshaw," Roland told her indignantly.

"No, my dear, I am sure you are not, but if you think it will help Jenny at all to be getting yourself involved in a duel, and very likely killed, you are quite mistaken. Oh, confound the man! Why could he not have offered for one of the silly females who have been setting their caps at him all these years?"

This question being unanswerable by anyone save Mr. Ravenshaw himself, another heavy silence settled over the room. The situation was fraught with difficulties, and not even Miss Cresswell's quick wits and fertile imagination could discover a solution to them.

The Linleys and the Wildes were neighbours; their estates in Hertfordshire adjoined each other, and for many years a close bond of friendship had been maintained between the two families, though this was now in danger of suffering a serious rupture. The cause of it all was the report which had reached Mr. and Mrs. Wilde, some months earlier, that their only son had been killed in action against Bonaparte's armies in Spain, and severe as this blow was to the Captain's stricken parents, it fell with even more shattering effect upon Jennifer Linley. From her earliest childhood there had existed between her and Roland, despite the six years difference in their ages, an extraordinarily deep affection which had strengthened with the passing of time, until it was taken for granted by both families that as soon as Jenny was old enough a marriage would be arranged between them. Lady Linley, a formidable widow, was satisfied, for Roland was heir to a snug fortune as well as whatever wealth and honours he might acquire in the course of a promising military career, while Mr. and Mrs. Wilde could think of no one whom they would rather welcome as their son's wife.

The tragic news from Spain put an end to these comfortable plans. Overnight, it seemed, Jennifer changed from a merry, high-spirited girl into a quiet young woman who regarded the whole world with an air of gentle aloofness, and seemed in danger of slipping out of it altogether from sheer indifference. Her mother, with the laudable intention of diverting her mind, immediately began making plans for her début, and as soon as the London season began, carried her unprotesting daughter off to town and plunged her into a whirl of balls, parties and similar entertainments. Lady Linley had very little hope of her engaging the interest of any eligible gentleman until her grief for Roland Wilde had abated somewhat, and so was all the more surprised to receive, within a few weeks of Jennifer's first appearance in the Polite World, an offer for her hand which was not merely satisfactory but dazzling.

Mr. Guy Ravenshaw had been a bachelor for so long that even the most persistent of matchmaking Mamas had regretfully abandoned hope of him, and her ladyship could scarcely believe her ears when he made formal application to pay his addresses to Miss Linley. Recovering from the shock with commendable promptness, she gave him to understand that he had not only her approval but her blessing, and that Miss Linley would be most happy to accept his very flattering proposal. She felt almost overwhelmed by her own good fortune, for though she had married off two elder daughters with success, this was by far her greatest triumph. Guy Ravenshaw was a man of immense wealth and irreproachable birth, while the fact that he had hitherto regarded all the blandishments of the fair sex with an indifferent but comprehending eye gave an added piquancy to the achievement. That he was generally held to be a hard man—even heartless—was a trifle which her ladyship could not be expected to consider in the face of the worldly advantages he offered her daughter.

She half expected some protest from Jennifer and was prepared to overcome it, but the girl received the news of Mr. Ravenshaw's offer with the unnatural docility which had marked her every action since the news of Roland's death. On this occasion Lady Linley gave thanks for it, published an announcement of the betrothal, and began to talk of bride-clothes.

Such was the situation when Captain Wilde himself arrived in England to refute those reports of his untimely death. He had indeed been wounded, almost mortally, and owed his life to a family of Spanish peasants who had hidden him from the French, tended his hurts, and finally, when he had sufficiently recovered his strength, led him back in disguise to the safety of the British lines. Since he owed his recovery more to his own excellent constitution than to the skill of his nurses, and was still very far from well, he had been sent home on sick-leave and so returned unheralded to England, forestalling by several days the news of his miraculous escape.

Upon Jennifer the effect of his return was as startling as that of his supposed death, for it was as though she, too, had been suddenly restored to life. Roland had travelled direct from the coast to Hertfordshire, but as soon as the news of his survival reached his sister in London she set off immediately to see him, pausing on her way out of town to tell the Linleys the glad tidings. Lady Linley was out when she called, but Jennifer, as soon as she had assimilated this astounding news, delayed only long enough for her maid to pack a few necessities before joining Letitia on her journey, never doubting that this would mean the end of her engagement to Mr. Ravenshaw and reunion with her true love.

Her mother soon put an end to these happy dreams. Though genuinely glad at Roland's return, Lady Linley had no intention of permitting it to interfere with her own plans. It was not, she pointed out, as though there had ever been a formal betrothal between him and her daughter; in fact, Roland had never even sought her permission to address Jennifer. Since Jenny had been only fifteen at the time of the Captain's last visit to England this was felt by everyone to be grossly unfair, but her ladyship was as impervious to criticism as to persuasion. Jenny was betrothed to Guy Ravenshaw, and Guy Ravenshaw she should marry. Anything else was out of the question.

From this determination nothing could shake her, although everyone who might be thought to have the least influence with her was pressed into service by the distracted young couple. At Roland's urgent request, Sir Reginald Linley tore himself away from the pleasures of the bottle and the gaming-table long enough to plead his sister's cause, but without effect. Mr. John Linley, who as her late husband's only surviving brother might be thought to wield some influence with her ladyship, met with a like fate.

The only person closely concerned who remained unaware of the turmoil was Mr. Ravenshaw himself, who for the past month had been residing at his ancestral home in Sussex, making certain, no doubt, that it was in readiness to receive his bride. He was expected, however, to return to town within the next few days, a fact which had prompted Lady Linley's plan to whisk her intransigent daughter off to Hertfordshire before his arrival in the hope of keeping him in ignorance of her rebellion. Jennifer, by this time a virtual prisoner in her own home, had enlisted the aid of her devoted abigail to carry to Mrs. Fenton's house, where Roland was at present staying, a letter informing him of this intention, assuring him of her undying devotion, and begging him to find some way of rescuing her. The date set for the wedding, she reminded him, was drawing near; already the cards of invitation had been sent out.

Caroline Cresswell had arrived in Brook Street soon after the letter. She was fully acquainted with the situation, and had even acted as go-between for the lovers on one or two occasions, braving Lady Linley's unconcealed hostility in order to visit her friend. Her ladyship would have liked very much to put a stop to these visits, for it did not suit her sense of importance to receive a young woman in Caroline's unfortunate circumstances. It would not be so bad, she confided to her sister-in-law, if the girl were residing in some genteel household, but the vulgarity of her present background could well be imagined. However, since Caroline, as well as being the childhood playmate of her own children, was still upon terms of intimacy with the Wilde family, there was nothing that she could do about it, particularly as Miss Cresswell had never sought to introduce any of her appalling relatives to her old friends. Lady Linley certainly suspected Caroline of carrying messages from Roland to Jenny, but lacking proof of this, was powerless to prevent it.

"I wonder," Caroline said suddenly now, "whether you could enlist Reginald's aid in this. If you eloped with Jenny, Lady Linley would certainly command him to go after you, and if he agreed, with no intention of overtaking you, surely that would serve to prevent any other pursuit."

Mrs. Fenton looked admiringly at her, and even Roland seemed impressed by the suggestion, but after considering it carefully, shook his head.

"It's a good notion, Caro, and might serve, but for one thing. It would be the devil's own work to persuade Reginald to set out on such a journey in earnest, and if he knew beforehand that it was to be a wild goose chase, he would never consent to go."

"He need not follow you all the way to Scotland," Caroline pointed out. "He could put up at a comfortable inn for a few days, just far enough out of London to lend colour to his story."

Captain Wilde grinned ruefully. "Can you imagine Reginald amusing himself at a country inn for days at a stretch? He would be so bored after the first evening that he would come straight back to town next day."

"That is very true," Letitia agreed sadly. "I do not dislike Reginald, but there is no denying that he is the most selfish creature alive. Besides, after that talk he had with his mother he said that nothing on earth would induce him to meddle in the affair again."

"There's another thing, too," Roland added. "He's devilish indiscreet. Dashed if I ever knew such a loose-tongued fellow in my life, and the more he drinks, the more he talks. As like as not he would be telling the whole tale all over town as a very good joke."

"What is more," Letty concluded, with an air of clinching the matter beyond all doubt, "I have just recollected that he and Pelham Ravenshaw are close friends. I think Roland will be well advised to keep any plans he may make secret from Reginald."

"Then," Caroline said regretfully, "I can think of no other scheme. Jenny will just have to remain firm in her refusal to marry Mr. Ravenshaw."

"But that will not solve the problem," Roland reminded her. "Sooner or later I shall have to rejoin my regiment, and then Heaven knows when I shall be in England again. I cannot expect Jenny to hold out against her mother indefinitely."

Since this was undeniably true, neither lady could think of any reply to make, and before any of them could speak again, Letty's husband came into the room. He appeared to be the bearer of unusual tidings, and as soon as he had greeted Miss Cresswell he said gravely:

"Now here's a shocking thing! I met young Linley at White's, and he tells me that his uncle's house was broken into during the night, and a quantity of valuables stolen."

"What, John Linley, the Nabob?" Roland exclaimed. "Then I'll wager the thieves made a very pretty haul. That house was crammed with Eastern treasures."

"Their booty was less than it might have been," Mark Fenton told him, "for one of the servants, hearing suspicious sounds, went to investigate and so disturbed the robbers. He gave the alarm, but in order to make their escape, the scoundrels set upon the poor fellow and killed him."

Captain Wilde gave a low whistle. "Murder, too!" he commented. "That's bad, Mark, devilish bad!"

"Bad indeed, Roland, when robbery and murder can take place upon our very doorstep, as it were. However, Sir Reginald tells me his uncle does not despair of the criminals being brought to book, as many of the articles stolen are of an unusual nature. He mentioned particularly an especially fine ruby which Mr. Linley brought back from India, and which he has just had set in to a pendant made to a design executed especially for him. It came home from the jeweller only a few days ago, and was intended as a wedding-gift for Miss Linley."

Miss Cresswell, who had listened intently to this interchange, rose to her feet.

"I think," she remarked, "that I will just step round to Mount Street and call upon Jenny, for it seems to me, Roland, that a family upset of this nature may afford you just the opportunity you have been looking for."

"Caroline, how can you be so unfeeling?" Letty protested. "I declare I shall not sleep soundly for many a night to come after this dreadful occurrence, yet you talk calmly of a family upset, as though it were no more than the merest trifle."

"Well, it is all very shocking, to be sure," Caroline replied, pulling on her gloves with a determined air, "but one should never allow oneself, Letty, to be blinded by sentiment. You may depend upon it that poor Mrs. Linley is in the gravest agitation, and she is certain to turn for reassurance and support to Lady Linley. Therefore her ladyship will have less time to attend to Jenny, and we may contrive something between us. Believe me, it is the only chance we shall have!"

2

The Bride

WHEN Caroline arrived at Lady Linley's house in Mount Street, she found that matters were very much as she had supposed. The butler informed her that her ladyship was not at home, and that Miss Linley would no doubt be delighted to see Miss Cresswell. Then, taking advantage of many years' acquaintance with this visitor, he ventured to inquire whether she had heard of the recent shocking events at Mr. John Linley's house.

"Yes, I learned of it at Mrs. Fenton's, not ten minutes since," Caroline replied briskly. "It has thrown the whole family into the greatest disorder, I have no doubt. Now tell me where I may find Miss Jennifer, for I will not put you to the trouble of announcing me."

This, however, the butler would not permit, and preceded her in a very stately way up one pair of stairs to a small sitting-room at the back of the house, where Miss Linley was discovered listlessly turning the pages of The Lady's Monthly Museum. She cast the journal aside when Miss Cresswell was announced, and jumped up with outstretched hands to greet her.

"Caro!" she exclaimed delightedly. "Oh, how happy I am to see you! I have been moped to death sitting here by myself, for Mama would not let me go with her to my uncle's house, and told me not to receive anyone while she was out, as in all likelihood they would have come merely to pry into this dreadful affair. But perhaps you have not yet heard what happened last night?"

"Indeed I have," Caroline replied cheerfully, "for Mr. Fenton came in with the news while I was sitting with Letty just now, and you see me positively agog with curiosity. So you perceive that your Mama was quite right."

Jennifer laughed, and led her friend towards the sofa, but when they were seated she said seriously:

"There is very little that I can tell you. Early this morning my uncle sent us word of what had happened, and begged Mama to go at once to Aunt Louisa, who was utterly prostrated by the shock. She went, of course, and that was when I sent the letter to Roland, for I had been waiting since yesterday afternoon for an opportunity to do so. The servants did not then know what had happened at my uncle's house, but I suppose it must be all over the town by now. When Mama returned she said that Dr. Matthews was of the opinion that as soon as my aunt had composed herself a little it would be advisable for her to come here for a time. Mama has gone back to fetch her now."

"I see!" Caroline said thoughtfully. "In that event, you will not be going into the country."

Jennifer shook her head ruefully.

"That is what I thought, but I was wrong. Mama, of course, must remain with Aunt Louisa, but I am to be sent out of London none the less. Miss Fawley is at Westbridge, you see, with the children, and Mama has told her to expect us the day after tomorrow." She jumped to her feet as though she could not endure sitting still, and added rebelliously. "I tell you, Caro, it is beyond all bearing! If I am old enough to be married, then I am too old to be treated like a schoolgirl, and put into the charge of my governess again!"

Miss Cresswell regarded her affectionately, but with a trace of amusement. Jennifer was eighteen, a charming brunette with a winsome, heart-shaped face, soft dark eyes and a general air of fragility which was wholly deceptive. Though Caroline would have been the first to admit that Jenny undoubtedly knew her own mind and heart, the fact that she was grown up was easily forgotten by one who was eight years her senior, and had known her since babyhood.

"So Miss Fawley is cast for the part of gaoler," she remarked. "Well, my dear, I fear you will have small hope of evading her vigilance, for she will watch you even more closely than your Mama has done."

"I know, and there is not the least hope of winning her over, for she has not the smallest trace of romance in her nature, and can think only of what a splendid match Mr. Ravenshaw will be."

"Governesses, my dear Jenny, can rarely afford the luxury of romantic fancies!" There was a trace of bitterness in Caroline's voice. "Do not blame Miss Fawley for thinking first of worldly considerations. I daresay she has had to do so all her life."

"Oh, Caro dear, forgive me!" Jenny's voice was contrite. "I did not mean—! But *you* enter fully into my feelings in this matter, so why cannot she?"

"Possibly because her present livelihood depends upon not displeasing your Mama," Caroline said drily, "or perhaps because she is a good deal older than I. In any case, I have an incurably romantic disposition, as you very well know. However, that is by the way! We are agreed that it is impossible to draw Miss Fawley into the affair, so we must think of something else. You would not, I take it, be averse to an elopement?"

"I would not be averse to anything which meant that I could marry Roland," Jenny said despairingly, "but how can we possibly contrive it? Mama means to keep me at Westbridge until a few days before the wedding, for she thinks that if matters have gone that far I shall be obliged to marry Mr. Ravenshaw. Well, I will not! I do not care how great a scandal is created, and Roland may carry me off from the church door if he chooses!"

Miss Cresswell chuckled. "It is an enchanting idea, Jenny, but scarcely practical," she replied. "No, we must try to find some way of making use of this change of plan. If you are to make the journey to Westbridge alone. . . ."

"I had thought of that," Jennifer broke in, "but even if Roland met me somewhere on the road and we set off at once for Scotland, someone would be bound to come after us. The servants would soon set Mama on our track."

"It is all a question of time," Caroline pursued thoughtfully. "If only there were some way of preventing the news of your flight from reaching Lady Linley, all would be well." Jennifer started to speak, but was checked by a dramatically uplifted hand. "Wait, Jenny! I believe I have the glimmering of an idea! I wonder?" She broke off, and sat for a moment or two lost in thought, while Miss Linley, no stranger to Caroline's ingenuity, waited with breathless anticipation. At last the elder girl chuckled again, and looked up at her friend with wickedly dancing eyes.

"I believe I have it!" she announced triumphantly. "Jenny, can you trust that abigail of yours?"

"Oh, yes!" Jennifer assured her earnestly. "She would do anything to help Roland and me. Her father is a tenant of Mr. Wilde's, you know, and Agnes is devoted to both of us. Her one fear is that if I marry Mr. Ravenshaw, she will be turned off in favour of someone more fashionable."

"Then listen to me!" Caroline reached out to clasp Jennifer's hand and draw her down beside her on the sofa; her voice was lowered to a conspiratorial whisper. "Somewhere between London and Westbridge, you must make a halt at an inn. At much the same time Roland, too, will arrive there, escorting a lady who is heavily veiled."

Jennifer leaned forward eagerly, her eyes sparkling. "You, Caro?" she asked breathlessly.

"Myself," Caroline agreed solemnly, "but when he leaves the inn, Jenny, the veiled lady will be you, while I, making some excuse to hide my face, take your place in the chaise bound for Westbridge. It is fortunate that we are much of the same height."

"Yes, Caro, but I do not see that we shall gain very much time by such a trick, for it will be discovered as soon as you reach Westbridge."

"I do not think so. I shall alight from the chaise weeping bitterly into my handkerchief, refuse to speak to anyone, and retire at once to my bedchamber in a fit of the sullens. Miss Fawley will not consider that remarkable, since she knows the reason for your visit, and if I pretend to sleep late the next morning I should be able to fob her off until noon at least. Even then word will have to be sent to London before any pursuit can begin, and so you and Roland should be more than twenty-four hours ahead of it. In fact, it will probably be considered useless to go after you at all."

Jennifer clasped her hands beneath her chin and regarded Miss Cresswell with shining eyes.

"It is a wonderful idea!" she said reverently. "When you do disclose your identity, Caro, you must be sure that everyone knows where I have gone, and with whom. Then there will be no chance of keeping it secret and Mama will have to countenance my marriage to Roland, because otherwise I should be completely ruined and neither Mr. Ravenshaw nor anyone else would wish to marry me."

"Jenny, you are incorrigible," Caroline told her with a laugh, "but what you say is very true. You may depend upon me to shatter your reputation completely."

Miss Linley groped suddenly for her handkerchief and dabbed her eyes with it, saying in a stifled voice: "What a silly goose I am to be crying at such a time! Oh, Caro, how good you are! I shall never be able to thank you enough."

Caroline took her hand between her own and pressed it hard, but merely said in a rallying tone: "If you want to show your gratitude, take care not to come to our rendezvous dressed in pink or red. I love you dearly, Jenny, but not even for your sake will I wear those colours."

Jennifer gasped, gave a little laugh that choked on a

sob, and promised to do no such thing. This stipulation on
the score of colour was easily understood, for Miss Cresswell's hair was an unfashionable shade of red; not auburn
or Titian, but just plain red, and not even its glossy thick-
ness, or its deep natural curl, could be held to outweigh
this defect. In fact, Miss Cresswell was no beauty. Her
face was too thin and her chin too pointed, and when she
smiled, which was often, her mouth was seen to be a trifle
crooked. She was certainly blessed with that dazzling complexion sometimes seen with red hair, but though her eyes
were large and of a limpid grey-green, the darkness of
brows and lashes owed more to artifice than to nature,
while the fact that she was long-legged and as slim as a
willow-wand made her appear taller than she actually was.
Her taste in dress was excellent, and had she possessed the
means to indulge it would have rendered her extremely
stylish, but she was not seen to advantage in clothes which
more often than not were made over from the cast-offs of
her aunt and cousin. At rare intervals she would accept
the gift of a simple gown or pelisse from Mrs. Wilde, but
this, as she assured her benefactress, was merely in order
that she might continue to visit the fashionable friends
without giving them cause to be ashamed of her.

"And while we are speaking of clothes," she continued
now, "you must remember to wear something which will
enable me to hide my hair. A cloak with a hood would
serve admirably, if you have such a thing."

"Yes, I have, though I have not worn it since I came to
town," Jenny assured her, adding, with a mischievous
glance: "It is dark blue, so it should become you very
well. Where do you think we ought to meet?"

"Where do you usually change horses when you travel
to and from Westbridge?"

"In Barnet, always. At the Red Lion."

Caroline shook her head. "That will not do. You will be
known there, and so, perhaps, may Roland. We must run
no unnecessary risks." She paused, considering, and added
after a little: "There is a small inn a mile or so this side of
Finchley Common. I stopped there once with Papa, and

though it is not a posting-house, it is clean and respectable. I think it is called the Cap and Bells."

"I remember it!" Jennifer agreed eagerly. "I have been past it several times, and noticed it particularly because of its odd name. I will pretend to feel unwell just before we reach it, and that will provide an excuse to stop there."

"Excellent!" Caroline said with satisfaction. "Now let us have Agnes in, and take her into our confidence."

Agnes pledged her aid willingly enough. Only one thing appeared to trouble her, and when, the scheme having been explained, Caroline inquired if she could perceive any defect in it, she said slowly:

"Well, miss, I cannot but wonder what will become of us when Miss Fawley finds out the trick we've played on her. Like as not she'll turn us out of the house, and even if she don't, I'd as lief not stay to face her ladyship."

Neither of the young ladies had thought of this, but after a moment's consideration Caroline said firmly: "Simple enough! I will take refuge with Mrs. Wilde at Brightstone Park, and you, Agnes, may come with me, or go to your father's house, just as you choose. Brightstone is only a few miles from Westbridge, so it will be no great hardship even if we have to go on foot."

Reassured on this point, the handmaiden repeated her assurances of unswerving loyalty and then withdrew, leaving Jennifer and Caroline to discuss their plans down to the smallest detail, since it would not be advisable for Caroline to come to Mount Street again for fear of arousing Lady Linley's suspicions. Miss Cresswell then bade her friend goodbye, and walked briskly back to Mrs. Fenton's house to inform Captain Wilde of the arrangements made on his behalf.

She found Roland and his sister anxiously awaiting her. They received with astonishment and some dismay her calm exposition of the scheme to outwit Lady Linley, but though the Captain was persuaded without much difficulty to fall in with it, Letitia was less easily convinced.

"I agree that if Caroline can maintain the deception long enough, your difficulties, Roland, will be over," she said uneasily, "but what of hers? When the story leaks out, as it is bound to do, it will do her no good at all."

"You forget, Letty, that I do not move in fashionable circles," Caroline reminded her. "And it does not matter in the least what the Polite World thinks of me."

"Your aunt may not agree with you," Mrs. Fenton pointed out. "I warn you, Caro, that if you indulge in this escapade your situation in her house may become intolerable."

Caroline shrugged. "In that event I should be obliged to seek a refuge elsewhere. Believe me, I am not entirely without resources."

"Indeed you are not," Roland agreed warmly. "You know, for my mother has assured you of it a score of times, that there is a home awaiting you at Brightstone whenever you choose to go there."

Caroline smiled, but shook her head. "As companion to your Mama, Roland, who has no need of one as long as her sister resides with her. I am deeply obliged to Cousin Esther, but I cannot accept her charity. In my present situation I at least have the satisfaction of knowing that such small services as I am able to perform are really necessary. My aunt would be obliged to employ a governess if I were not there."

"And a companion and a lady's maid, for I am sure you are expected to do the work of all three," Letty said indignantly. "Oh, Caro, I do wish you would do as my mother desires!" Miss Cresswell shook her head, and Letitia added accusingly: "Very well, then, tell me this! How do you propose to account to your aunt for an absence of several days?"

"Yes, I shall have to make some sort of excuse to Aunt Lizzie," Caroline agreed. "I was thinking about that as I came from Mount Street, and I am sorry to have to tell you, Letty, that both your Mama and your Aunt Amelia have become indisposed, and your Papa has sent to beg you to come home for a short visit. Unfortunately you are out of town, and Roland, being quite at his wits' end, has begged me to go in your place. He will naturally escort me to Brightstone, and that will account for my setting out in his company."

"But I am not out of town," Letitia protested dazedly.

"No, but Aunt Lizzie will not know that," Caroline pointed out. "Now you are not to be vexing yourself over that, Letty! You will have other things to think about, for I shall be obliged to leave the procuring of a suitable disguise in your hands. It will be as well, I think, if I pass myself off as a very old lady. Yes, that is the very thing! I will be your grandmama, Roland, so see to it that you accord me a proper respect."

For a little while they discussed the details of the costume which Mrs. Fenton was to obtain, a discussion treated with levity by Miss Cresswell and Captain Wilde, and with some misgiving by Letitia. When Caroline at length rose to go, she said anxiously:

"Will you at least promise us one thing? If, as I fear, this escapade puts you quite out of favour with your aunt, will you accept Mama's offer, and go to live at Brightstone?"

Caroline shook her head. "No, Letty, I will not promise that, but you must not worry about me. I have said nothing of this before, for I have not yet entirely made up my mind to it, but I may shortly be leaving my uncle's house and setting up my own establishment." She hesitated, and then added with a hint of defiance: "Mr. Horace Firkin is obliging enough to wish to marry me."

Brother and sister stared at her; Roland said blankly: "Who the deuce is Horace Firkin?"

"A very worthy man, an old friend of my aunt." Caroline was smoothing her gloves over her hands, her gaze upon them rather than upon her companions. "To be sure, he is past sixty and sadly troubled by rheumatism, but he is in a very prosperous way of business as a corn-chandler, so I should be quite comfortably set up in the world."

Letitia gave a gasp of relief. "Oh, you are jesting!" she exclaimed. "It is too bad of you, Caro! For one moment I almost believed that you were in earnest."

"I am, Letty! Make no doubt about that." Caroline

looked up sharply, her eyes flashing. "Mr. Firkin's offer may seem ludicrous to you, but to me it is my one chance of independence. *You* cannot conceive what it means to be a poor relation, wholly dependent upon the whims and tantrums of one's more prosperous connections, and to live, moreover, in a house where one's very presence is a source of jealously and resentment."

"But, Caro, think!" Letty wailed. "A tradesman, and old enough to be your grandfather!"

"Hush, Letty!" Roland spoke rather sternly, and moved to set a brotherly arm about Miss Cresswell's shoulders, adding in a softened tone: "We know what you mean, Caro, and it is not to be wondered at that you long to escape it, but that way will not serve, my dear. Nothing would please your friends more than to see you comfortably established, but you could do better than this."

"Could I?" Caroline's voice was hard, and she stood rigid within the circle of his arm. "Whom do you suggest, Roland? One of your brother-officers? Some eligible bachelor selected by Letty? I do not possess the attributes necessary to make such a match. It is true that I am well-born and that, thanks to your Mama, my education has been more than adequate, but I have not a penny to my name, and you know as well as I do that a dowerless female has to be blessed with an extraordinary degree of attraction to contract a respectable alliance. I am very nearly twenty-seven years old, and even in the first flush of youth had not the least pretension to beauty." She paused, but Captain Wilde, brought up short by the undeniable truth of her words, could find nothing to say. After a moment Caroline's tense attitude relaxed, and she reached up to pat his hand, saying more lightly: "But it is your marriage which concerns us at this present, and not mine. I may accept Mr. Firkin, or I may not, but upon one thing I am determined. Nothing is going to prevent your marriage to Jenny."

The rallying tone of these last remarks showed that she was not prepared to discuss her personal problems any further, and both Roland and his sister knew her too well to attempt it. Farewells were said, and Captain Wilde escorted Miss Cresswell downstairs and saw her set off in a hackney coach for her uncle's house in the City. Then, returning to the drawing-room where Letitia sat gazing pensively into the fire, he said with strong feeling:

"It's a damned shame about poor Caro, for I am sure a better-natured girl never lived. Cannot you do anything for her, Letty? We cannot let her make this preposterous marriage."

"I would do anything for her, Roland. You know that," Letitia replied with a sigh, "but what she said is true, you know. *We* are aware of her worth, and her many amiable qualities, but it is a sad fact that a penniless female has very little hope of establishing herself creditably. The only way I can think of to help her is to persuade her to come here. Theodore is old enough for a governess, and Nurse would be glad, I dare say, to be relieved of the charge."

Captain Wilde frowned. "Would Caro come to you, do you think?"

"She might be persuaded, since she would realize that I really need someone to take charge of Theodore, and am not merely inventing a post for her, as Mama has tried to do. You know, Roland, if she did come it could be a permanent arrangement, for when the children have grown up, *I* shall be glad of a companion."

"It might serve," Roland agreed doubtfully, "though she would still be a dependent."

"You cannot suppose that I would ever treat her as anything but a friend," Letitia said earnestly, "and I assure you that in my house she would receive every consideration. Surely it would be a thousand times better to be a dependent in the kind of household in which she was brought up, than the mistress of some shop-keeper's establishment?"

"I suppose so," her brother said slowly, but there was still doubt in his voice. "The thing is, Caro has some devilish odd notions, and may not see matters in quite the same way as you or I. But ask her, by all means! It is the least that we can do."

3

The Bridegroom

ON the morning which saw the birth of Miss Cresswell's ingenious plan for the elopement of Jennifer Linley with Captain Wilde, Miss Linley's betrothed might have been discovered in the library of his Sussex home. The estate of Fairings had been in the possession of the Ravenshaw family for many generations, but the present owner's grandfather, infected by the spirit of his day, had caused the old house to be pulled down, and had erected in its stead a mansion in the Palladian style, with an immense pillared portico, and flanking pavilions connected to the main building by colonnades. Since cost had been of trifling importance, the foremost architect of the day had been employed upon the enterprise, and the room in which Mr. Ravenshaw now sat was rich in that beauty and elegance for which the name of Adam was renowned. The tall windows looked out upon formal gardens and beyond them to parkland and woodland rich in game, the vista being bounded in the distance by the noble outline of the downs.

The master of this handsome house and these broad acres was seated at the inlaid writing desk between two of the windows, but his chair was turned from it and he sat with one arm resting along its back, while the fingers of the other hand beat an impatient tattoo on the polished surface of the desk. The unfavourable estimate of his character expressed by Letitia Fenton was that commonly held by the wide circle of his acquaintance, though the few who could account themselves his intimates did not share it. His friendship, once given, was given unreservedly, but to the world at large he presented an unyielding front. Mr. Ravenshaw was a man of iron will, and a disregard for the opinions of others which amounted to arrogance.

Had his detractors been able to see him on that cold, blustery morning in early April, they would have perceived no reason to alter their judgment of his nature. Guy Ravenshaw was not a handsome man, though there was a certain compelling quality in his dark-complexioned face with its harsh, rather irregular features, and cool grey eyes beneath heavily marked black brows. At times, when laughter glinted in those eyes and softened the sternness of his mouth, the whole character of the man was presented in a very different light, but this was an expression which few were privileged to see and which at that moment was certainly not in evidence. His lips were grimly compressed, and his brows contracted. He looked, as indeed he was, a man at the end of his patience.

The cause of his exasperation was seated opposite to him in the elegant person of his cousin, Pelham Ravenshaw. Pelham was in every way a contrast to his kinsman, being a slight, fair young man with a clear-cut, boyish face upon whose good looks a life of startling dissipation had as yet left no visible mark, and an engaging air of candour which had been known to deceive even the most worldly-wise. He had discovered the value of these two assets before he reached his teens, and had been trading upon them more or less successfully ever since. His cousin, however, had long since ceased to be taken in by them, and Pelham, knowing this, was taking no pains to be pleasant. There was a sulky look about his mouth, and resentment in his brown eyes as he stared at his relative. The elder Mr. Ravenshaw met that sullen regard with a look of cold dislike.

"It would appear," he said sarcastically, "that you have forgotten my parting words to you on the occasion of our last meeting." The younger man made no response beyond shifting ill-humouredly in his chair, and Ravenshaw went on: "I warned you then that I had assisted you for the last time, and that when next you found yourself in difficulties you must extricate yourself from them without my help. You know that I do not threaten idly."

"And you know damned well that unless you do help me, I shall find myself in a debtor's prison," Pelham retorted sullenly, adding as an afterthought: "Unless I blow my brains out first."

"Both possibilities," said Guy deliberately, "leave me unmoved. Either one of them would relieve me of a burden which has become increasingly irksome with the years."

Pelham sneered. "What of the precious Ravenshaw honour?" he demanded. "A fine scandal there would be if you left your heir to rot in prison because you are too damned close-fisted to pay his debts."

Guy's hands went to the arms of his chair as though he would have risen, and such a flame of anger leapt into the grey eyes that even Pelham's insolence was momentarily tempered by alarm. Then slowly the elder man relaxed, and when he spoke again his voice was as deliberate as before.

"Do not place too much dependence upon family loyalty, Pelham," he said. "There are times when the cost of it is too high. For ten thankless years I have been helping you out of difficulties and crushing scandals of your making, and I am heartily tired of the whole sordid business. As far as I am concerned, your race is run."

He rose to his feet and walked across to the fire-place and there turned, a commanding figure, to face his cousin again. The prevailing fashion for close-fitting, long-tailed coats, skin-tight pantaloons and glossy Hessian boots was one which many men found difficult to wear, but it suited Guy Ravenshaw to admiration. He was tall above the average and very powerfully built, a true Corinthian in his dress as well as in his proficiency at all sporting pastimes, and much of Pelham's dislike of his kinsman had its root in jealousy. Guy was, in so many ways, exactly what Pelham himself would have liked to be.

"Folly and youthful wildness I could forgive," Mr. Ravenshaw continued after a few moments, "but that is less than half the tale. You are vicious through and through, a liar, a thief and a cheat, with not one redeeming feature and no thought whatsoever beyond the gratification of your own selfish desires. You have so far succeeded in imposing a very different picture of yourself upon the world, but you cannot impose it upon me."

Beneath the goad of that scathing denunciation, and the contemptuous tone in which it was uttered, Pelham, too, came to his feet. A dark flush of mortification stained his cheeks, for he had as little liking for unpleasant truths as any man, but before the scornful regard of those cold grey eyes, the indignant words he had been about to utter died on his lips. No matter who else he might be able to deceive, the immediate members of his family were not among them.

"Quite right!" Guy said sardonically, as though reading his thoughts. "Heroics would be wasted upon me. Reserve your histrionic abilities for your creditors, who may perhaps be deceived by them."

"Small chance of that!" Pelham retorted sulkily. "Confound it all, Guy, you cannot refuse to help me, when it is your fault that I find myself in this infernal position!"

"My fault?" Blank astonishment drove all other expression from Mr. Ravenshaw's face. "Good God! Am I responsible for your spendthrift ways?"

"You are responsible for setting this pack of duns at my heels," Pelham retorted hotly. "Until this damned betrothal of yours was announced, my credit was sound enough."

There was a brief silence, broken only by the cheerful

crackle of the fire, and the twittering of birds in the gardens outside. The two men faced each other across the room, Pelham flushed and angry, one hand gripped hard on the back of the chair from which he had risen, his cousin seemingly unmoved, but with that in his face which belied the relaxed stillness of his powerful body.

"So that is what rankles!" Guy said quietly at last. "I should have guessed it! My brother's death made you my heir, but your talent for self-deception must be even greater than I supposed if you imagined that I would condemn myself to perpetual loneliness merely to ensure that you remained in that enviable position."

An ugly sneer twisted Pelham's mouth. "My God, what a hypocrite you are!" he burst out. "Perpetual loneliness! You know damned well that if Terence were still alive you would never have offered for Jennifer Linley or anyone else."

Guy received this charge with equanimity, his anger seeming to subside as Pelham's increased. The heavy brows lifted a fraction, and the faintest of ironic smiles etched itself about the strong lines of his mouth.

"You see, Pelham," he said calmly, "I could contemplate with perfect composure the prospect of Terence, or a son of his, inheriting my possessions, but it was quite another matter when chance set you in his place. Did you really expect me to resign myself to that? I hope that my sense of responsibility is too great."

"Devil take your sense of responsibility!" Pelham retorted passionately. "For the present, at least, I am still your heir, and I can guess, if you cannot, what will be said if you let me be flung into prison without lifting a finger to help me."

"Certainly I can guess!" Guy's voice was mocking. "The world will regard me as a heartless, unnatural tyrant and you as my hapless victim, but what consolation will that be to you? As for myself, I have suffered too often from similar misapprehensions for accusations of that nature to trouble me."

"They may trouble Miss Linley. I fancy she lacks your cursed arrogance."

"Is that a threat, Pelham?" Ravenshaw asked softly. "If it is, here is one to answer it. Let it come to my knowledge that you have done anything to cause Miss Linley even one instant's disquiet, and a debtor's prison will seem a veritable paradise by contrast to what will happen to you. Do I make myself clear?"

He spoke very quietly, without moving from his position before the fire, but some of Pelham's high colour faded, and he passed his tongue uneasily across his lips. He said defiantly:

"You make it clear what a damned bully you are! You think that because you hold the purse-strings you may insult me as you choose."

"I do not think it. I know I may," Guy retorted contemptuously, "and our respective fortunes have nothing whatsoever to do with it. Now be good enough to take yourself off, and do not come whining to me again with your troubles. This time I do not intend to take the burden upon my shoulders. To carry it alone may teach you a much needed lesson."

For a few moments longer Pelham stood staring at him with an expression of resentment and dismay, as pale now as he had been flushed before. With the optimism of a thoroughly selfish nature, he had hitherto succeeded in persuading himself that Guy's threats were intended merely to alarm him, and that when it came to the point, his cousin would rescue him from his present difficulties as he had so often rescued him in the past There would be an unpleasant scene, of course, and he might even find himself banished from London for a while, but that anything worse could befall his precious person was unthinkable. Now, however, conviction was forced upon him against his will.

"Confound it, Guy, you cannot refuse to help me!" he exclaimed, panic rising in his voice. "I have no hope of settling my debts unless you do. It will be for the last time, I swear it! I'll never trouble you again, but for God's sake give me one more chance!"

Mr. Ravenshaw shook his head. "I have been giving you one more chance ever since you were sixteen," he said flatly, "and now I have reached the end of my patience.

Change your ways, and I may change my mind, but until then spare me these promises which we both know that you have no intention of keeping. I will not pay your debts. That is all I have to say."

In proof of this he went back to his desk, took a letter from the pile of correspondence awaiting his attention, and sat down to read it, paying no further heed to his cousin's presence in the room. Pelham stood for a little while longer gnawing at his lower lip and glaring at the broad shoulders and exquisitely disordered black hair thus presented to his gaze, then, realizing the futility of further argument, turned and flung petulantly out of the room, slamming the door with a violence which made the windows rattle.

Mr. Ravenshaw read to the end of the letter and then let it fall and rested his chin on his clenched fist. Once more the fingers of his other hand drummed irritably upon the desk, for the conversation with his young kinsman had put him thoroughly out of temper. This was a mood which had descended upon him with increasing frequency during recent weeks, provoking surprise in his friends and consternation among his servants, for in spite of the harsh streak in his nature he was not normally a bad-tempered man. In this instance, however, ill-humour was the direct result of a strong and self-willed character being forced by the demands of duty into a course repugnant to it. In short, Mr. Ravenshaw had not the smallest desire for a wife.

This was a fact which, until that day, he had thought to be known only to himself, but Pelham's malicious words had shown him how mistaken he was; and if Pelham had guessed the truth, others might well have done likewise. Just when and how his aversion to matrimony had come into being Guy did not know, though his Aunt Augusta, a lady notable more for frankness than for tact, maintained that it sprang from the indefatigable pursuit of him by ladies too numerous to mention.

"For the past fifteen years," Lady Dinsmore would assert, with even more than her wonted emphasis, "Guy has been one of the most eligible bachelors in England, and the number of females who have set their caps at him is great enough to have turned the most amiable of men into a confirmed misogynist. And Guy has never been the most amiable of men."

Whatever the cause, however, its effect troubled no one save the ladies themselves, for Mr. Ravenshaw had a brother, seven years his junior, who had made a very suitable marriage with a young lady of birth and fortune, and even when their first child died within a few days of its birth, Guy, though sympathetic to their sorrow, was not unduly disturbed. Terence and Jane were young; there would be other children. What he had not bargained for was an accident in the hunting-field a short while later which left Jane a widow, and placed the ne'er-do-well Pelham in direct succession to the Ravenshaw fortune.

Guy had realized then, as soon as the first shock of his brother's death had passed, that his own intention to remain a bachelor must be set aside, for the master of a fortune such as his had responsibilities which must come before his own inclinations. It was not long before the mothers of marriageable daughters began to realize it, too, and the attempts to capture his interest, which had languished somewhat of late years, were renewed with redoubled energy. A whole bevy of young ladies, all well-bred and blessed in varying degrees with wealth, or beauty, or both, was paraded before him on every possible occasion.

Mr. Ravenshaw looked them over without enthusiasm, for the prospect of binding himself irrevocably to a lively damsel approximately half his age did not appeal to him. He was by no means a woman-hater, and various actresses and opera dancers had enjoyed his protection from time to time, but the daughters of polite society, fresh from the schoolroom, attracted him not at all. Yet it was from among these that convention demanded he should choose his bride.

He had still not made his choice when Lady Linley launched her third daughter into society, and contrived, though without much hope of any result, to introduce her to Mr. Ravenshaw. Jennifer, still numb and dazed by the shock of Roland's supposed death, made not the smallest attempt to catch his attention, and for that very reason succeeded in doing so. Guy, not knowing the cause of that quiet indifference, and mistaking it for the outward sign of a placid and undemanding nature, decided that he need look no farther for his bride. Miss Linley, it was plain, would expect no romantic transports; she would accept his offer in the spirit in which it was made, from a sense of duty and because it was convenient to them both.

As the date set for the wedding drew nearer, however, the prospect of taking even so docile a wife, as Jennifer seemed likely to be, grew steadily more irksome. They were still strangers to each other, Lady Linley's sense of propriety precluding them from ever being alone together, and even on the one occasion when Guy had taken his betrothed driving in the Park, the presence of his groom prevented anything but an exchange of impersonal small-talk. Jennifer was shy of the dark, unapproachable man so soon to be her husband, while he had not the slightest idea how to win her confidence and liking. Both were relieved when the outing was over, and they could go their separate ways.

With the memory of this not very happy portent for the future to bear him company, Mr. Ravenshaw had betaken himself to Sussex, on the pretext of seeing that all was in readiness for the coming of his bride. His childhood had been spent at Fairings, to which he was more deeply attached than to any other of his several residences, and he lingered there a good deal longer than was strictly necessary. At length, however, it became obvious that his return to London could be delayed no longer, and the knowledge, implying as it did the approaching end of his days of untrammelled freedom, exacerbated his temper even further.

In this dangerous mood he was found by his cousin Pelham, who had come posting down from London the previous day. Mr. Ravenshaw was not pleased to see him, but he greeted him with civility if not with warmth. He had no intention of being turned from his decision to refuse all further aid, and neither the possible consequences to Pelham, nor the certainty that the younger man would curry sympathy by making public the refusal, troubled him in the least, but the recent interview had disturbed him none the less. He was a man who hated to fail in anything, and where Pelham was concerned he felt that he had failed most lamentably. He sat for some while deep in thought, and then shrugged impatiently and returned to his correspondence.

The younger Mr. Ravenshaw, meanwhile, had stormed up to his bedchamber, summoned his valet and ordered him to pack.

"And don't be all day about it," he added irritably. "I've no wish to stay in this house any longer than need be."

Mr. Samuel Meake had been in Pelham's service long enough to know that any verbal response would turn his employer's ill-humour upon himself, so he merely bowed and moved softly to do his bidding. He was a thin, pallid man of indeterminate age, with narrow shoulders and a slight stoop which created an impression of cringing servility. In fact he was far from servile. Observant, unscrupulous, and with more than his fair share of cunning, he had on a number of occasions proved useful to Pelham in ways not generally included in the duties of a gentleman's gentleman, and he was fully conversant with the present ruinous state of his young master's affairs. He knew why Pelham had come to visit his wealthy kinsman, and he now concluded that the errand had proved unsuccessful. It was regrettable, he reflected, but not, to him, unexpected. Mr. Meake had never underestimated Guy Ravenshaw, and on more than one occasion had taken the liberty of warning his master that some day he would try his cousin's patience too far.

The journey back to Town was accomplished under the same conditions of ill-suppressed fury. Pelham passed the entire journey in brooding savagely over the injustice of a fate which had given him so little worldly wealth, and Guy so much, and in wishing passionately that he could hit upon some way of restoring his fortunes and at the same time avenging himself upon his cousin, but beneath the jealousy and the self-pity he was a badly frightened man. Disaster loomed hideously before him, and this time, it seemed, there was no way of escape.

He stopped to dine on the road, and arrived back at his rooms in Duke Street midway through the evening, and it was characteristic of him that once in London again he ceased to brood over his misfortune, but changed his dress and set out in search of something to divert his mind from it. This quest led him eventually to a discreet gaming house in the neighbourhood of St. James's, where his arrival was greeted with slightly inebriated enthusiasm by a dark, raffish young man lounging before a card-strewn table.

"Pel! Where the devil have you been these two days past? Dashed if I hadn't begun to think you must have fled the country!"

Pelham laughed, and dropped into the vacant chair beside him. "It may come to that yet," he retorted humorously, "unless my luck takes a turn for the better. I have been down to Sussex, Lin, to see your future brother-in-law."

"Oh?" Sir Reginald Linley shot him a swift glance. "I thought he intended to return to Town this week?"

"He does, but my business with him was urgent." Pelham hesitated for a moment, and then added with a wry grin: "I might have spared myself the trouble, for as usual I met with nothing but sermons and reproaches. I wish you joy of your closer relationship with him, Lin, but here's a word of advice. Never turn to him for help if you find yourself in trouble of any kind."

Two or three other gentlemen joined them before Sir Reginald could reply, and the subject was dropped. It was not, however, forgotten, and some hours later, when the two young men left the house together and began to walk homeward in the first grey light of dawn, Pelham referred to it again. He had sensed a certain uneasiness in his friend when Ravenshaw's name was mentioned, and his curiosity was aroused.

"I suppose I should have known better than to look to

Guy for sympathy or help," he remarked with a sigh, "but the truth is, Lin, I'm in devilish deep, and I was fool enough to think that his engagement to your sister might have mellowed him a trifle." He paused, and then added, as though struck by a sudden idea: "I wonder if Miss Linley—but no! I have no right to ask such a thing of her."

Sir Reginald cast him a sapient glance. He might have been obliged to grip his friend's arm to steady his slightly wavering steps, but he was not too fuddled to grasp the sense of that unfinished remark.

"Think Jenny might succeed where you failed?" he suggested. "Well, I dare say she'd try if I asked her, for she's a good little soul, and not one of these strait-laced, sanctimonious females, either." He chuckled. "Not likely to be with a brother like me! Thing is, though, she's going out of Town tomorrow, so I don't suppose she'll have the opportunity."

"Going out of Town?" Pelham repeated in a tone of mild surprise. "With the wedding less than a month away?"

Sir Reginald looked a trifle embarrassed. "Well, you know how it is," he said vaguely. "Too many balls, and parties and so forth, and then the excitement of her wedding being so near—! She's quite worn out, m'mother says, so she's sending her down to Westbridge for a while. Best thing she could do!"

Pelham murmured agreement, reflecting with malicious amusement that apparently distaste for the approaching marriage was not all upon the bridegroom's side. He was not surprised. No doubt the little bride was showing reluctance and her careful mother sending her out of Town until she came to her senses. Having once captured such a matrimonial prize as Ravenshaw, Lady Linley would make short work of any threat to her plans.

"M'mother would have taken Jenny to Westbridge herself," Reginald continued after a moment, "but with my Aunt Louisa on her hands, and going into strong hysterics at every sound, she feels she can't leave London at present. Did you hear about that shocking affair at my uncle's house last night? Damned outrage, if you ask me! Don't know what things are coming to!"

Pelham replied that he had learned of the crime on his return to London, but seemed to be more interested in Miss Linley's proposed visit to Hertfordshire. Was he to understand, he asked, that she was to make the journey alone?

"Well, what's wrong with that?" Miss Linley's brother demanded belligerently. "Dash it all, it's only a few hours' journey, and her maid will be with her, and she'll travel in my mother's chaise, with our own servants. M'mother wanted me to escort her, but I can't see the need for it, and told her so. Don't see what harm Jenny can come to—in broad daylight, too! Only one stop to change horses, and that's at the Red Lion at Barnet, where we've all been well known ever since I can remember. Fine figure of fun I should look, trailing all the way to Westbridge for such a paltry reason!"

Pelham agreed to this, a trifle absently, and for a while they strolled on in silence. Then Reginald, who had apparently been turning the conversation over in his mind, said abruptly:

"Don't see that Jenny could be much help to you at present, anyway. She's never left alone with Ravenshaw, and it's not the sort of subject she could broach in front of m'mother. Wait till after the wedding, and if you haven't come about by then we'll ask her to see what she can do. Dare say Ravenshaw might agree to it then. Young bride, y'know—anxious to please her! Depend upon it, Pel, Jenny's the one to help you out of your difficulties."

Pelham's lips had curled contemptuously at the picture thus presented to him of his cousin in the role of adoring bridegroom, but Reginald did not observe the sneer, and when Pelham spoke there was nothing in his voice but hopeful satisfaction.

"The one to help me," he repeated softly. "Do you know, Lin, I believe she is!"

4

Curious Happenings at a Country Inn

IT was not to be expected that Mrs. Henry Cresswell would accept with complaisance her niece's intention to go out of London. In fact, it was seldom that any of Caroline's actions met with her aunt's approval, for to Lizzie Cresswell the younger woman's presence in her house was a constant irritation. Jealousy and disappointment lay at the root of her resentment, for she had long cherished social aspirations which had not yet been gratified, and probably never would be. Twenty years ago, when she had married Henry Cresswell in the teeth of her father's opposition, she had believed that the marriage would automatically open to her the doors of fashionable society.

It had taken less than a month for her to discover the truth. In the eyes of his own world, Henry Cresswell had committed the unpardonable sin, and as far as that world was concerned had ceased to exist. Even his elder brother,

Richard, though not above accepting financial assistance from time to time, had made it quite clear that he desired to have as little as possible to do with his sister-in-law and her family. Cheated of the social success she craved, Lizzie had avenged herself on her husband by slighting him at every opportunity, so that it was not surprising that over the years a character always pliable and easy-going had become a colourless nonentity. No one in the Cresswell household, from Henry himself to Becky, the little maid-servant, had any doubt as to who was the real ruler of the establishment.

When Richard Cresswell died, and his orphaned daughter sought refuge with them, Lizzie's ambitions revived. Most of Caroline's childhood had been spent at Brightstone Park, and though lack of means had prevented her from entering the Polite World, she was still on the closest of friendly terms with the Wilde family and their neighbours, the Linleys. Agreeable visions floated before Lizzie Cresswell's eyes, in which her niece's fashionable friends frequented the house, and repaid the hospitality by invitations to their own homes. So she made Caroline welcome, and assured her repeatedly that she was free to entertain her friends whenever she wished.

Caroline thanked her gravely, but at twenty-one she had seen enough of the world to recognize the reasons behind her aunt's generosity, and though she continued to visit her old friends, never invited them to return the calls, or introduced her relations to them. Mrs. Cresswell, seeing her hopes dashed for the second time, and being the more bitterly disappointed because she now had a growing family to consider, soon ceased to treat her niece with even a semblance of consideration. Caroline was given to understand that in return for a home she was expected to take complete charge of the children, and to perform in addition any other duty which Mrs. Cresswell might desire, and since Lizzie's ingenuity in inventing such tasks seemed inexhaustible, she was soon in a fair way to becoming nothing less than a drudge.

Now, some six years after her arrival, the family had

begun to emerge from the schoolroom, George, the eldest, being nineteen, and Sophy sixteen, but Caroline's responsibilities were increased rather than diminished. It did not suit Mrs. Cresswell's notions of gentility for her daughter to be unchaperoned, and this duty fell upon Caroline's shoulders in addition to all the rest. Even her close friends, such as Letty and Roland, had only a hazy idea of the kind of life she led; had they known the whole truth, Caroline reflected bitterly, they would have been less surprised and shocked by her reaction to old Mr. Firkin's proposal of marriage.

In accordance with the plans they had made together, Caroline said nothing of her intention to go to Hertfordshire, but early on the chosen day the Cresswell household was thrown into unwonted confusion by the arrival of Captain Wilde. He asked for Miss Caroline, but the manservant who admitted him, taking in with one awed glance the visitor's style and elegance, and being in no doubt of his own duty, ushered him into the drawing-room and then hastened in search of the mistress of the house.

Mrs. Cresswell could scarcely believe her ears, but did not allow astonishment to dull her wits. Instructing Silas to refrain from informing Miss Caroline of the Captain's arrival, she hurriedly thrust her eldest daughter into a new and fashionable gown, refurbished her own appearance, and with Sophy at her heels swept into the drawing-room to greet the unexpected but very welcome guest.

"Captain Wilde, this is indeed a pleasure! We have long hoped to make your acquaintance, and I am sure I have been telling Caroline for ever that she should have her friends to call upon her."

Roland bowed, and asked her pardon for calling upon her at so unreasonable an hour. This was brushed aside, as with one hand Mrs. Cresswell drew her daughter forward.

"My dear sir, you are welcome to call at any hour, for I assure you that I do not mean to stand upon ceremony with such an old friend of my niece. Now let me make you known to my little girl. Sophy, my love, make your curtsy to the Captain."

Miss Sophy, a stout blonde with very round blue eyes and a high complexion, obeyed ungracefully, blushing and simpering. Her mother regarded her with a doting eye.

"So shy and retiring," she said fondly. "She is not yet out, of course, and has not learned how to go on in the world, though I will own that I find a gentle modesty in a young girl very pleasing."

"Miss Sophy, ma'am, could not fail to please, in any company," Roland replied with more gallantry than truth. He found the young lady singularly unprepossessing, but Caroline had warned him to do all he could to ingratiate himself with her aunt.

He could have chosen no more certain way of doing so. Mrs. Cresswell beamed upon him, begged him to be seated, and invited him to take some refreshment. He declined, and ventured to inquire again for Caroline.

"I am reluctant to seem importunate, ma'am, and do not wish to put you, or Caroline, to the least inconvenience, but the matter which brought me here is of some urgency. If I might see her for a few moments—?"

"Of course, my dear sir!" Mrs. Cresswell assented quickly. "I do not know why that foolish fellow has not told her of your arrival. Sophy, love, run up to the schoolroom and ask your cousin to join us. Caroline is devoted to the little ones, Captain Wilde," she added. "I do not know what we should do without her."

Roland made a polite rejoinder, and reflected that Mrs. Cresswell would soon have an opportunity to find out. His hostess chattered on, enumerating the ages and accomplishments of her offspring, and lamenting the fact that her son, George, was not at home. She would so much have liked the Captain to make his acquaintance. Roland expressed regret that this pleasure was to be denied him, and hoped secretly that Caroline would not delay her appearance too long.

To his relief only a few minutes passed before the door opened and Miss Cresswell came into the room. She was wearing a very plain and somewhat shabby gown of a dull maroon colour which did not suit her in the least, its high neck, long sleeves and general lack of ornamentation in marked contrast to her cousin Sophy's sprigged and flounced muslin and fringed silk shawl. The difference in their attire as much as Mrs. Cresswell's patronizing manner marked Caroline unmistakably as a poor relation, but this fact did not seem to oppress her unduly.

"Well, Roland," she greeted him briskly, "this is unexpected indeed! Is anything wrong?"

Recognizing his cue, the Captain embarked upon the prearranged story of his mother's supposed illness, and begged that Mrs. Cresswell would be kind enough to spare Caroline to her for a few days. Lizzie, who would gladly have endured a far greater inconvenience than this if it meant placing the Wilde family under an obligation to her, assured him that she would be happy to do so, and Caroline added: "It will be as well if I come with you at once, Roland. Just to give me time to change my dress and pack a valise. I shall not keep you waiting above half an hour."

She whisked out of the room again, leaving Roland to reflect thankfully that when Caroline said half an hour, she meant thirty minutes, and no longer. He was finding Mrs. Cresswell's spurious gentility almost as hard to bear as her daughter's clumsy attempts at coquettishness.

Caroline, pausing only to ask the maidservant, Becky, to help her with her preparations, quickly mounted the stairs to her bedchamber at the top of the house. This was little better than an attic, and next door to the one shared by Becky and the cook, but Miss Cresswell had long since grown accustomed to its lack of comfort. She took from the cupboard a battered valise which had belonged to her father, and asked the maid to pack it while she exchanged her old dress for the one she habitually wore when visiting her friends.

Becky, who had caught a glimpse of Captain Wilde as he entered the house, was quite overcome by the prospect of her beloved Miss Caroline going off in company with so modish a gentleman. She showed an alarming tendency to weave a romance out of the situation, until Caroline brought her firmly back to earth by saying with a laugh:

"There is no cause for these high flights, Becky, I assure you. I have known Captain Wilde since we were both in the nursery, and regard him as I would a brother. Besides, he is very deeply in love with a lady who is far younger and prettier than I am."

Becky sniffed. "That's as may be, miss, but it ain't right for a lady like you to be at the beck and call of the likes of the missus yonder. You deserve to have servants to wait on you, and a fine house of your own."

Caroline laughed, not without a trace of wistfulness, and patted the girl's shoulder. Becky was the only person in her uncle's house for whom she felt the least degree of affection.

"Well, if ever I do, Becky, depend upon it that I shall take you into my service immediately. Now stop talking nonsense, there's a good girl, and fetch my muff for me. You know where it is."

Becky sighed, and fetching a large fur muff from the cupboard, laid it reverently on the bed, stroking it with one roughened hand. The muff, which had been a birthday gift from Mrs. Wilde, was Caroline's one luxurious possession, and Becky admired it tremendously. Now, however, she perceived that a small accident had befallen it.

"Oh, miss, the lining's torn!" she exclaimed in dismay. "I'd best stitch it up for you."

"Not now, my dear, there is not time, for I must not keep Captain Wilde waiting." Caroline tied the strings of her bonnet beneath her chin, picked up her gloves and stretched out her hand for the muff, adding with a chuckle: "He is in great haste to be off, for he has a very important engagement to keep."

Becky picked up the valise and followed Miss Cresswell down the four flights of stairs to the hall, where they found young George Cresswell standing in an attitude of indecision. He had apparently just entered the house, and, hearing the sound of voices from the drawing-room, was wondering whether or not to go in. Like Sophy, he had his mother's blue eyes and florid complexion, but his slender build and more patrician cast of countenance were inherited from his father. He was a weak-willed and rather ineffectual youth, and Caroline's attitude towards him was one of tolerant indifference. He returned her greeting absently, and looked with faint surprise at the valise which Becky had set down beneath the table which stood against the wall.

"You are not going away, are you, cousin?" he inquired, and Caroline nodded.

"Cousin Esther is ill, and Roland has come to ask me to go to her for a few days. He is in the drawing-room now with your Mama." She laid her muff and gloves on the table, and made a discovery. "Oh, how foolish of me! I have left my reticule upstairs. No, Becky, I will fetch it myself, for Cook will scold you if you do not go back to her at once. Goodbye, and thank you."

Becky said goodbye and scurried off to the kitchen, and Caroline turned to mount the stairs. Glancing back as she reached the top of the first flight, she saw George still standing in the hall, gnawing at a fingernail and staring blankly before him. Probably, she thought as she went on up the next flight, he was in trouble of some kind. Caroline suspected him of having fallen into bad company. He was on close terms with a certain Mr. Bartholomew Trench, who often visited the house and whom Caroline had had no hesitation in classing as a rogue. He had attempted gallantry with her, and been dealt a sharp set-down.

When she descended to the hall again, George had disappeared. Caroline picked up her muff and gloves and went into the drawing-room, where she found him in uneasy conversation with Captain Wilde. The Captain greeted her with a look of undisguised relief, and, rising immediately to his feet, began to take leave of his hostess. Silas was sent to procure a hackney, Roland explaining to Mrs. Cresswell that they would transfer to a post-chaise at his sister's house, and a few minutes later he and Caroline were being driven through the busy streets with the first part of their plan successfully accomplished.

Later that day the landlord of the Cap and Bells, that comfortable but unpretentious hostelry in the neighbourhood of Finchley, was surprised and gratified to see a private chaise pull into the inn yard. Gratified, because he was not in the general way called upon to cater for carriage trade, and surprised because this was the second such vehicle to halt at his house within the hour. The first was a post-chaise-and-four from which had descended first a good-looking young gentleman of military appearance, and then a bent and obviously aged lady, her face completely concealed by the black lace veil which was attached to the brim of her bonnet and hung to her knees. Her gown of heavy, violet-coloured silk was almost hidden beneath a voluminous cloak of a darker shade; with one gloved hand she leaned heavily upon a silver-knobbed ebony cane, the other was buried in the depths of a large fur muff.

Tenderly supported by her companion, this venerable dame tottered slowly into the inn, the young gentleman instructing the post-boys to stable the horses and then to refresh themselves at his expense. To the landlord he explained that his grandmother desired to lie down and rest for a while, adding that they intended to stop at Barnet, where her ladyship's abigail, who had set forth earlier in the coach carrying the baggage, was no doubt anxiously awaiting them, but that the old lady had been unable to endure any longer the jolting of the chaise. He then assisted his aged relative up the stairs to the bedchamber hastily prepared for her by the innkeeper's wife, and on her signifying that she desired to be left alone, assured the good woman in a discreet undervoice that the poor old soul was extremely eccentric and must be humoured at all costs.

When the landlord stepped out of his front door to greet the occupants of the second chaise, he was wondering uneasily whether these travellers would be content to use the coffee-room, since his only private parlour was now occupied by her ladyship's grandson, or whether, if there were ladies in this second party, he should request the young gentleman to give up the room to them. This thorny problem, however, did not materialize, although a lady certainly descended from the chaise, a pretty, dark-eyed child in a blue cloak, the hood of which was thrown back on her shoulders to reveal a profusion of dusky curls. She was accompanied by a plump maidservant upon whom she leaned heavily and who announced that Miss was feeling poorly and would be glad to rest for a while.

So for the second time the landlady of the Cap and Bells made ready a room for an ailing lady, who thanked her prettily but appeared to be on the verge of tears. The abigail said that Miss was often made to feel unwell by the motion of a carriage, but would soon be feeling more the thing, if only she could have some rest and quiet. The landlady, taking the hint, withdrew, saying that she would be below stairs if anything were needed.

Five minutes passed, and then the door of one bed-chamber opened, and the bent and shrouded figure of its occupant appeared on the threshold. Leaning heavily on her stick, she hobbled across the landing, tapped softly on the opposite door, and entered without waiting for a reply. There was a gasp from within, and a ripple of laughter, hastily stifled, and then the door closed behind her and all was quiet again.

Half an hour later the veiled figure was once more to be seen, this time descending the stairs with the assistance of Miss Linley's abigail, who informed the startled landlady in an aside that she had found the poor old lady coming down on her own. Her ladyship thanked her in a quavering voice, and requested the landlady to fetch her grandson to her, and to have the horses put-to. This was soon done, the shot was paid, and the young gentleman helped his companion to enter the chaise. He followed her, the steps were put up, and the vehicle moved sedately away along the Great North Road.

Inside the chaise, as soon as the inn was left behind, the bent figure straightened, the long veil was thrown back, and a pretty, glowing face turned towards Captain Wilde.

"We have done it!" Jennifer said exultantly. "We are really on our way to Scotland! Oh, Roland, I can scarcely believe it!"

"Nor I!" agreed the Captain, taking her in his arms. "We're not home yet, sweetheart, but by God! we are over the worst of the fences."

"It is all thanks to Caro," Jennifer reminded him, misty-eyed. "We shall never be able to repay her, never!"

"I'm more grateful to Caro than I can say," Roland replied firmly, "but at this present, my darling, I am far more interested in you. Take off that devilish bonnet, so that I may kiss you properly."

5

The Captive

WHEN Agnes returned to the bedchamber with the news that the Captain and his bride were safely on their way, she found Miss Cresswell seated on the edge of the bed and pensively regarding the fine diamond ring on the third finger of her left hand.

"What I am expected to do with this trinket when our deception is revealed, I cannot imagine," she remarked. "Of course, I can understand Miss Jenny's reluctance to elope with Captain Wilde with another man's ring on her finger, but I would prefer not to have charge of so costly a jewel. Did you speak to the landlady here as I told you to?"

Agnes chuckled. "Yes, miss, I told her that my mistress was really ill with weeping and worry because she was being compelled to marry a man she couldn't abide, just because he was rich, instead of the one she truly loved.

She was near weeping herself before I'd done, and the things she said about her ladyship would have done your heart good to hear."

"Would they indeed?" Caroline said dryly. "Well, they were probably not nearly as harsh as the things her ladyship will say of us when she learns how she has been tricked—and to us, also, if the chance offers. I hope you are prepared for that, Agnes. She will have to vent her anger on someone, and Jenny and Roland will be beyond her reach."

"Hard words can't hurt us, miss," Agnes pointed out practically, "and even if her ladyship turns me off, I shan't worry. The Captain's promised that I shall go back to Miss Jenny as soon as they come home from Scotland, and that's all that matters to me. No, I'm not afeared of her ladyship, but I'll tell you this: If it was Mr. Ravenshaw I had to face, 'twould be a very different matter."

Caroline's brows lifted. "Dear me, what a monster the man must be!" she said lightly. "Everyone appears to be afraid of him. However, one must in justice admit that he will have every right to be angry, for not only has he lost his chosen bride, but he will be made to look exceedingly foolish by this affair."

"Serve him right!" said the rebellious Agnes. "Anyway, miss, it's her ladyship that'll have to break it to him, Heaven be thanked, and not us. Shall I go down and tell William to have the horses put to?"

"Yes, for I think we have given Captain Wilde sufficient time to get well ahead of us, and you had better settle our score as well," Caroline agreed. "When the chaise is at the door, come back to me."

When Agnes had gone, Miss Cresswell rose to her feet and studied herself critically in the looking-glass. Jennifer's simple gown of pale blue cambric fitted her well enough, and the fact that it had been made for a slightly plumper lady would pass unnoticed beneath the cloak. She put this garment on, pulling up the hood and tying the strings firmly beneath her chin, so that her face was closely framed in a frill of dark blue cloth. One or two strands of red hair were still visible, but when she tucked these out of sight and held a lace-edged handkerchief up to her eyes, she decided that the disguise was sufficient for the few minutes it would be needed. Once within the chaise, she would be safe from detection until Westbridge was reached.

It was not long before Agnes came back to say that the chaise was at the door. Miss Cresswell nodded, and was subjecting herself to a final close scrutiny in the mirror when the abigail uttered an exclamation and pounced on something lying beside the bed.

"It's your muff, miss," she said. "Miss Jenny's gone without it."

Caroline sighed. "How very like her," she said resignedly, "though I suppose that at this of all times we cannot expect her to remember trifling details. Carry the muff down under your cloak, Agnes, and put it among your own belongings for the time being. You can return it to me later."

The landlady of the inn, deeply moved by the heartrending tale recounted to her by the abigail, was not at all surprised to see the young lady weeping bitterly when she came downstairs. With the utmost delicacy she refrained from speaking to her, merely curtsying respectfully as the cloaked figure went past her out of the house, and when the chaise had bowled away in the direction of Finchley Common, she returned to the kitchen to inform her husband that any mother capable of treating that pretty dear so cruelly was not worthy of the name.

The stretch of the Great North Road which crossed Finchley Common had long been notorious as the huntingground of highwaymen, but these were not now so numerous as they had been during the previous century, and even the romantically-minded Miss Cresswell had no expectation of being held up by one. In fact, such a thought had not even entered her head, and when, rather more than halfway across the Common, there was a sudden commotion comprised of pounding hooves, shouts, and, finally, the crack of a pistol-shot, her first reaction was complete astonishment. The chaise halted so abruptly that she and Agnes were almost thrown from their seats, and by the time they had recovered themselves the door had been flung open, and a bulky figure in a frieze great-coat, with a mask across his face and his hat pulled low over his eyes, was framed in the aperture.

He surveyed the two young women for one tense and silent moment, then nodded to himself and stepped back a pace, making a slight but meaning gesture with his pistol.

"You, missie," he said gruffly, nodding at Caroline. "Down you come, and step lively about it."

With his free hand he reached out and lowered the steps, but neither the pistol nor the eyes behind the mask wavered for an instant from the two girls. Through the open door Caroline could see a second masked figure, mounted on a good-looking roan and covering with his pistol the two postillions. Clearly no assistance would be forthcoming from that quarter. She looked again at the first man, who jerked his head impatiently. Caroline rose to her feet.

"Oh, miss, don't you do it!" Agnes gasped, clutching her arm to detain her. "They might murder you, the villains!"

"I imagine they are more likely to murder me if I do not do as they wish," Caroline retorted calmly. "Let me go, Agnes! One cannot argue with a pistol."

She stepped down from the chaise, remembering even in the stress of that moment to keep her back towards the other servants in case they looked round and saw her face. The first highwayman put up the steps and slammed the door, and then some kind of heavy cloth was flung over Miss Cresswell's head from behind, and her instinctive movement to free herself frustrated by a pair of muscular arms.

The impression which she afterwards retained of the next few minutes was hazy in the extreme. She was aware of a cord being passed round her body over the muffling cloth, pinioning her arms to her sides, and another being lashed about her ankles. Then she was hoisted up and slung anyhow across the withers of a fretting horse, and held there firmly by its rider as the animal was wheeled round and urged at a rapid pace away from the chaise.

Fortunately for Caroline, the distance they covered thus

was not great, but even so she was shaken and dizzy when at length her captor drew rein, and rough hands once more laid hold upon her. This time she was carried for a few yards and then lifted over some obstruction and set down, none too gently, on what seemed to be a pile of sacks. She could hear voices somewhere close at hand, but either they were speaking in lowered tones, or the thick covering over her head prevented the words from reaching her distinctly. Then the floor on which she lay gave a violent lurch forward, and she realized that she was in a vehicle of some kind.

After that she lost all count of time. The thick folds of cloth that covered her to the waist were heavy and stifling; she found it increasingly difficult to breathe, her head began to pound in a sickening fashion, and her last coherent thought before she lost consciousness was a hope that Agnes would have sense enough to say nothing of the exchange of identity which had taken place at the Cap and Bells.

When she came to her senses again the cart was at a standstill, and once more a murmur of voices reached her ears. After a minute or two she felt herself lifted, slung like a sack over a brawny shoulder, and carried forward a short way and then up a flight of stairs. At last she was dropped on to what felt like a bed, and hands began to fumble at the ropes confining her; they fell away, and the stifling folds of cloth loosened a little, but a voice spoke sharply beside her, and this time the words came clearly to her ears.

"Wait, you fool, don't let her see me!" It was a firm, imperious voice, with the cultured accent of an educated man. "Give me the ring!"

Someone seized her left wrist, her glove was ripped off and Jenny's betrothal ring dragged from her finger. Then came the sound of swift, receding footsteps, and at long last the muffling cloth was pulled from her head.

She lay gasping for breath and blinking in a light which, though in fact far from bright, seemed to dazzle her eyes, while the rope was hacked away from her ankles. Too stiff and cramped to move, she could only lie there helplessly while a slightly-built youth peered at her and then moved away to the far side of the room. There was the sound of liquid being poured out, and then he came back and, slipping a hand beneath her head to raise it, held a mug to her lips.

"Here, dearie, drink this!" To Caroline's surprise the voice was feminine. "There's no call to be afraid. No one's going to do you any harm."

Caroline swallowed obediently, and choked over a fiery liquid which seemed to sear her throat. The draught was not without effect, however, and after a little her head cleared sufficiently for her to realize that in spite of cropped hair, frieze coat and breeches, and stout boots, her companion was a young woman of about her own age. Considerably reassured by this fact, she endeavoured to sit up, but found this beyond her power. Falling back against the pillow, she said huskily: "Where am I? Why have you brought me here?"

"Never you mind the 'where' and 'why' of it all, miss. You behave yourself, and you'll come to no harm, that I promise you. You're just going to stay here for a day or two, and as soon as we've got what we want you can go home again, back to your Ma, and the fine gentleman you're to marry. Meantime I'm here to look after you. Nancy's my name, and that's all you need to know." She held out the mug again. "Take another sup o' this, dearie! It'll do you a power of good."

Caroline pushed the proffered mug away. "No, thank you, but I would like a drink of water."

Nancy shrugged, and swallowed the contents of the mug herself before going away and locking the door behind her. Caroline made a supreme effort, struggled into a sitting position and looked about her. The room was small and rather dark, the only light coming from a dormer window set in the sloping roof, and she judged it to be the principal bedroom of some small cottage. Its furnishings were poor, the narrow bed on which she sat, a chair with a broken back, and a cupboard bearing a basin and ewer with a small mirror hanging above it, comprising the sum total.

Miss Cresswell lowered her feet cautiously to the floor and stood upright, supporting herself by the bed-post. Her legs showed a disconcerting tendency to give away beneath her, but she managed to reach the window and peered through the grimy panes. What she saw told her nothing, for the view consisted merely of a depressed-looking patch of garden beyond which a thick wood loomed black against the pallid evening sky; it could have been almost anywhere in England, and since she had no means of knowing how long she had lain unconscious in the cart, or in which direction they had travelled, she could not even hazard a guess as to her whereabouts. Finding no comfort in the cheerless prospect confronting her, she made her way back to the bed and sat down on the edge of it.

She was still sitting there when Nancy came back into the room with a glass of water in her hand. Giving this to Caroline, she looked with some concern at her white, drawn face.

"Now, miss," she said with a certain rough kindliness, "it's no good fretting yourself over what can't be helped. You must be fair shook to pieces, so why not take off your cloak and lie down? Maybe you could get some sleep."

Caroline looked at her for a moment before replying. Nancy's face, though homely, was good-natured, and she seemed eager enough to please. Caroline leaned forward and put the empty glass down on the chair.

"Will you not tell me why I have been brought here?" she begged. "How can I rest until I know what you intend by me?"

Nancy shook her head. "I've told you all I can, miss, but you've naught to fear, I give you my word. We've handled you a bit rough, I know, but there was no help for that, and it's the worst that's going to happen to you. Now lie down, do, and I'll be up again in an hour or so with a bite to eat."

It was clear that she meant to say no more, and Caroline, realizing the futility of further argument, allowed the other woman to help her to lay aside her cloak and shoes. She was, in fact, quite exhausted by her recent experiences, and glad enough to lie down again upon the bed, but even when Nancy had gone, she found it impossible to sleep. The events of the day were too disturbing, the questions they posed too portentous, to allow her mind to rest.

Someone, it was plain, had known of Jennifer's proposed journey, and had planned to kidnap her. That someone was presumably the man whose voice she had heard when she was first brought to the cottage, and who had wrested Jenny's betrothal ring from her, but though it seemed likely that had he seen her face he would have realized that something had gone wrong with his scheme, Nancy at least, had no suspicion of the truth. Therefore, unless and until the instigator of the outrage returned to the cottage (and provided, of course, that Agnes held her tongue), there was no need to suppose that anyone else would discover it, and Jenny and Roland could continue their flight to the Border with no fear of pursuit. Miss Cresswell forced her mind to dwell on that consoling thought, and tried to keep at bay others less reassuring, most prominent of which was the burning question of what the mysterious kidnapper would do when he found that he had carried off, not Miss Jennifer Linley, but a totally unimportant stranger.

On one point at least, Caroline need not have worried. Agnes, as soon as she recovered from the shock of seeing her supposed mistress carried off by a gang of masked ruffians, realized that no good, and possibly a good deal of harm, would be done by revealing the fact that the captured lady was not Miss Linley. Therefore, since her fellow servants had no suggestion to offer, the resourceful abigail took charge of the situation, demanding to be driven instantly to Whetstone, the nearest village, in order that an information might be laid against the miscreants.

This, after some delay, was duly done, though there was small hope of identifying the highwaymen. When asked for a description of the kidnapped lady, Agnes, hoping devoutly that she was acting in the best interests of both Miss Linley and Miss Cresswell, painted a vivid word-picture of the former.

Darkness had fallen by the time they arrived back in

Mount Street, and her ladyship was found spending a quiet evening with her brother-in-law, John Linley, and his wife. The story which Agnes had to tell cast the earlier shocking events at Mr. Linley's house quite into the shade, but her ladyship bore up under the shock with commendable fortitude, and said firmly that someone must go instantly to Whetstone.

"I'd be happy to oblige, ma'am," Mr. Linley assured her. "Damme! I'd set out at once, but these Bow Street fellows have especially desired me not to leave Town at present on account of this other affair."

"Reginald must go!" said Reginald's mother decidedly. "I will send round at once to his lodging. Oh dear, if only Mr. Ravenshaw were in Town! He would be the very man to deal with a crisis of this sort."

"Very man to deal with a crisis of any sort, ma'am," Mr. Linley agreed bluntly. "You'd best send for him."

"I believe that will not be necessary, for he returns to London tomorrow. I will have a note taken round to his house first thing in the morning, so that he will receive it the instant he arrives. Meanwhile, Reginald must do the best he can."

Mr. Linley looked as though he placed very little dependence upon his nephew's capabilities, but merely said: "In that case, ma'am, I'll fetch the boy myself."

Sir Reginald, however, was not at home, and since his habits were as erratic as they were deplorable, the night was well advanced before his exasperated uncle finally ran him to earth. By that time, Reginald was in no condition to set out upon a journey, though the shock of Mr. Linley's news, when at length he could be persuaded to attend to it, sobered him considerably. He agreed to return at once to Mount Street, and there assured his mother that he would snatch a few hours' sleep and set out for Whetstone as soon as it was light.

With this she had to be content, but she had now had leisure to ponder the situation, and certain doubts had raised themselves in her mind. She remembered the presence in London of Captain Wilde, and as soon as she found herself alone with her son, asked anxiously if he thought the supposed abduction could possibly be a ruse to cover an elopement. Reginald considered the theory for a minute or two, but finally shook his head.

"Shouldn't think so, ma'am," he said positively. "Depend upon it, if they had been planning a trick of that sort, Roland would have been one of the men who held up the chaise. From what you tell me, those rogues handled poor little Jenny damned roughly, and he would never allow that. Thinks the world of her!"

Upon reflection, Lady Linley was bound to admit that he was right, but the conviction brought no reassurance at all. With Roland Wilde she could at least be sure that Jenny would come to no harm, but what might have befallen her at the hands of her unknown captors, her mother could not bear to contemplate. She had no great faith in Reginald's ability to accomplish anything useful, and could only hope that Mr. Ravenshaw would reach London at an early hour.

In this she was not disappointed, for Guy had never been a man of sluggardly habits, and in the country it was his habit to rise betimes. He arrived at his house in Grosvenor Square early in the afternoon, having driven from Sussex in a curricle-and-four, for he was a notable whip. By this time the news of Miss Linley's abduction was known all over Town, for the postillions who had witnessed it had wasted no time in describing it to their colleagues in the stables, whence it had spread with astonishing rapidity. Mr. Ravenshaw's butler, therefore, had no doubt of the contents of the note which had been brought round from Lady Linley's house that morning, and ventured to hand it to his master as soon as he set foot in the house, and before he had even put off his driving-coat.

Mr. Ravenshaw ripped the letter open there and then, and as he read it, the butler and his two attendant footmen saw the thick black brows draw quickly together, and the firm lips set in a grim line. Guy made no comment, however, but thrusting the letter into his pocket, and picking up his hat and gloves again, said briefly:

"I am going at once to Mount Street. It is unlikely that I shall be dining at home."

He ran quickly down the steps, and set off at a brisk pace towards Lady Linley's house.

He was conducted at once to her ladyship, who was in a state of almost unbearable anxiety. Since it was her belief, however, that no well-bred person betrayed emotion, she was able to greet her prospective son-in-law with tolerable composure, merely betraying by her convulsive clasping of his hand the extent of her agitation.

"I am deeply thankful that you are here, Mr. Ravenshaw," she said earnestly. "So deeply thankful!"

"I have but this instant arrived in London, ma'am, and came as soon as I had read your letter," he replied. "Is there any further news?"

"None!" her ladyship told him despairingly. "Reginald went to Whetstone this morning to discover what is being done, but we have had no word from him."

"It was scarcely to be expected yet, ma'am," Guy reassured her. "Will you be good enough to tell me the whole story? I know no more than you told me in your note."

Lady Linley pressed a hand to her forehead. "Of course, sir. Forgive me! I am so distracted with worry that I scarcely know what I am doing. It was Jennifer's abigail who brought the news to me, for she witnessed the entire event, and had the good sense to lay an information against the villains before returning to London."

Mr. Ravenshaw looked faintly surprised. "She would appear to be a woman of sound commonsense," he remarked. "Is she in the house at present?" Lady Linley assented, and he went on: "In that case, ma'am, will you be kind enough to send for her? I should like hear her story at first hand."

Agnes, summoned to her mistress's presence, and informed that Mr. Ravenshaw was with her ladyship, presented herself with some misgivings. Finding that she was merely required to tell her story again, her courage revived and she was able to do so lucidly enough, and even to answer the gentleman's searching questions without blundering. When she had been dismissed again Mr. Ravenshaw stood staring before him for a time, his grey eyes thoughtful, and his brows contracted into that frown which lent his dark countenance so forbidding an expression. At last Lady Linley found the silence unendurable, and said with some asperity:

"Well, sir, what are we to do? What can be the purpose behind this dreadful occurrence? I scarcely dare to think of what may have happened to Jennifer by now!"

The frowning regard transferred itself to her; Mr. Ravenshaw said quietly: "I believe the purpose of the crime is simple enough, ma'am, and I do not think that Miss Linley will have suffered any harm beyond the shock inseparable from such an experience. She is not a great heiress, so it is unlikely that she has been carried off by a needy adventurer who intends to force her into marriage. No, the reason is not far to seek. It is ransom."

"Ransom!" her ladyship repeated blankly. "But why Jennifer? As you say, she is not an heiress."

A slightly saturnine expression came into Ravenshaw's face. "The demand, I fancy, will come to me, and not to your ladyship. I am surprised that I have not received it already." He paused, as a fresh thought occurred to him. "Wait, though! Perhaps I have received it! My butler handed me your letter as soon as I entered the house, and I did not stay to read any other which might have been awaiting me. I had best go home immediately."

Lady Linley looked up at him with hope and doubt struggling for mastery in her eyes. "Do you indeed believe that, Mr. Ravenshaw? I pray to Heaven that you are right!"

"I am convinced of it, ma'am." Guy took the hand she put out to him and held it for a moment between his own, adding more gently, "Try not to worry too greatly. It is my belief that your daughter will soon be safely restored to you. I will send word to you immediately of any news that may reach me."

He went out, leaving her insensibly cheered and comforted by their conversation. She reflected that what he said was very likely true, and that if anyone could find Jennifer and bring her safely home, it was Guy Ravenshaw. He was a man who usually accomplished what he set out to do.

Mr. Ravenshaw himself, reaching his own house some ten minutes later, was greeted with the information that his cousin, Mr. Pelham, had called and was waiting to see him. The butler broke this news apologetically, for it was well known to him that the younger Mr. Ravenshaw's visits were at all times an irritation to his cousin, and that this one must seem unusually inopportune. Mr. Ravenshaw, however, gave no sign of displeasure, but merely stood for a moment looking at his servant with an arrested expression in his eyes, and then said softly: "Is he, indeed? Where may I find him?"

"Mr. Pelham is in the Yellow Saloon, sir. I told him that you were not expected to return, but he insisted upon waiting."

Guy nodded, dropped his driving coat into the hands of the waiting footman, and strode across the wide hall. As he entered the Saloon, the slender, foppish figure of his kinsman rose from the chair before the fire where he had been lounging.

"I can give you five minutes, Pelham," Guy greeted him curtly, "for I have many things to do which are of far greater importance than listening to your everlasting demands and reproaches. What is it this time?"

Pelham smiled, the swift, boyish grin which had captivated so many people. He looked charming, candid, and very eager to please.

"What is it at any time, cousin, between you and me?" he asked with engaging simplicity. "It is money, of course! I have come to ask you for twenty thousand pounds."

6

Disobliging Behaviour of Mr. Ravenshaw

IN the long moment of silence which succeeded this remarkable statement, Guy walked slowly forward until he was confronting Pelham across the width of the fireplace. The bright light from the flames flickered impartially over them both, and the faint sounds which drifted in from the Square emphasized rather than disturbed the stillness of the room.

"I see!" Guy said quietly at length. "So I was right in supposing you responsible for Miss Linley's abduction."

Pelham smiled again, and shrugged. "Let us say rather that this time I took precautions to ensure against a refusal. Miss Linley has come to no harm. I have her safely bestowed at a charmingly secluded spot in the country, and without assistance, my dear cousin, neither you nor anyone else is likely to find her. She will be returned to you when you pay me the sum I ask."

Guy's lips twisted contemptuously. "A very one-sided bargain," he said coldly. "I am to give you twenty thousand pounds, with no better assurance than your word—*your* word, Pelham—that Miss Linley will be restored to me safe and unharmed. With no better assurance, in fact, that she is in your hands at all. How am I to know that you are not merely making use of her disappearance in order to extort money from me, when in reality you have no more idea than I have where she is?"

Pelham was still smiling, but his lips had thinned a trifle, and there was an unpleasant glitter in his eyes.

"You have no choice but to take my word that twenty thousand will buy her safety and her freedom," he retorted. "As for proof that I know where she is, perhaps this will satisfy you."

He put his hand into his pocket, and then held it out towards the other man with something glittering in the palm. Guy took the small object and looked at it, and the set of his lips grew perceptibly harder. He had no difficulty at all in recognizing the very fine diamond ring which he had given to Jennifer Linley to mark their betrothal.

"Well?" Pelham said softly. "I took that from her finger myself not four-and-twenty hours ago. You have no choice, you see, but to pay me what I ask, if you wish to recover your bride."

Guy slipped the ring into his pocket. He had not really doubted that Pelham had planned Jennifer's abduction. He had suspected it from the first, and been certain of it from the moment the butler told him that his cousin was waiting to see him, but the sight of the ring had brought home to him, as nothing else had yet done, what that abduction must have meant, in terms of suffering and terror, to a gently-bred young girl. He remembered the abigail's vivid description of the rough way in which her mistress had been carried off, and a deep, fierce anger took possession of him. No outward sign betrayed it, however; he stood quite still, one hand resting lightly on the marble mantelpiece, his gaze fixed thoughtfully upon Pelham's face.

"What if I refuse?" he asked after a moment.

Pelham shrugged. "Surely you can guess? If the money is not forthcoming, I can no longer guarantee Miss Linley's safety. It is as simple as that."

"Is it?" Guy said sardonically. "I know you to be capable of most things, Pelham, and I suspect that you would not hesitate even at murder if you stood to profit from it, but in this case I do not see what you could hope to gain. I know you to be behind this affair, and you could not possibly escape the gallows."

This blunt speech seemed to offend Pelham; he looked pained. "I said nothing of murder, cousin! Miss Linley's life is in no danger at my hands, I give you my word." He paused to see the effect of this, and then went on softly: "Now her honour is a very different matter. At present no one knows that she is in my hands, but they will, Guy. Oh yes, they will! The world will learn that, consumed by a burning passion for my cousin's bride, I carried her off to that secluded spot I spoke of, and that, in spite of appearances, she was by no means unwilling. In short, I will ruin her! I do not think your pride will permit you to marry her after that, and if *I* am to be persuaded to do so, rest assured that it will cost you a great deal more than twenty thousand pounds."

He paused, looking inquiringly at his cousin, but Mr. Ravenshaw neither moved nor spoke. Pelham waited for a moment or two, and then added provocatively: "Devil take it, I believe that would be the more profitable course! Besides, she is a charming little creature, and you do not appreciate her as you should."

He was watching his cousin closely as he spoke, and he had an instant's warning from the sudden blaze of anger which lit the grey eyes. He fell back a pace, his hand going swiftly to his pocket, but Guy, when he chose, could move with a speed astonishing in so big a man, and Pelham's fingers had barely touched the hidden weapon before two iron hands seized him by the throat. He was lifted clean off the floor and shaken to and fro as a dog might shake a rat, until his teeth rattled in his head and he could think of nothing but trying to break the grip of the merciless fingers which were choking the life out of him. He clawed ineffectually at them, struggling frantically for breath, and when at last they loosed their hold as suddenly as they had taken it, he crashed helplessly to the floor and lay gasping like a newly-landed fish.

Guy dropped to one knee beside him, and after a brief search found the little silver-mounted pistol and transferred it to his own pocket. Then he grasped Pelham by the lapels of his elegant coat, and heaved him up and flung him into a chair. He was breathing heavily, but more from anger than exertion.

"You miserable little worm!" he said between his teeth. "So that is what you have in mind, is it? Yes, I can well believe it! You would have no qualms about forcing yourself upon a girl who was your helpless prisoner, but at present, Pelham, you are not dealing with a girl. You are dealing with me, and that is something very different."

Pelham dragged himself more upright in the chair and put a trembling hand to his throat. It felt as though it had been mauled by a wild beast, and he could still only breathe in hoarse, choking gasps, while speech was quite beyond him. Guy studied him contemptuously for a moment or two before he spoke again.

"You have been very free with your demands and with your threats," he said at last. "You have told me at great length what you intend, but now it is my turn to speak, and I am going to tell you what is really going to happen. You are going to tell me, here and now, exactly where Jennifer Linley is imprisoned."

Pelham tried to speak, found it beyond his power, and shook his head vigorously instead. Mr. Ravenshaw, ignoring this, went across to the door, locked it, and dropped the key into his pocket. Then he took off his excellently tailored coat and placed it, together with his waistcoat, across the back of a chair, while Pelham watched these ominous preparations with starting eyes. Guy came back and stood in front of him, hands resting lightly on his hips, his eyes grey and bleak as ice beneath the thick black brows.

"You will tell me, Pelham," he said softly, "because I am going to thrash you until you do."

Pelham cowered in the chair, staring up at him with sheer horror. He was ready enough with a pistol, and was, in fact, a very fine shot, but any more personal form of violence filled him with revulsion.

"You could not," Pelham stammered hoarsely. "You would not dare! The servants—"

A satirical smile curved Mr. Ravenshaw's lips without softening the expression in his eyes.

"I am the master of this house, Pelham," he reminded him, "and my servants know better than to interfere in my affairs. No doubt they will come to investigate any unusual sounds issuing from this room, but as you no doubt observed, I have taken the precaution of locking the door. I fancy they will not venture to force it, if I call out to them, as I shall most certainly do, that they are not to concern themselves with what may be happening in here."

Pelham, knowing this to be true, could find no answer to it. For the second time Guy laid hold of the front of his coat and, apparently without much effort, hoisted him to his feet.

"Well," he said curtly, "which is it to be? Do you tell me now, or must I beat the information out of you? I confess that to do so would afford me infinite satisfaction."

The thought of affording his kinsman any satisfaction at all, coupled as it was with the certainty that he would be forced to give way in the end, obliged Pelham to acknowledge defeat. Thus, at least, he could save his person from violence.

"Let me go! I'll tell you," he said sullenly, adding, with what was almost a sob: "Damn you! Damn you!"

"Very well!" Guy released him so suddenly that he lost his balance, and dropped down again into the chair. "Where is Miss Linley?"

"At a cottage not far from Barnet." Pelham was cherishing his bruised throat again; his voice was a hoarse and sulky murmur. "It belongs to Meake's brother."

"Meake?"

"My manservant. He helped me to arrange the whole affair."

"Indeed?" Guy's voice was sardonic. "How very useful

such a servant must be to you. How many men at the cottage?"

"Only Meake's brother and his son. His daughter is there, too, of course. She is looking after Miss Linley."

"Very obliging of her," Guy said shortly. "Now I will tell you what I mean to do. You will take me at once to this cottage near Barnet, and if I find Miss Linley there, safe and unharmed, and if she assures me that she has been treated with reasonable consideration, I will see that no charges are brought against you. That is not out of concern for you, but because I have no wish for this unsavoury affair to be made public. If, however, Miss Linley *has* suffered any harm beyond the rough handling which I know she received from your hirelings, then I give you my word that no considerations of family pride will save you. I will see you punished to the uttermost limit of the law, if I have to drag the name of Ravenshaw through every court in England to do it. Do I make myself clear?"

Pelham made no reply to this, but remained slumped in the chair, tenderly fingering his throat. Mr. Ravenshaw regarded him in silence for a moment, then turned away, resumed his coat and waistcoat, unlocked the door, and rang for a servant. When a footman appeared, he said briefly: "Send word to the stables to have the greys put to the curricle immediately, and inform me as soon as it is done. My cousin will accompany me, and I do not require the attendance of a groom." He glanced at Pelham, who at the servant's entrance had risen unsteadily to his feet and gone to the mirror which hung upon one wall, where he was trying, without much success, to repair the damage to his neckwear. The mocking note deepened in Mr. Ravenshaw's voice. "Mr. Pelham has had the misfortune to disarrange his cravat. Be good enough to desire Trotter to bring him another. Then fetch writing materials to me here."

Mr. Ravenshaw's servants were too well trained to betray surprise or curiosity, or to accord the oddest commands anything but prompt obedience. In a very few minutes, pen, ink and paper were laid before him, and almost immediately afterwards his valet came into the room with several starched neckcloths hanging over his arm. This privileged person did permit an expression of the utmost disapproval to appear in his face, but as Mr. Ravenshaw left the room almost as soon as Trotter entered it, this entirely failed of its intended effect.

Pelham was still too much shaken by his recent experience to attempt anything but the simplest of styles, and even so his fingers shook so much that he ruined two of the cravats. He had barely succeeded in achieving a passable result when his cousin re-entered the room, nodded dismissal to Trotter and sat down at the table. For several minutes only the scratching of his pen disturbed the silence, then he sanded the paper, folded and sealed it, and wrote a brief direction upon it. As he did so, the door opened to admit the footman, who brought the information that the curricle awaited Mr. Ravenshaw's pleasure. Guy nodded, and glanced at his kinsman.

"Come, Pelham," he said curtly. "The sooner we are on our way the better." He handed the footman the letter he had written, adding briefly: "That to Lady Linley at once."

In sullen silence Pelham followed him out of the room, received his hat and greatcoat from the footman in the hall, and went after Guy down the steps to where the curricle, with four magnificent and perfectly matched greys harnessed to it, was awaiting them. The groom in charge of the team said warningly that they were a trifle fresh, an obvious understatement of a fact which was apparent to the most inexperienced eye, but Mr. Ravenshaw merely nodded in response to this as he mounted to the box-seat. When Pelham had taken his place beside him, and the footman had cast a light rug over their knees, Guy nodded again to the groom, who at once sprang away from the horses' heads. The greys plunged forward, were brought immediately under control, and the curricle swept away from the house and out of the Square by way of Duke Street.

For a time Mr. Ravenshaw was too much occupied in guiding his team through the press of traffic, and Pelham too possessed by fury, to have either the time or the desire for conversation. When they reached the outskirts of the town, however, and were approaching the Tottenham Court turnpike, the younger man asked sullenly: "What did you tell Lady Linley?"

"Merely that certain information had reached me, and that I hoped to restore her daughter to her in the near future," Guy replied briefly. "She will have to be told the truth, of course, but time enough for that when we know the outcome of the affair."

At this ominous remark Pelham relapsed into silence, and for the rest of the journey neither man spoke more than was strictly necessary. Highgate and Finchley fell behind them, the notorious Common was crossed without incident, and they swept through Whetstone without a halt. Some while after this, Pelham broke a long silence to say sulkily: "There is a road to the left a short way ahead. We take that."

"To the left?" Guy glanced at him in quick suspicion. "Miss Linley's abigail told me that her mistress was carried off in an easterly direction."

"So she was, but that was simply to mislead possible pursuit. There was a farm-cart waiting a quarter of a mile away, and once she was hidden in that it crossed the main road again and headed west. Meake's brother knows his business."

"So it would appear, and it is not difficult to guess what that business is. A pretty kind of rogue you have in your service."

The road indicated by Pelham was a narrow one, and led them presently into a tangled maze of lanes. Guy did his best to memorize the route they followed, but it was by no means easy, and even Pelham hesitated once or twice. He excused this by explaining that he had visited the cottage only once before, and then with Samuel Meake to guide him.

They came at length to a narrow, muddy and deeply rutted lane bordered on one side by a dense wood, and Pelham said reluctantly: "The cottage lies just around the next bend. What are you going to do now?"

"One thing I do not intend to do is to advertise my approach," Guy replied curtly, bringing his team to a stand-still. "Get down and lead the horses over to that tree by the roadside and tether them there." He watched his cous-in swing down from the curricle and added mockingly: "If you are thinking of making a bid to reach the cottage ahead of me and rouse your henchmen, I should not ad-vise it. I fancy that I can run a trifle faster than you can."

Pelham made no answer to this, but obeyed his cousin's earlier command in a seething silence. Mr. Ravenshaw sprang to the ground, drew a pistol from his pocket, and with his free hand took a firm grip on Pelham's arm.

"Now we go forward," he said shortly, "and if you utter one sound before I give you leave, it will be the worse for you."

The cottage, when they came in sight of it, proved to be a dilapidated place with a sagging roof, and pieces of rag stuffed into several broken window-panes. A dull after-noon was now giving place to early twilight, and a feeble light shone faintly from one of the lower windows. The cousins walked up the muddy path, and at Guy's com-mand Pelham rapped sharply on the door. There was a brief silence, and then a man's voice demanded gruffly to be told who knocked.

"It is I, Pelham Ravenshaw. Open the door!"

A bolt grated and the door creaked back, revealing the man who had opened it as a bulky silhouette against the light. Guy released Pelham's arm and gave him a vigorous push in the back which sent him staggering heavily against the dim-seen figure, and as they reeled together into the house sprang in after them, slamming the door again and leaning his shoulders against it.

The startled conspirators found themselves covered by a pistol in the hand of a very tall, broad-shouldered gen-tleman with a singularly uncompromising cast of counte-nance. Cold grey eyes looked them over with grim deliber-ation, and the strong mouth curled satirically.

"A very pretty little nest of scoundrels," Mr. Raven-shaw remarked after a moment, "but you chose the wrong pigeon to pluck, my friends, when you lent an ear to my cousin's ingenious schemes. Yes, I am Guy Ravenshaw, and I have come for the lady whom you so ill-advisedly carried off yesterday afternoon. Be good enough to fetch her, one of you! I trust that you have treated her with consideration, for it depends very largely upon what she has to tell me whether or not this affair brings you all to prison."

The inhabitants of the cottage exchanged glances. There were three of them, the big man who had opened the door, a second man who was a younger and slimmer edition of the first, and a well-built young woman in shirt, breeches and riding-boots. After a silence big with suppressed emotion, the elder man jerked his head towards the girl.

"Fetch the wench down!" he told her, and added bitterly: "This is the last time I works with a flash cull, damme if it ain't! Sam and his fine promises! I'd promise him summat if he was here."

While he was speaking, Nancy had taken up one of the two candles burning on the mantelpiece and gone out of the room through a door which opened on to a steep and twisting stair. A faint murmur of voices drifted down to the waiting men, and then the candlelight brightened again on the stair, and a light footstep was heard descending. The skirt of a crumpled, pale-blue gown came into view, and a moment later Guy and Pelham were staring with equal astonishment at a very slender young woman with magnificent red hair above a thin, pale face which neither of them had ever seen before. Guy was the first to recover his voice.

"What the devil——" he exclaimed thunderously, and rounded upon his cousin. "What trickery is this?"

One glance sufficed to tell him that if trickery had been practised, then Pelham, as well as he, was the victim of it. The younger man's face was a study, in which astonishment, mystification and wrath struggled for supremacy. After one pregnant moment, wrath triumphed and found strangled utterance.

"God in Heaven!" he said feelingly. "The damned, blundering fools have kidnapped the wrong woman!"

7

A Crisis and a Confession

THE elder Mr. Meake, his professional pride cut to the quick by the imputation of blundering, was quick to defend himself. His ruddy countenance took on a deeper tinge, and he said indignantly: "The wrong woman, is it? This is the gentry mort as we took from the chaise Sam pointed out to us, my bully, and if she ain't to your liking that's no fault of ours!"

"Then that block-headed brother of yours picked the wrong carriage," Pelham replied furiously. "This is not Jennifer Linley. We have never seen this woman before in our lives."

"One moment, Pelham!" Guy broke in sharply. "Who this young woman may be I have no idea, but she was certainly taken from Lady Linley's chaise, and her abduction reported by her ladyship's servants. Moreover, there is the ring you took from her finger. It is, without the shadow of a doubt, that which I gave to Miss Linley."

"But I don't understand," Pelham said blankly. "What was she doing there? Where is Miss Linley?"

"That, I fancy, is something which only the lady herself can tell us." Guy's voice was grim. "We have both been duped, along with a number of other people." His commanding glance returned to Miss Cresswell, who was still standing on the lowest stair with Nancy's astonished and bewildered face peering over her shoulder. "Enlighten us, ma'am, I pray! Elucidate this mystery."

Caroline drew a deep breath. Nancy had hustled her downstairs without any explanation, and she had been considerably taken aback to behold two fashionably-dressed gentlemen, the elder of whom was apparently holding her captors at pistol-point. Pelham's voice she had recognized instantly, though she was still not quite certain who he was. Of his companion's identity the brief conversation had left her in no doubt whatsoever. This tall, black-browed stranger was the formidable Guy Ravenshaw himself.

"It is really very simple," she said after a moment, with a calmness which she was far from feeling. "Jennifer and I changed places just before the chaise was held up."

Mr. Ravenshaw's brows lifted a fraction, as though the refined accents of her voice came as a surprise to him. He left his position by the door and moved farther into the room, looking at her very hard. Pelham said impatiently: "Why the devil should you do such a thing? Where is Jennifer Linley now?"

Caroline looked him straight in the eye. "Who you may be, sir, I do not know," she told him roundly, "except that you are the instigator of this deplorable affair, and I shall certainly not explain to you either Miss Linley's actions, or my own. They are no concern of yours."

A gleam of amusement lit Guy Ravenshaw's eyes for a moment, and was gone. He said with ironic courtesy:

"Perhaps you will be good enough to explain them to me, ma'am. As Miss Linley's future husband, my interest, as I trust you will agree, is not altogether impertinent."

"Certainly I will tell you, Mr. Ravenshaw," Caroline said with dignity, "but *you* will agree, I think, that this is neither the time nor the place for such an explanation."

Whether or not he would have agreed was never known, for at that moment the conversation was brought to an abrupt conclusion. The younger Mr. Meake had been standing somewhat apart from the rest of the group, and by Guy's movement from the door was now just out of Mr. Ravenshaw's range of vision. While the others talked, he had been cautiously and unobtrusively edging his fingers towards a heavy riding-whip which lay on the table beside him; now at last they closed about it, and at the same moment he sprang forward, bringing the whip down with all his strength across Guy's right arm. With an involuntary gasp of pain Guy dropped the pistol, and before he could retrieve it, the elder Meake had grappled with him. His son leapt to his assistance as Guy broke free and sent his assailant sprawling, and in an instant all was confusion, while Pelham backed into a corner out of harm's way, and the two women stood as though rooted to the stairs by astonishment and dismay.

Mr. Ravenshaw was giving a good account of himself, and it began to look as though, despite the odds against him, he would emerge victorious from the conflict. Pelham's glance went longingly to the pistol which had been kicked beneath the table, but with so fierce a fight going on in that confined space he did not care to risk leaving his refuge to possess himself of it.

Suddenly a new and unexpected element added itself to the struggle. The outer door of the cottage opened a little way, and through the narrow aperture a thin, stoop-shouldered man slid into the room. He had a pistol in his hand, but he was grasping it by the barrel, and, moving forward with a silent cat-like movement, he brought the butt of the weapon down in a terrific blow on the back of Guy's head before the other man even suspected his presence.

Mr. Ravenshaw crashed to the floor, and in a moment

the younger Meake was kneeling astride his prostrate figure, while the elder, wiping a trickle of blood from his
chin with the back of his hand, said breathlessly: "Well
done, Sam! Who'd have thought a flash cull like that could
put up such a fight? I'd like to see him in the Ring, damme
if I wouldn't!"

"I apprehend," replied Samuel Meake in the precise
voice which contrasted oddly with his brother's rough
tones, "that Mr. Guy Ravenshaw is well known as an am-
ateur pugilist. That is why I had no hesitation in striking
him down from behind."

"And a good job you made of it," his nephew informed
him, getting to his feet. "Out like a light, he is! He won't
give us no more trouble yet awhile."

Pelham moved swiftly forward, picked up Mr. Ravenshaw's pistol, examined it briefly, and then turned towards
his cousin's inanimate form with so murderous an expression in his face that Caroline uttered an involuntary cry of
alarm and protest, and the eldest Mr. Meake, apparently
sharing her fears, seized Pelham by the arm and wrested
the weapon from him again.

"No, you don't, my buck!" he said grimly. "Highway
robbery and a trifle o' kidnapping's one thing, but murder
I don't hold with, and never will."

"And you could never profit by such a deed, sir, even
though you are your cousin's heir," Samuel pointed out
reasonably. "It is known to a number of persons that you
left London in Mr. Guy's company, and you would be the
first to be suspected if he disappeared."

Pelham jerked his arm free of Meake's grasp and
walked across to the fireplace, saying sullenly over his
shoulder: "I know that, confound you! How did you arrive so opportunely, anyway?"

The valet spread his hands in a deprecating gesture.
"As you are aware, sir, I could not help feeling that you
were a trifle too complacent in your estimate of Mr. Guy's
reaction to your demand, so I took the liberty of following
you to his house. When I saw you set out together, I knew
that my fears had been justified. Fortunately, the busy
state of the streets enabled me to keep the curricle in sight

long enough to discover in which direction you were travelling, and as soon as I felt certain of your destination, I obtained a horse and followed you. Naturally, I had no hope of overtaking those greys, but I know this neighbourhood very well, and by going across country was able to arrive here not very long after you."

"Never mind all that," his brother broke in impatiently. "I'll not deny you done us a good turn, Sam, coming when you did, but it's what's to be done next as is most important now. Seems to me as this flash cove here ain't the sort to take kindly to being knocked on the head, and I'd as lief not be by when he comes to his senses."

"Can't we hold him to ransom?" his son suggested eagerly. "He's well-breeched, ain't he?"

Pelham considered this suggestion, biting his lips and glaring at Guy's recumbent form, but eventually shook his head.

"Too risky," he said regretfully. "Any number of people saw me drive out of Town with him, and I dare say we were remarked on our way here, also. It's not often a turn-out like those greys is seen in such a God-forsaken part of the country." He walked across to his cousin, grasped his shoulder, and rolled him over on to his back. Mr. Ravenshaw lay inert, with no sign of returning consciousness, and Pelham stood upright again. "Our wisest course is to leave before he comes round. Are your horses here?"

The Meakes assured him that they were, and were advised to saddle them without delay. The young man went at once to do this, and Pelham added to the elder: "Take Samuel's horse with you. He will come with me in the curricle, and I desire to leave no convenient mount for my cousin's use. Presently we will appoint a rendezvous, where I will pay you for your part in this, though I fear the sum will not be as great as we had hoped."

Mr. Meake jerked his head towards Miss Cresswell. "What about her?"

"Ah, yes! The fair unknown!" Pelham turned to face the stairs, where Caroline was still standing. "I was forgetting her. Bring her over here."

Thrust forward by Nancy, Caroline advanced into the

room until she stood face to face with Pelham. He set upright a stout wooden chair and pushed her roughly into it. "Tie her up," he said briefly. "We'll leave her here as consolation for my cousin when he comes to his senses."

He watched this command obeyed, Nancy fetching a length of stout cord from a cupboard and first lashing Miss Cresswell's arms together behind her, and then passing another cord round her body and the back of the chair. Caroline endured this indignity in silence, merely casting a very speaking glance at Pelham where he stood leaning against the overturned table. He met it with his disarming grin.

"I wish I could spare the time to find out who you are," he remarked, "and why Miss Linley found it necessary to exchange identities with you, though since the exchange took place on the road to the Border, I might perhaps hazard a guess as to its purpose. However, you will have ample opportunity to discuss the matter with my cousin, and he, after all, is more closely concerned than I." He laughed softly. "I would give much to hear that conversation. His head will ache abominably and he will be in the devil's own temper, while you, unless I am much mistaken, have a spirit to match your hair."

On one point at least, Pelham had judged accurately. When Mr. Ravenshaw began to come round, the first thing of which he was aware was a pounding agony in his head which made it feel several sizes too large. He opened his eyes, but a light of incredible brilliance seemed to be shining directly upon his face, and he hurriedly closed them again. After a little while something cool and damp was laid across his forehead, and a woman's voice said encouragingly: "Come, sir, try again! I have moved the candle, and its light will not trouble you any more."

Cautiously he opened his eyes again, and this time the blinding light had faded to a gentle radiance, against which the outline of a head and shoulders seemed to swim into his vision. The light gleamed ruddily on red hair, and Mr. Ravenshaw's memory returned. He struggled to sit up, and was assisted to do so by an arm about his shoulders.

He found that he had been lying on the dirty floor of a small room which looked as though it was suffering from the effects of an earthquake, its meagre furnishings broken and overturned. Almost the only piece of furniture remaining upright was a plain wooden chair which stood nearby with a tangle of cord lying beside it. Mr. Ravenshaw fixed his gaze upon it and said thickly to the woman who knelt beside him: "Help me up!"

She obeyed him in silence, but the room spun round him and the pounding in his head was sickeningly increased. He reeled into the chair with a groan which would not be stifled, and leaning his elbows on his knees, took his throbbing head in his hands. Miss Cresswell, standing beside him, laid gentle, exploratory fingers on the thick waves of black hair.

"There is no wound," she said reassuringly after a moment, "and I do not think any serious injury has been done, though there is a very large bump indeed. I dare say your head aches exceedingly, but it will be better directly."

Mr. Ravenshaw winced, and moved away from her hand. "That is the most fatuous remark I have ever heard," he said disagreeably. "Good God, ma'am! do you have to speak to me as though I were in the nursery?"

"Your cousin said that you would be in the devil's own temper when you came round," Caroline remarked equably, "and I see now that he was perfectly right. Not that I am blaming you, of course. You have every reason to be ill-humoured." She went across the corner cupboard, adding over her shoulder: "I have found some brandy. I dare say it is a very poor sort, but it may help you to feel more the thing."

Mr. Ravenshaw accepted the thick, chipped glass with a grudging word of thanks, and sat sipping its contents and trying to recall the details of the events which had followed his arrival at the cottage. Miss Cresswell picked up a three-legged stool which lay on its side near the hearth, set it on its feet and sat down, clasping her hands in her lap and fixing her gaze upon the smouldering logs. After some minutes had crept by in silence, Guy said abruptly: "Who knocked me on the head?"

Caroline looked up. "Your cousin's servant had followed you from London, and slipped into the cottage while you were defending yourself from the other men. I do wish I had cried out to warn you, but he was so quick that it was all over before I realized what was happening." She seemed to feel that this needed some excuse, and added apologetically: "You were all fighting so very violently, and I had never seen such a thing before, and although not precisely alarmed, I felt a good deal bewildered."

He made no comment on this, merely saying: "What has become of my cousin and his confederates? Why have they left us alone?"

She told him all that she had been able to discover of Pelham's intentions, concluding apologetically: "Before he left, your cousin went through your pockets, and took all your money and valuables, even to the signet ring you wore on your finger. Just as he was leaving he gave me a message for you." She hesitated, but Mr. Ravenshaw did not speak, merely continuing to regard her with those exceedingly hard and penetrating grey eyes. Caroline's chin lifted a little, and she added with some relish: "He said, 'tell Guy that it will be good for him to be obliged to depend for once upon his own wits, instead of upon wealth and consequence.'"

"Impudent young dog!" Guy spoke without heat. "He will learn, if he has not done so already, that I am not so easily defeated. However, that can wait! You say they left you bound to a chair. How did you contrive to free yourself?"

"It was not very difficult, though it took a little time. Nancy tied me up, and I think she must deliberately have knotted the cords so that I should be able to escape from them. She is really quite a good sort of girl, and has been very kind to me since they brought me here."

"Since they brought you here," Guy repeated coldly. "It is time, I think, that you told me how that came about. You said that you changed places with Miss Linley. Why? Where is she now?"

Caroline clasped her hands more tightly together, and

drew a deep breath. This was the moment she had been dreading.

"Yes, it is time," she said in a low voice. "I am sorry to have to tell you, Mr. Ravenshaw, that Jennifer is at present on her way to Gretna Green with the gentleman whom she truly desires to marry."

There was a long and, to Caroline, nerve-wracking pause. Guy Ravenshaw sat very still, leaning forward with his elbows on his knees and the empty glass balanced between his hands; his eyes had widened a fraction, but that was the only change in his expression and it was in vain that Caroline searched the strong, dark face for some hint of the emotions aroused by her confession.

"I see!" he said at last, and though his voice was quiet, she felt as though the lash of a whip had curled about her body. "Miss Linley fancies herself in love, and you, prompted by the usual feminine weakness for what is commonly regarded as romance, have assisted her to make what is probably a highly unsuitable match."

"It is nothing of the kind!" Now that the unbearable silence had been broken, Caroline felt able to defend herself. "Captain Wilde is eligible in every way, and Jenny was as good as promised to him long before you ever set eyes upon her."

This time his expression did change; he said abruptly: "If that is so, ma'am, why did she consent to become my wife? Or, having consented, why did she suffer yet another change of heart?"

"It is a long story, sir," Caroline replied quietly, "but, if you will consent to hear it, you will agree, I think, that neither Jennifer nor Captain Wilde is to be blamed. Chance played a cruel trick upon them, and then——" she broke off, looking inquiringly at him. "Well, Mr. Ravenshaw? Shall I tell you the whole?"

He nodded, putting the glass down on the floor by his chair. "'I beg that you will, ma'am, but first I should like to know your name."

"It is Caroline Cresswell, sir. I am distantly related to Captain Wilde, and have known both him and Jenny for many years."

He bowed slightly in acknowledgment of this information, and Caroline launched at once into a full description of the situation. Guy heard her to the end without interrupting, and even then sat for some moments in silence before he made any comment.

"Why was I not told of this?" he said at last. "Good God! does the poor child think me such a monster that I would hold her to a betrothal entered into under such a misapprehension?"

He had spoken, it seemed, more to himself than to her, but nevertheless Caroline ventured to reply.

"Forgive me, sir, but I do not think Jenny was ever given the opportunity to know you well enough to guess what your reaction to such news might be. Besides, what could you have done, even if you were sympathetic to her distress? *You* could not in honour have cried off from the engagement, and I assure you that *she* would not have been permitted to do so."

He directed another of his hard, penetrating glances towards her. Caroline met it levelly, and after a moment he nodded.

"I understand you, I believe. Measured by material standards, Captain Wilde's resources do not compare with mine." He rose a trifle unsteadily to his feet, moved nearer to the fire, and kicked with one booted foot at the sullenly smouldering logs. There was contempt in his voice. "Too many people judge by those standards, and by those alone."

"That is very true," Caroline agreed gravely. She hesitated, and then added with some diffidence: "I have to ask your forgiveness, sir. I do not regret what I did, for Jenny could never be happy with any man but Roland, but I am exceedingly sorry if I have caused you pain."

He glanced quickly down at her. "Do not disturb yourself, Miss Cresswell. I was not in love with Jennifer Linley, and if my pride has suffered a jolt, no doubt it will do me more good than harm. The world will enjoy a laugh at my expense, but that does not unduly trouble me."

Caroline regarded him approvingly. "I must say, sir, that you have taken this remarkably well. I confess that had I known it was to be my lot to make known the truth to you, I should have been less ready to play my part."

Guy turned more fully to face her; his expression was ironic. "If, as you assert, Miss Linley can find happiness with no one but Captain Wilde, then in assisting their elopement you have done me a service as well as them. I should say that you have had by far the worst of the bargain. You have been kidnapped, insulted, imprisoned, and now find yourself in a situation which is far from enviable."

"Oh?" Caroline eyed him rather warily. "How, sir, am I to take that?"

He raised his brows. "Have you forgotten, ma'am, that we are marooned in an isolated cottage with no means of conveyance, with the prospect of a long and tiring walk through muddy lanes before we can obtain assistance? Also that I have been robbed of every penny, and every article of value which I might have sold or pledged when we do reach a town or village? And I have no doubt that you are in like case."

"Yes, I am," Miss Cresswell admitted regretfully. "In fact, the only article of value I had with me when I was carried off was Jenny's diamond ring, and that your cousin took from me yesterday."

"Precisely. However, nothing is to be gained by delay. If you will fetch your cloak, ma'am, we will set off at once."

Caroline regarded him in silence for a moment, and then transferred her gaze to the window. It was now quite dark, and rain was lashing against the panes.

"Are you familiar with the roads in these parts, sir?" she inquired thoughtfully.

He was not, and remembering the confusion of narrow lanes through which he had come, was conscious of a qualm of doubt. Scorning to betray it, he said briefly: "I shall find the way, never fear! Will you come, ma'am?"

"How far do you suppose we shall have to walk?" she asked, not moving from her seat by the fire.

"Some three or four miles, I should imagine."

"Three or four miles," Caroline repeated pensively. "I see. In that case, Mr. Ravenshaw, I must decline your invitation. I shall remain here."

"Pray do not be absurd, ma'am," he said impatiently. "I cannot leave you alone in a place like this."

The green-grey eyes met his in a wide, direct stare; she said simply: "Why not?"

"Why not?" he repeated blankly, and then went on with growing exasperation: "This man Meake and his family are professional thieves. You cannot spend the night alone in a house which is probably a rendezvous for every highwayman who frequents Finchley Common."

"I shall dislike it excessively, of course," Caroline agreed candidly, "but I should dislike it even more to spend the night tramping about unfamiliar countryside in pitch darkness and pouring rain. I am sensible of your concern for my safety, but I dare say I shall contrive tolerably well on my own. Goodnight, Mr. Ravenshaw!"

She moved from her stool to kneel by the hearth, stirring the embers to life and placing fresh logs upon them from the pile in the inglenook. Guy stared at her for a moment or two with an astonishment which rapidly gave way to anger. Miss Cresswell picked up the bellows and plied them vigorously. Mr. Ravenshaw directed a final, smouldering glance in her direction and then looked about him for his hat; finding it in a corner of the room, he picked it up, brushed it with the sleeve of his coat, and saying savagely: "Goodnight, ma'am!" strode across to the door.

Caroline made no reply to this beyond advising him to see if the cottage could provide him with a lantern, but instead of following this excellent advice, Mr. Ravenshaw flung open the door. A violent gust of cold wind hurled icy raindrops against his face, and the darkness of the storm-swept night yawned blackly before him, except where, just outside the door, the light from the interior of the cottage showed a foot or so of the garden path as a swirling rivulet of liquid mud.

He hesitated, and cast an involuntary glance over his

shoulder. The fire was now blazing merrily, and Miss Cresswell, apparently satisfied with it, was inspecting the contents of the larder.

"Ham, cold beef, eggs, butter, cheese," she remarked as though to herself. "Nancy is a better housekeeper than she is a cook. I wonder where she keeps the bread?" She raised her voice a little to add over her shoulder: "Pray make haste and close the door, Mr. Ravenshaw! The fire is beginning to smoke."

Guy looked again at the uninviting prospect outside, while his inherent dislike of being bested struggled with a variety of other emotions. He remembered the difficulty with which Pelham had found his way to the cottage even in broad daylight; he allowed himself to admit that his headache, which he had been trying to ignore, was in fact exceedingly unpleasant; he recollected that he had not dined that day. Another assault by wind and rain clinched the matter. He closed the door, tossed his hat on to a chair and his driving-coat after it, while Caroline, turning from the cupboard, viewed these actions with apparent surprise.

"So you are not going after all," she remarked cordially. "Oh well, no doubt you know best!"

Guy walked across the room towards her and stood looking down into those wide and apparently guileless eyes. His own countenance was unsmiling, but the set of his lips had become less grim, and the beginnings of rueful laughter lurked in his eyes.

"There is no necessity to turn the knife in the wound, Miss Cresswell," he informed her gravely. "Permit me to tell you that you are a designing female, and that it will not be wonderful if your murdered corpse is found here by the next person to visit this place."

Caroline chuckled. "That is a great deal better," she said approvingly, "for what is to be gained, in a situation such as this, by standing upon one's dignity? Now just help me to set the table on its legs again, and then sit down by the fire, like a sensible man, while I see what I can contrive for our supper."

8

April Morning

WHEN Mr. Ravenshaw awoke the following morning, it was some moments before he could recollect where he was. He was accustomed to waking in surroundings of extreme luxury, but now a cracked and stained ceiling, walls badly marked with damp, and a window uncurtained by anything but cobwebs met his affronted gaze. He lay regarding these depressing objects for a moment or two until an incautious movement against the lumpy pillow served, by informing him that the back of his head was extremely tender, to remind him of the events of the previous day.

He sat up, thankful to discover that the raging headache with which he had fallen asleep had now gone, and observed that beyond the dirty window-panes a clear blue sky gave promise of a fine day. Apparently the storm had blown itself out during the night, and Miss Cresswell's judgment was thus proved to be better than his. The long walk which lay before them, though still far from desirable, would be infinitely less unpleasant than it would have been in the rain and the darkness.

He flung back the blankets which covered him and swung his feet to the floor, becoming aware as he did so that a delicious aroma of frying bacon was drifting up from the kitchen. He had lain down in shirt and breeches, and as he had not so much as a comb in his pocket, there was little he could do about his appearance; he washed his hands and face in the very small basin which stood on a table in one corner, smoothed his hair as much as possible, and did the best he could with a limp and crumpled cravat. Then he pulled on his boots, resumed his coat and waistcoat, and went downstairs.

In the kitchen the table was already set for breakfast, and Miss Cresswell, singing softly to herself, was busy by a bright fire. Her cambric gown was soiled and creased, and one of its flounces torn, but her beautiful hair was becomingly arranged, and altogether she looked so fresh and neat that Mr. Ravenshaw, acutely aware of his own unshaven and generally dishevelled appearance, felt unreasonably irritated. She greeted him with a smile, and expressed the hope that he was feeling better.

"Thank you, ma'am, I feel perfectly well," he replied curtly, "though I will own that I am not in quite such excellent spirits as you appear to be."

"Well, you cannot imagine how delightful it is not to be imprisoned any longer in that poky little bedroom," Caroline replied cheerfully. "Besides, it is such a beautiful day."

He made no reply to this, but opened the cottage door and looked out. It was indeed a very fine spring morning, with fluffy white clouds sailing across the blue sky, and a brisk breeze shaking the branches with their mist of new green leaves. Mr. Ravenshaw observed and appreciated these facts, but since he was a practical man he noticed also that the garden and the lane beyond were dotted with large puddles and inches deep in mud. Glancing over his shoulder at Miss Cresswell, and seeing that she was shod only in the lightest of blue kid sandals, secured with satin ribbons, he reflected ironically that her opinion of the beauty of the day was not likely to survive more than the first hundred yards of their journey.

He closed the door and returned to the table, where he consumed in silence the excellent breakfast set before him. Caroline apologized for the fact that ale was the only drink she could find to offer him, the Meake family apparently holding in contempt such beverages as tea and coffee; she herself was drinking water. Guy said absently that ale would do very well, and lapsed again into silence, for he was considering the plight in which they found themselves and liking it less with every passing minute.

It was not the theft of his money and other valuables that he resented, or even of his carriage and horses, though he was conscious of a pang of regret at the loss of his cherished greys. He knew that Pelham, seething with fury at the failure of his plot, had been concerned not merely to escape, but also to place his cousin in the most humiliating situation he could devise. He had succeeded very well. Alone, Guy would have had not the smallest hesitation in making the whole journey to London on foot, but with Miss Cresswell to consider this was out of the question. Nor could he abandon her, in spite of the trick she had played upon him. Pelham would have done so without a qualm, but he had read his cousin's character accurately enough to be sure that such a thought would never even enter Guy's head.

Caroline had made one or two attempts at conversation, but finding these answered quite at random, fell silent and applied herself to her own breakfast. Only when the meal was over did Mr. Ravenshaw seem to become aware of her presence; then, leaning back in his chair, he said with a slight smile: "I make you my compliments, ma'am. You are an excellent cook. It seems to me, however, that you are unusually silent this morning."

Caroline laughed. "I kept house for my father, sir, long enough to know that when a gentleman gets up in the morning in a certain mood, it is wiser to wait until he has eaten his breakfast before talking to him."

"That, Miss Cresswell," he replied gravely, "is an example which every woman should follow. I have an aunt who prides herself on her frankness, and invariably chooses breakfast-time for the most devastating exhibitions of it. If ever I have the misfortune to be staying in the same house with her, I make a point of avoiding her until noon at least. But I am sorry that I appear to you in so disagreeable a light."

Caroline shook her head, and made a laughing disclaimer. She did not find Mr. Ravenshaw at all disagreeable, nor was she cast into alarm by his frequently mordant remarks; it was difficult for her to see why such people as Jenny and Letitia considered him overbearing and harsh. Miss Cresswell could detect no sign of it. During the previous evening, while she struggled to free herself from her bonds, and he lay unconscious almost at her feet, she had had a unique opportunity to study him, and she had liked what she saw. He was very different from the mental picture of him which she had formed from the opinions of her friends. Strong-willed, certainly, and disliking very much not to get his own way, but, as she had proved to her own satisfaction, it was possible to turn him from a chosen course if one set about it in the right manner. She remembered Letty's indulgent references to Pelham Ravenshaw, and decided that the world was very much at fault in the judgment it had made between the two cousins.

"If I have seemed silent," Guy resumed after a moment, "it is because I have been trying to decide what will be the best course for us to follow, for, to be frank with you, I was in no case to consider it last night. I think that as soon as we reach another house I will ask to be directed to the nearest magistrate, to whom I will spin some tale of us having been set upon and robbed, and request his help. Once I can get a message to my house in London, our difficulties will soon be over."

Caroline agreed to this, though she could not help feeling that while it might be true of Mr. Ravenshaw's problems, her own might prove to be less easily solved. Not wishing to appear tiresome, she merely said: "Will that not put the authorities on your cousin's track? I know he deserves to be punished, but surely any public scandal will be excessively distasteful to you?"

"Extremely so, ma'am, though I am being brought rapidly to the conclusion that even that would be a small price to pay to be rid of the young scoundrel once and for all. I have borne with a good deal from him over a period of years, but this time he has gone too far."

Caroline rested her elbows on the table and her chin on her linked hands, her wide, thoughtful gaze on her companion's face. "Were you his guardian, sir?"

Guy nodded. "Yes, for my sins I occupied that unenviable position for six years, and when he came of age I gave thanks that our association was at an end at last." An expression of self-mockery came into his face. "I found that I had rejoiced too soon. While he was my ward I had been able to exert some authority over him, but once he was his own master it was a very different matter. My only hold upon him lay in the fact that he has very little money of his own, and yet is wildly extravagant. As long as I would pay his debts I could, to a certain extent, compel him to obey me."

"And I suppose," Caroline said reflectively, "that this time you refused to pay them?"

"Precisely, and you perceive what has come of it." Guy pushed back his chair and rose to his feet. "Well, Miss Cresswell, I believe that nothing is to be gained by lingering here. We had better take advantage of the present delightful weather, for I fancy it is a deal too fine to last."

"What a depressing thing to say," Caroline remarked as she got up. "Still, I have no desire to stay here any longer, so I will fetch my cloak immediately."

She went upstairs, and when she came down again a few minutes later, Mr. Ravenshaw was waiting for her by the open door. Caroline hesitated on the doorstep, eyeing the morass before her with some dismay, but she made no comment, and merely picked her way carefully between the puddles with her skirts caught up in one hand. Despite all her care, however, they had not walked a hundred yards along the lane before her shoes and stockings, as well as the lower flounces of her dress, were soaked through and liberally splashed with mud, and Mr. Ravenshaw, going dry-shod in riding boots, waited for some complaint. It did not come, and when Miss Cresswell did at length break the silence, it was merely to remark with determined brightness upon the beauty of a clump of larch trees in all the glory of their spring foliage.

Some three-quarters of a mile from the cottage they came to a point where the road swept in a wide curve about the foot of a hill, while straight before them a narrow path wound upwards through meadowland to disappear over the crest of the rise. Guy paused, remembering the spot from his drive with Pelham the previous day.

"I believe that path would shorten our journey considerably," he remarked. "Unless I am much mistaken, it rejoins this same road on the other side of the hill."

"Then let us take it, by all means," Caroline replied promptly, "for it appears to be considerably less muddy than the lane."

In this she was presently proved correct, for though the path itself was wet and slippery, the grass on either side of it, sodden though it was with rain, was far easier to walk upon than the miry, stone-strewn surface of the road. It was a steep climb, but when the summit was reached a broad view of rolling countryside lay before them, and in the distance, bowered in trees, the spire of a church could be seen. Guy released Caroline's hand, which he had taken to help her up the last few yards of the climb, and pointed towards the spire.

"That, I fancy, is the nearest village. We passed through it yesterday on our way to the cottage. There is an inn there which appeared to be quite tolerable."

Caroline received this information in silence, and refrained from pointing out to him that in their present penniless state it could matter very little whether the inn were tolerable or not. It was plain to her that Mr. Ravenshaw was so much in the habit of going where he liked and giving what orders he chose, that he had forgotten that in this out-of-the-way place, where neither his name nor his face were known, his credit could not be as sound as it was elsewhere. It would be time enough to remind him of that when they reached the village.

She looked again towards the church spire, and stifled a sigh. It seemed to be a very long way off, and if other houses lay between they were not visible from where she stood. The good spirits with which she had faced the new day were fading rapidly. She was not dressed for country walking, and though she had felt warm enough as she climbed the hill, here on the summit the wind bit keenly, penetrating her light cloak; her skirts clung dankly about her ankles, and though the wet grass had washed most of the mud from her shoes, they were still soaked through and her feet numb with cold. She shivered, and said, trying to sound less discouraged than she felt: "Shall we go on our way, then? It will take some time to reach the village."

She set off down the hill without waiting for a reply, and Guy followed her without making one. The path led them presently into a thick copse, where the sunlight filtered through the branches to dapple mossy banks thick with primroses and violets, but Miss Cresswell was no longer in a mood to enjoy the beauties of nature. When Mr. Ravenshaw, with a note of unmistakable amusement in his voice, solemnly drew her attention to them, she paid no heed whatsoever, merely walking on ahead of him with head held high and shoulders very erect. A moment later she stepped on a root of a tree protruding from the path, and uttered an involuntary exclamation as it bruised her foot through the thin sole of her shoe.

"I cannot imagine why women wear such preposterous footgear," Mr. Ravenshaw remarked with maddening superiority. "If those absurd sandals are suitable for any surface less smooth than a drawing-room floor, I shall be very much surprised."

It was too much. Caroline stopped dead in her tracks and swung round to face him, a faint, becoming colour in her cheeks and her eyes fairly blazing.

"That, sir, is a remark as obvious as it is uncalled-for!" she said furiously. "Had I known, when I set out from London, that I should be put to the necessity of tramping for miles across country, I would have dressed myself accordingly. As I had not then made the acquaintance of the peculiar standards of behaviour obtaining in your family, I did not foresee the need to equip myself against them."

She turned her back on him and went on down the hill, and as Guy followed her he was smiling faintly to himself. Her failing spirits had not escaped his observation, and he hoped that after that outburst, which he had deliberately provoked, anger would, for a time at least, keep her mind from the difficulties of their uncomfortable journey.

At the foot of the hill the road once more came in sight, and the path ended at a stile. Guy vaulted easily over this and turned with outstretched hand to assist Miss Cresswell. She ignored him, and gathering her skirts together stepped daintily over, but the dignified effect of the gesture was ruined by the fact that her foot slipped on the damp wood, and only her companion's ready arm saved her from a fall.

"The just reward of ill-humour!" Mr. Ravenshaw said sardonically, setting her on her feet again. The expected retort did not come, and looking down at her, he saw that her face was white and her lower lip caught between her teeth. "What is it?" he added quickly. "Did you hurt yourself?"

"My ankle!" Caroline's voice shook a little. "But it is nothing. It will be better directly."

Mr. Ravenshaw paid no heed to this. Lifting her up to sit on the stile, he said imperatively: "Which one?"

"The left," Caroline replied, "but indeed—" she broke off, for it was obvious that he was not attending, and a moment later she found herself suffering the embarrassment of having her foot taken in a light, firm clasp, her sandal untied, and the damaged ankle examined by gentle fingers.

"I do not think any serious harm has been done," he said at length, "though you must certainly have wrenched it rather badly. Sit still and rest for a while."

He loosely tied the ribbon of the sandal and then stood upright, wiping the mud from his fingers with his handkerchief and looking thoughtfully about him. Miss Cresswell fought a short struggle with herself, but in the end her sense of justice triumphed over injured feelings and she said in a small voice: "I am very sorry. It was entirely my own fault, and you have every right to be angry with me."

He shot her a quick, suspicious glance, then, seeing that she was in earnest, his expression relaxed and he said with a smile: "I am not angry, ma'am, and in any event the accident was largely my fault for teasing you as I did. What *is* worrying me is how I am now to convey you to the village."

"I shall walk there, of course," Caroline declared stoutly. "My foot needs only to be rested for a little while. Indeed, it feels distinctly better already."

If he had doubts on that score, he did not voice them, and for a while there was silence. Then Caroline said, rather diffidently: "There is one question, Mr. Ravenshaw, which has been plaguing me ever since last night, and though you will probably consider it vastly impertinent, and give me a sharp set-down, ask it I must. If you do not feel a strong romantic attachment for Jenny, why did you offer for her?"

He laughed, and leaned one hand on the topmost bar of the stile. "Impertinent or not, it is a very logical question. I offered for her because eighteen months ago my only brother died childless, and Pelham became my heir. By far the greater part of my fortune is entailed, and would inevitably pass to him." He shrugged. "You have met Pelham, Miss Cresswell, and been privileged to see him in his true colours rather than in the disguise he usually assumes. Need I say more?"

"No, indeed!" Caroline shook her head. "But why Jenny? You offered for her almost as soon as she appeared in Society."

Guy shrugged again. "Unlike most young ladies, she seemed to me to be a quiet and sensible sort of girl, one who would indulge in no nonsensical romantic fancies, but would be content with an arrangement of duty and convenience. To me the most astonishing aspect of this whole affair is the fact that she allowed herself to be persuaded into anything as unconventional as a flight to Gretna Green."

Caroline was regarding him with growing amazement. "Good gracious!" she exclaimed. "I see now that I have done you a greater service than I supposed. My dear sir, if a quiet and dutiful wife is what you desire, Jenny would not do at all. Why, she is the greatest madcap imaginable, full of romantic notions and for ever getting into some kind of scrape. She will plunge headlong into any venture that appeals to her, with no thought for the consequences."

"I would never have supposed it," he replied, beginning to laugh. "I cannot allow her to be unique, though, in impetuosity and disregard for the consequences. Permit me to tell you, Miss Cresswell, that upon *your* lips that criticism is sadly out of place."

Caroline was disconcerted to feel the colour rising in her cheeks. She could not account for it at all. She had more than once found herself the object of undesired gallantry, and had dealt with it efficiently and without agitation. Why then should she blush like a schoolgirl because Guy Ravenshaw looked at her with laughter in his eyes, and made a remark which not even the most vivid imagination could regard as anything more than a friendly jest? Clearly it was time to bring to as speedy an end as possible the dangerous isolation in which they found themselves.

As though in answer to that unspoken thought, the sound of plodding hooves and creaking wheels came faintly to her ears, and in a very short while a farm-cart, drawn by a stout horse and with a skinny youth riding on one of the shafts, came into view around the bend of the lane. Mr. Ravenshaw uttered an exclamation of satisfaction, and strode forward to meet it.

From her seat on the stile Caroline could not hear what he said, but when it became evident, as it did after some discussion between the two men, that the custodian of the cart was prepared to assist them, she stepped carefully to the ground and limped towards them. Guy came to meet her, taking her arm and saying in a low voice: "He is going to the village, and is willing for you to ride in his cart. He seems to be very slow-witted, for he did not even inquire how we come to be in this plight."

"I hope everyone will be equally incurious," Caroline remarked as they reached the cart, "though I cannot feel that it is very likely. Am I to ride on the shaft, as he is doing?"

"Certainly not! You will ride in the cart itself, and I trust that you will not be too greatly jolted. There is a crate there which will have to do duty as a seat." He picked her up and lifted her over the side of the cart, adding as he did so: "I regret that I cannot provide you with a more luxurious form of transport. Let us hope that I can do better when we reach the village."

"Any transport, sir, is better than none," Caroline assured him, settling herself on the crate. "Are you not going to join me?"

He shook his head, resting one hand on the side of the cart and looking up at her with a smile.

"I think not. There is, after all, only one crate, and *my* footgear, Miss Cresswell, is perfectly capable of withstanding a walk through the mire."

At this point the cart moved forward with a jerk which almost made her lose her balance, and by the time she had recovered the opportunity for a retort was lost. The cart was lumbering slowly along the lane, and Mr. Ravenshaw walking beside its owner and endeavouring, with moderate success, to obtain from him some information regarding the local magistrate.

Caroline, balancing herself precariously on the crate, wondered idly what his friends would think if they could see the wealthy Mr. Ravenshaw at that moment. Or, for that matter, what her own friends would think if they could see her.

It could, of course, have disastrous consequences for her if it became known, but she had complete confidence in Guy Ravenshaw's ability to deal with any difficulties confronting them. It was strange, she reflected, how quickly one could learn to trust and to depend upon another person, for she did not doubt for a moment that her reputation was safe in his keeping. They were within sight of the village before the thought of Pelham Ravenshaw occurred to her to shatter her peace of mind.

9

Adventure's End

THE obliging farm-lad set Miss Cresswell down at the
crossroads by the White Lion; and Guy, paying no heed to
her attempted protests, immediately escorted her into the
inn. They had barely set foot inside the door, however,
when they were confronted by a portly dame who had
watched their approach from the tap-room window. She
regarded them with a hostile eye.

"You'll be wanting the Rose and Crown, further down
the street," she announced by way of greeting. " 'Tis them
as caters for the likes of you."

Caroline was leaning on Guy's arm, and felt him stiffen
with anger. He said in his most biting tone: "Mend your
manners, my good woman! I have business with Colonel
Morecambe at the Hall, and desire a private parlour
where this lady may rest until I have seen him."

The landlady gasped, and a dark flush mounted to her

plump cheeks. "Bless my soul if I ever heard such impudence!" she exclaimed. "Business with the Colonel, indeed! The only business his Honour might have with you, my man, is to clap you in the lock-up for a vagabond knave, and your fancy-piece along with you. I saw her get down from Joe Potter's cart! Imposing on a poor, simple lad as don't know no better! Now be off with you, before I call my man or the ostler to send you about your business."

Caroline clung frantically to Mr. Ravenshaw's arm.

"Please, please," she whispered desperately, "let us go to the other inn. It will only cause trouble if we try to remain here. I would not wish to stay, anyway, after being spoken to in that fashion." He glanced impatiently down at her, and she added with all the entreaty of which she was capable: "Mr. Ravenshaw, please!"

"Very well!" he said shortly, and without another glance at the landlady turned on his heel, adding savagely as they stepped out again into the sunshine: "When this wretched affair is over, it will give me great satisfaction to return to this place and inform that woman how her customers should be treated."

Miss Cresswell was too thankful that the storm had been averted to argue with this decision. Limping beside him along the street, she said: "The poor woman cannot really be blamed, for we look a shockingly disreputable pair. Perhaps it will be best if when we reach the Rose and Crown you allow me to make the first approach." She saw that he was still frowning thunderously, and added with attempted lightness: "*You* have always been able to do as you please without the least need to be conciliating, but *I* have been obliged to learn that a deal more may be accomplished by requesting than by demanding."

"I do not make a good beggar, ma'am," he said contemptuously. "I have not the nature for it."

Caroline bit her lip but made no reply, and they walked on in silence until they reached the other inn. There Guy halted, and looked down at her with a rueful smile.

"Forgive me," he said quietly. "That was an unpardonable thing to say. This time I leave everything to you, for I am sure that you possess the tact which I so sadly lack."

The Rose and Crown was a very different establishment from the White Lion, a seedy, down-at-heel little tavern which obviously catered only for pedlars and labourers. Mr. Ravenshaw eyed it disparagingly, but remained silent while Caroline entered into negotiations with the couple who owned it. Whether her persuasive powers won the day, or whether the proprietor of the Rose and Crown was more tolerant than his more prosperous colleague at the White Lion was difficult to tell, but the outcome of it all was that Miss Cresswell was installed by the fire in the big room which did duty as kitchen, dining-room and tap-room, with the assurance that she might stay there until her companion had transacted whatever business he had with the Squire. The innkeeper looked a trifle sceptical when this was mentioned, but directed Guy to the Hall and assured him that his good lady would be safe enough where she was until he returned.

Ignoring the latter part of this remark, Mr. Ravenshaw said quietly to Caroline: "I will be as quick as I can, but it is bound to take a little time to convince this Colonel Morecambe of the truth of my story, so do not be alarmed if I seem to be gone for some while." He looked impatiently about the room, and added in a troubled voice: "I wish I could take you with me. I do not like to leave you alone in a common ale-house."

Caroline, who had been gently rubbing her swollen ankle, looked up with a rather weary smile. "Do not trouble your head about me, sir, for I assure you that I am not at all nice in my notions. This corner by the fire will suit me very well, and indeed, I do not think I could walk any farther just at present."

The Hall, when Mr. Ravenshaw reached it, proved to be a square, solid-looking house, set in the midst of a pleasant garden. The butler who opened the front door in answer to his knock seemed to be of the same opinion as the landlady of the White Lion, and first advised him to go round to the back of the house, and then, the visitor be-

coming more insistent, threatened to call the other servants to eject him. Since Guy was fully prepared to force
his way in if necessary, it was perhaps fortunate that at
this juncture a stout, rubicund gentleman came into the
hall to demand, in tones of mingled joviality and annoyance, what all the confounded uproar was about.

Guy swept the butler aside and strode into the house.
Removing his somewhat battered hat, he said curtly to the
stout gentleman: "Colonel Morecambe?"

The Colonel, blinking at the apparition before him, admitted it. Guy said blightingly: "I believe, sir, that you are
a Justice of the Peace. It is a thousand pities that you do
not make some attempt to rid this neighbourhood of the
dangerous scoundrels who infest it."

Colonel Morecambe, astounded by this uncompromising greeting, opened his lips to order the instant ejection
of the offender, and then closed them again and took a
second and closer look at him. More perceptive than his
butler, he observed that in spite of the rough usage to
which they had obviously been subjected, the stranger's
clothes were tailored in the first style of elegance, and that
voice and manner had an authority which contrasted
strangely with his unkempt appearance.

"I do not know, sir, what business you have with me,"
he said quite mildly, "but obviously it cannot be discussed
here in the hall. Will you step into my study?"

Guy followed him into the room from which he had
emerged, but stopped short just within the door. A grey-
haired and rather frail-looking lady who was sitting beside
the fire was regarding him with astonishment and some
dismay. Mr. Ravenshaw bowed to her.

"I must ask your pardon, ma'am, for intruding upon
you in this state," he said courteously. "Necessity must be
my excuse." He glanced at the Colonel. "My name is Guy
Ravenshaw, and I was set upon and robbed not many
miles from here."

The lady uttered a shocked exclamation, but appeared
to be reassured by his manner. The Colonel introduced
her briefly as his wife, and then demanded to be told when
and where the robbery had occurred.

"Yesterday afternoon," Guy replied without hesitation. "I had engaged to drive my future wife from London to the house of a relative in this county and was misguided enough to attempt what purported to be a short cut. Unfortunately I mistook the road, and as dusk was falling halted at a small cottage to inquire where I was. Before I realized what was happening, I had been knocked on the head, and when I came to myself again I was imprisoned in an upper room of the cottage, watched over by an armed ruffian who informed me that my companion was also a prisoner, and that having discovered my identity by the simple expedient of going through my pockets, he proposed holding us both to ransom."

The Colonel made a strangled noise in his throat and took a turn about the room to relieve his feelings, while Mrs. Morecambe said anxiously: "Pray go on, sir! How did you make your escape?"

"Early this morning, ma'am, I saw three men ride away from the house, believing, no doubt, that their prisoners were secure enough. I contrived to break out of the room in which I was confined and released Miss Cresswell, and since my curricle and horses were nowhere to be found, we set out on foot in search of assistance."

"By Heaven, the scoundrels are making a regular practice of it!" Colonel Morecambe said explosively. "Was there anyone else in this cottage, sir? Any other prisoner?"

Guy shook his head. "Only Miss Cresswell and myself, sir. Why should there be?"

"Because three masked men kidnapped another young lady only two days ago. Took her from her chaise, sir, in broad daylight on Finchley Common. Must be the same fellows!"

Guy preserved his countenance successfully in the face of this information. Mrs. Morecambe said impatiently: "Never mind that now, my love, shocking though it is. Mr. Ravenshaw, you said that your betrothed escaped with you, but where is she now?"

"She is waiting for me in the village, ma'am," Guy replied, turning towards her. "She had the misfortune to injure her foot slightly during our walk, and, having been refused admission by the landlady of the White Lion, I was obliged to leave Miss Cresswell at the Rose and Crown, which is something I cannot be easy about. May I invoke your kindness on her behalf?"

"Of course, sir, with all my heart! The poor, poor child! What a dreadful experience for her! You must fetch her here at once. I will have my carriage brought to the door, and tell the housekeeper to prepare a room."

She hastened away, and Guy turned once more to the Colonel. "I cannot at present furnish you with any proof of my identity, sir," he said bluntly, "but if you will trust me sufficiently to send word of my situation to my house in London, I assure you that such proof will be immediately forthcoming. I regret the necessity which forces me to impose upon you in this manner, but those rogues have left me with not a penny in my pocket, nor an article of value to offer as security."

"My dear sir, do not speak of that!" Colonel Morecambe assured him. "This disgraceful affair occurred within my jurisdiction, and anything which I can do to assist you is poor recompense for that. Did I understand you to say that they stole your curricle and horses as well?"

"Yes, four match-greys, one of the finest teams it has ever been my pleasure to handle. I tell you, sir, the money and other trifles are of small account, but those horses are irreplaceable. I would give a great deal to have them restored to me."

"And so they may be, Mr. Ravenshaw, for it seems to me that in stealing them these scoundrels have overreached themselves. Jewels and money can easily be hidden, but a team of horses is a very different matter. Nevertheless, I will have particulars of the other articles stolen from you, and from the young lady. It will all make it easier to apprehend the thieves."

They were still occupied in this way when a servant came in to say that the carriage was at the door. Guy rose to his feet.

"Forgive me, Colonel, but this matter must wait. I shall not be easy until Miss Cresswell is safely under this roof."

Arriving some fifteen minutes later at the Rose and

Crown, he found that his uneasiness was justified. Neither the host nor hostess was in the kitchen, but on the settle by the fire, where he had left her sitting alone, Caroline was endeavouring to repulse the increasingly familiar advances of a brawny individual whose dress, and the tools of his trade in a bundle at his feet, proclaimed him to be a tinker. Guy took in the scene with one smouldering glance, and then strode forward, plucked the tinker from the settle by the scruff of his neck, and knocked him down amid a shower of pots and pans which had been standing on shelves against the wall.

The consequent appalling clatter brought the landlord speedily in from the garden, to find the tinker sitting dazedly among the shattered shelves with a hand to his jaw, and the rather odd stranger who had visited the inn earlier standing over him with the apparent intention of knocking him down again as soon as he regained his feet. In one corner of the settle, the red-haired young woman was sitting with her hands pressed to her white cheeks.

Neither knowing nor caring what the cause of the dispute might be, mine host at once began to exclaim vociferously at the damage to his property. Mr. Ravenshaw, having by violent action relieved his sudden fierce and somewhat unreasonable fury, cut him short by saying arrogantly: "Any damage I have done shall be paid for before I leave Colonel Morecambe's house. Send the reckoning to me there."

The landlord seemed prepared to continue the argument, but his wife, who had also come hurrying to the kitchen, gripped him by the arm.

"You do as the gentleman says, Matthew," she admonished him, adding in a warning whisper: "He's just come from the Hall, and the Colonel's own chaise is waiting outside now to take up the young lady."

The landlord's attitude immediately changed from hostile to propitiating, but Mr. Ravenshaw paid as little heed to the one as to the other. Turning to Caroline, he took one look at her white face and trembling lips, and without more ado picked her up in his arms and carried her out to the waiting chaise.

Miss Cresswell suffered this high-handed procedure without protest, being fully occupied in resisting a sudden and almost overwhelming desire to put her head down on the broad shoulder so temptingly close to it, and burst into tears. Considerably startled by this evidence of weakness in herself, she remained silent while Guy took his place beside her in the chaise and it moved away along the village street; she must, she decided, be more shaken than she had supposed by the events of the past few days.

Apparently her companion's thoughts were dwelling upon the recent unruly interlude, for after a minute or two he said quietly: "It occurs to me that twice during the past two days I have indulged in a bout of fisticuffs in your presence, and asked your pardon for neither. I do so now, most humbly."

Miss Cresswell made a praiseworthy and almost completely successful attempt to steady her voice, saying as lightly as she could: "It does not matter, sir, in the least, for I have told you that I am not at all nice in my notions. Indeed, I was very glad to see you deal with that odious person so effectively. Now tell me how you fared with Colonel Morecambe. You returned much sooner than I dared to hope."

He described his interview with the magistrate, and the details of the story he had told, adding in conclusion: "I have kept to the facts wherever possible, as you will have realized, for I believe that in a situation such as ours it is best not to deviate any farther from the truth than is absolutely necessary."

"I think you have blended the two most ingeniously," Caroline agreed, but added a trifle dubiously: "I suppose it *was* necessary to say that we are betrothed?"

"Certainly it was," Guy replied promptly, "for how else could I account for the fact that we were driving about the country without so much as a groom in attendance? No one, I think, would believe that we are brother and sister. I trust that you have learned by now that I may be depended upon not to take advantage of the situation."

"Oh yes, indeed! I did not mean—" she broke off in

some distress, twisting her hands anxiously together. "It is just that it is so excessively awkward, for—both of us."

"I do not find it so, and I am persuaded that you would not if you were not tired and overwrought. Remember that we are most unlikely ever to meet these people again." She did not reply, and after a moment he laid his hand reassuringly over hers, adding, with a teasing note in his voice: "Come, ma'am, it was your own notion to take Miss Linley's place, and it cannot be so dreadful to continue to fill it for a few hours longer."

Fortunately for Caroline's peace of mind, the chaise at that moment came to a standstill at Colonel Morecambe's door, and in the bustle of arrival she had an opportunity to recover from her agitation. The Colonel and his lady met them in the hall, Mrs. Morecambe coming forward in a flurry of goodwill to take Caroline's hand in both her own.

"My poor dear, what a shocking experience you have suffered," she exclaimed. "It is no wonder that you look fagged to death. I have had a bedchamber made ready and shall take you up to it immediately."

"Quite right, quite right!" her husband agreed genially. "Very happy to have you here, my dear, and there's no need to trouble your head any more, eh, Ravenshaw?"

"Quite so, sir," Guy replied calmly. "There is nothing whatsoever for Miss Cresswell to vex herself about now." He took Caroline's hand and kissed it. "Go with Mrs. Morecambe, my dear! You have been very brave, but now the ordeal is over."

She murmured something incoherent, turning quickly away to hide the sudden rush of tears to her eyes, and allowed her hostess to lead her across the hall and up the stairs to a comfortable bedchamber where her own maid, a pleasant, middle-aged woman, was waiting for them, and for the next hour the two elder ladies enjoyed themselves very much by fussing in the kindest manner imaginable about the younger. It was a very long time since Caroline had been cosseted and comforted in that fashion, and she could not help enjoying their concern for her. At last she was left alone, tucked up in the most comfortable bed she had lain in for many a day, her injured ankle swathed in a soothing bandage, and the curtains drawn to exclude the bright daylight which might otherwise have prevented her from sleeping.

Yet in spite of all this she did not sleep. Mrs. Morecambe's kindness made her feel guilty; she was conscious of being in a totally false position, and could not be easy about it.

In fact, she ought not to be easy about any aspect of the situation, but she found that her feelings were not at all what they ought to be. She should be overcome by the shocking impropriety of the whole affair; instead she had not the least difficulty in pretending that she was betrothed to Guy Ravenshaw.

"Folly!" said Miss Cresswell, aloud and very firmly, for she perceived that the time had come to take herself severely to task. She forced her mind to dwell upon the less attractive aspects of Mr. Ravenshaw's character, as enumerated by Letty Fenton only a few days before; harsh, tyrannical, hating to be crossed in any way; she could remember them all, but without effect, for she had found him to be none of these. She reminded herself firmly that for a woman of her years and in her position to be indulging in romantic fancies was the height of absurdity, but one's heart, it seemed, could not be influenced by the voice of reason. She recollected that Caroline Cresswell and Guy Ravenshaw inhabited different worlds, and that once this mad adventure was over were unlikely ever to meet again. This, at least, was not without some effect, for it caused Miss Cresswell to weep so bitterly that she eventually cried herself to sleep, and so was able to forget her troubles for a time.

By the following day she was outwardly in command of herself again, though when Mrs. Morecambe insisted that she should spend the morning in bed she did not protest. From her hostess she learned that the messenger sent to London had returned with the assurance that all Mr. Ravenshaw's instructions were being carried out, and that his chaise would arrive at the Hall later that day to convey him and the lady back to Town. Caroline expressed a satisfaction which she did not feel, and reflected wistfully that the adventure was almost over. Beyond it loomed the prospect of a return to her former dreary existence, or else—a thought even more appalling—marriage with Mr. Horace Firkin.

Soon after noon Mrs. Morecambe came bustling into the room to announce that the chaise had arrived, and behind her came her abigail, carrying several bandboxes and an expensive-looking valise. Caroline eyed these articles mistrustfully.

"Here are the clothes which have been sent from London for you, my dear," Mrs. Morecambe said brightly, "and I am sure it is just as well, for, do what we might, the things you had on when you arrived here could never be made fit to wear again. I see that some of these have come straight from the modiste, so I dare say your Mama thought you would like to have them at once. She is very right! I have always found that there is nothing like a new gown to restore one's spirits."

Caroline made no reply to this, but watched with growing uneasiness as the abigail set down her burden and began to open the bandboxes, which, as Miss Cresswell observed with dismay, bore the name of the most exclusive modiste in London. No lady with any pretension to good taste could fail to be delighted by the exquisite garments which presently emerged from them, but Caroline's pleasure was considerably tempered with disquiet. She did not know by what miracle Mr. Ravenshaw had provided her with this new and expensive attire, but she could not help feeling that in doing so he was carrying a necessary deception a great deal too far.

Since, however, she could obviously reveal nothing of this to Mrs. Morecambe, and since it was equally impossible to remain where she was, she got out of bed and submitted meekly to the ministrations of the abigail. She was relieved to find that her ankle was no longer swollen, and that she could put her weight on it without experiencing anything worse than a slight discomfort, and when at length she surveyed herself in the long mirror, could not help doing so with a somewhat guilty satisfaction. The gown of Italian crêpe was simple but extremely elegant, and of exactly that soft shade of green which made the most of her complexion and her hair, while its fit, though not meeting with the entire approval of the maid, was in Caroline's opinion extraordinarily good. She was conscious of looking her best, and in spite of the many disturbing reflections troubling her mind, derived considerable consolation from the knowledge.

There was a velvet pelisse of a deeper shade of green, and a high-crowned bonnet trimmed with bronze-coloured feathers, but since Mrs. Morecambe had said, before leaving the bedchamber, that her guests must partake of some refreshment before setting out, these were left lying upon a chair while the abigail conducted Miss Cresswell downstairs. She was conscious of considerable trepidation at the prospect of confronting Mr. Ravenshaw again, but soon discovered that this was unfounded. When he came in with the Colonel to the room where a light repast was being served, there was nothing in his manner that could make her feel in the least uncomfortable.

It was not until they had said goodbye to their kindly host and hostess, and were driving in the direction of the road to London, that Caroline had an opportunity to broach the subject which was troubling her mind. Having rehearsed to herself exactly what she wished to say, so that he would have no doubt of her gratitude even though being made aware of the impropriety of his conduct, she took a deep breath and plunged into speech.

"Mr. Ravenshaw," she began determinedly, "these clothes I am wearing—"

"Are charming!" he interrupted lazily. "You look delightful, Miss Cresswell. I knew I could depend upon Jane, for her taste in dress is always excellent."

Thrown completely out of her stride by this interjection, Caroline could only repeat weakly: "Jane?"

"My sister-in-law," he explained. "When I sent that letter to London yesterday, I wrote to her also, requesting her to obtain some suitable clothes for you, and giving her such guidance as I could in the matter of size and colour. I think I may say that between us we have been very successful."

Caroline eyed him uneasily. "I trust, sir, that you explained to your sister-in-law just how it was that I came to be in such a situation?"

His brows lifted. "That was scarcely possible in a letter, though I assured her that the whole matter would be made clear as soon as I had an opportunity of calling upon her. No doubt she is very much mystified, but you need not fear that she will talk of it all over Town."

"I hope not indeed," Caroline said fervently, "but even if she says nothing, what in the world must she think?"

"Certainly not what you are obviously afraid she will think," Guy said sardonically, "for in that event, ma'am, I should not have applied to any member of my family for help. It would be most improper."

This remark naturally reduced Miss Cresswell to scarlet-cheeked silence, but she refused to be turned from her purpose, and after a minute or two, in which she struggled to regain her composure, and he watched her with some amusement, she tried again.

"I would not like you to think, sir, that I am insensible of your kindness, but I do not think you can have given the matter much thought. Surely you must see that I cannot possibly accept such a gift from you."

"No?" There was laughter in his voice. "Tell me, then, what you propose to do about it."

"You know very well that I can do nothing about it," Caroline retorted crossly, "but how am I to explain it to my aunt when I arrive home dressed in the first style of elegance?"

"Would it have been any easier to explain why you were arriving home bedraggled and mud-stained? You are supposed to have been visiting your relatives in the country. Tell your aunt that the clothes were a gift from them."

"I suppose I could say that," Caroline agreed doubtfully. "To be sure, Cousin Esther has given me such presents from time to time, though never anything as fine as this." She heaved a sigh. "Oh dear, if only one did not have to give an account of all one's actions!"

Guy looked at her with understanding and a good deal of sympathy. In describing the trick by which Jennifer had succeeded in eloping with Captain Wilde, Caroline had been obliged to tell him a little of her own circumstances, and during their subsequent conversations had unwittingly disclosed a good deal more. Since he possessed a degree of perception for which few people gave him credit, he had had little difficulty in forming a fairly accurate picture of the kind of life to which she was condemned, and none at all in guessing how much she disliked it. Being a man of considerable decision, he had already made certain plans of his own to remedy this state of affairs, but it was too early as yet to speak of them, so he merely said lightly: "This is the inevitable result, ma'am, of that reckless disregard for the consequences of which you yesterday accused Miss Linley. Sooner or later, one has to face it."

"If we are to speak on that subject, sir," Caroline retorted promptly, "I would like to ask you what the consequences will be if Colonel Morecambe's activities lead to the apprehension of your cousin. I may be reckless, but I cannot view with anything but the strongest agitation the thought of all that he will disclose if he is arrested."

"You need have no fear of that," Guy replied firmly. "If Pelham has a grain of commonsense, or even an instinct for self-preservation, he will long since have rid himself of the evidence against him which my curricle and horses would provide, and by this time be well on his way out of the country. Even if he has the temerity to remain in England, you may depend upon me to see that he keeps silent." He paused, and then added gently: "Do not look so anxious, Miss Cresswell. I give you my word that Pelham will not be permitted to injure you in any way."

She did not doubt that he meant it, and succeeded in thrusting that problem, together with all the rest, to the back of her mind. For her, the journey passed all too quickly, and very soon, it seemed, the chaise was bowling through the busy streets of the capital. Now, indeed, it was time to step back into the reality of her own uncomfortable world.

She had asked to be set down at some little distance

from her uncle's house so that her arrival would occasion no remark, but this Guy firmly refused to do.

"Set you down at some street corner and then drive off, leaving you to complete the journey on foot?" he said coldly. "Certainly not, ma'am! I shall deliver you safely to your door."

Caroline could only acquiesce, and hope most fervently that none of her relatives would be entering or leaving the house at the time. It would obviously be useless to point out that she had long been in the habit of walking unescorted, and though it was very pleasant to be treated as though chivalry were something which she had every right to expect, she did not think that Mr. Ravenshaw fully appreciated the very inferior position she occupied in the Cresswell household.

The chaise drew up at last before the familiar and hated entrance, and Mr. Ravenshaw, descending, took her hand to assist her to alight. She looked up at him, trying to smile.

"Thank you for everything," she said in a low voice, "and I am truly sorry to have placed you in so awkward a situation. If I thought it would do the least good, I would come with you to explain matters to Lady Linley."

He smiled and shook his head. "That is very courageous, Miss Cresswell, but as I told you before, I do not think it would serve any useful purpose, besides being exceedingly unpleasant for you. No, I fancy I shall do better with her ladyship on my own, just as you feel you will do better here. We both have a deal of explaining to do, have we not?"

Caroline nodded, not trusting herself to speak. Guy hesitated, as though he would have said something more, but apparently changed his mind, and merely bowed as he released her hand, which since she alighted from the chaise had continued to rest in his. Then he sprang up into the carriage again and it moved away along the street.

Caroline watched it wistfully out of sight and then picked up her valise and turned towards the house, only to halt again in the utmost dismay. The front door was now open, with Becky's startled, round-eyed face peering around the edge of it, and on the threshold Mrs. Cresswell and Sophy stood as though rooted to the spot, their mouths open and their eyes almost starting from their heads with astonishment and curiosity.

10

Some Consequences of Deceit

THIS was reality, indeed. Caroline walked up the steps with as much composure as she could command, smiled at Becky and calmly bade her aunt and cousin good-day. Neither replied to the greeting, but after one or two attempts Mrs. Cresswell said in a strangled voice: "What, may I ask, is the meaning of this?"

Caroline looked at her with assumed surprise. "Why, merely that Cousin Esther's indisposition was less serious than we feared. She is up and about again now, and since my presence was no longer required, I have come back."

Mrs. Cresswell's already high complexion deepened unbecomingly. "Don't trifle with me, miss, for you know very well what I mean. Who was that stylish-looking man who brought you home?"

"I will tell you, Aunt Lizzie, but would it not be better

to go indoors? I do not think that our private concerns can be of interest to the whole street."

Following the direction of her glance, Mrs. Cresswell saw that several idlers, drawn by the unusual magnificence of the Ravenshaw equipage, were now standing in an interested group at the foot of the steps. Pausing only to favour them with a pithy description of their manners, she turned and swept back into the house, commanding Becky to close the door and Caroline to come immediately to the drawing-room. Once there, she faced her niece accusingly.

"Well, miss, what have you to say for yourself? Who was your fine beau?"

"That was a neighbour of Mr. Wilde's who chanced to call at Brightstone yesterday to inquire after Cousin Esther's health. It was mentioned in his hearing that I intended to return to London, and since he was making the journey to-day he was kind enough to offer to take me up in his chaise. Roland desired to remain for a few days longer in Hertfordshire, and so I accepted the invitation."

Mrs. Cresswell looked as though she would have liked very much to argue with this story, but was not quite sure of her ground. Instead she sniffed, and said scornfully: "I am surprised that your cousin thought it proper for a young, unmarried woman to make such a journey without a chaperone. Fine goings-on, indeed, and would not do for a daughter of mine! What's the name of the obliging gentleman?"

This was a question which Caroline had not foreseen. It was impossible to give Guy's own name, since Mrs. Cresswell had heard of Mr. Ravenshaw's engagement to Jennifer, and she could not immediately think of a substitute. Fortunately, before her hesitation could be remarked, a welcome interruption came from Sophy. That stolid damsel had been staring in silence at her cousin ever since her arrival. Now, at last, she said eagerly: "Wherever did you get those clothes, Caroline? I've never seen anything half so fine!"

"Why, from Cousin Esther, of course! You know that she is kind enough to give me such presents from time to time."

Mrs. Cresswell uttered a short, angry laugh. "Mrs. Wilde must know very well that a female in your position can have no use for such a stylish rig."

This aspect of the matter had already occurred to Caroline, and she had an answer ready.

"In the ordinary way, that would of course be true, but she gave them to me in order that I might have something suitable to wear at Jennifer Linley's wedding."

"But you said you had not been invited to it," Sophy objected, staring.

"Of course I have not, but Cousin Esther felt sure that I would be, since we had all been such close friends as children." She gave a rueful laugh. "I could have told her how mistaken she was, for I knew that Lady Linley would never send an invitation to anyone as unimportant as myself. However, Cousin Esther had already purchased the clothes, and insisted that I should have them."

This explanation apparently satisfied her aunt, but as her mind was of a tenacious habit, and rarely abandoned any topic until nothing remained to be discovered about it, she demanded again to be told the identity of Miss Cresswell's escort. This time Caroline answered without hesitation.

"It was Sir Nicholas Renfrew. He lives at Coppice House, between Brightstone Park and Westbridge."

These facts were true enough. Sir Nicholas was an aged and gouty knight who rarely stirred beyond the confines of his own garden, and Caroline had no hesitation in borrowing his identity for Mr. Ravenshaw's use. Mrs. Cresswell said tartly that it was a pity Sir Nicholas had not taken the trouble to step in and make himself known to her.

"He could not spare the time to do so," Caroline explained, improvising recklessly. "He is going on into Kent to visit his sister, and had already turned aside from his road to bring me home. I could not impose any farther upon his kindness."

Sophy tossed her head. "I don't suppose you even asked him," she said crossly. "You will never let your smart friends visit us, will she, Mama?"

"Oh, I have long since ceased to look for any consider-

ation from your cousin, Sophy love," Mrs. Cresswell
agreed unpleasantly. *"We* are good enough to house and
feed her, but not to meet the fine ladies and gentlemen she
likes to call her friends." She rounded again upon Caroline. "Well, miss, why are you standing there? This is not
Brightstone Park, you know, with a score of servants waiting to do your bidding! You'd best put off those fine feathers and then go to the schoolroom, for I'm sure I have had
no time to inquire what mischief the children have been
getting up to while you have been gadding about the country."

Caroline went, thankful to have escaped so lightly and
hoping that Guy would fare equally well with Lady Linley,
though there was probably no need to worry on his account. Her ladyship could be formidable when she chose,
but that was not likely to overawe Mr. Ravenshaw. Probably, Caroline thought with a little smile, he would take
Lady Linley to task for saying nothing to him about Captain Wilde.

When she reached her own room, she found that Becky,
having carried her valise upstairs, was waiting with ill-
concealed excitement to ask the same questions already put
by Mrs. Cresswell. Caroline repeated her story, but added
with a sigh: "I did not suppose that my aunt would be
pleased at Sir Nicholas driving me home, but I cannot see
what is in that circumstance to put her so greatly out of
temper."

Becky sniffed. "Oh," she said scornfully, "she was out
of temper before ever you arrived, on account of Mr.
George. Her Pa came here this morning looking for him,
because he's not been near the counting-house for days,
and a fine rage old Mr. Perkins was in on account of it.
Called him idle, and dissolute, and Lord knows what besides. You was well out of it, miss, and that's a fact!"

Caroline was carefully hanging the green velvet pelisse
in the cupboard, but paused to glance over her shoulder
with a slight frown.

"What excuse did George make?"

"He never made none, miss, not being here at the time.
He hasn't slept in his own bed these two nights past, and

that didn't put his Grandpa into any better temper when he heard about it. Not that it's the first time, not by a long way, since he took up with that Mr. Trench. You mark my words, miss! Mr. George'll find himself in bad trouble before he's much older, and that Trench'll be the cause of it."

From what she knew of George, and had seen of Bartholomew Trench, Caroline felt inclined to share this opinion. Mr. Trench was a good deal older than George, a big, flashily-dressed man who smiled too readily and whose manner was obviously designed to impress.

"I dare say you are right, Becky," she replied, "though George is very foolish, for it will be excessively awkward for him if he becomes estranged from his grandfather. So that is why my aunt was so angry! I had hoped to arrive home without being remarked, and wished to be set down before we reached the house, but—but Sir Nicholas would not hear of it."

Becky was only too glad to seize the opportunity thus offered to return to the intriguing subject of Miss Cresswell's escort, and said hopefully that perhaps the gentleman would call upon her when he returned to London.

"Really, Becky, you are foolish beyond permission!" Caroline replied sharply. "Of course he will do no such thing!" She turned quickly back to the cupboard, adding in a stifled voice: "He has been exceedingly kind to me, but it is not likely that I shall ever see him again."

To be spoken to in such a manner by Caroline Cresswell was something quite new in Becky's experience, but as she was no fool in spite of her tender years, she realized at once that this was a subject which must not be pursued. She had a horrid fear that Miss Caroline was crying, and so she sidled out of the room and ran downstairs again, wishing earnestly but hopelessly that she could do something to help.

Caroline found it all too easy to slip back into the familiar, dreary round of life in her uncle's house, and by the following afternoon she had begun to feel that her recent adventures, and even her meeting with Guy Ravenshaw, were no more than a dream. She was in the schoolroom, trying to persuade fourteen-year-old Drusilla to practise her needlework and at the same time endeavouring to settle a dispute between the two youngest children, when Becky appeared to tell her that her aunt demanded her instant attendance in the drawing-room. Miss Cresswell, in her old maroon gown and with her hair somewhat ruffled by her efforts to prevent Master Harry from kicking little Aurelia, turned a harassed face towards her.

"Oh, Becky, what does she want now?" she asked, raising her voice above the clamour of Aurelia's screams. "I cannot leave the children just at present."

"I think you'd better, miss," Becky yelled in return. "In a fair fury, the missus is, if you don't mind my saying so."

Caroline sighed and got to her feet, holding a struggling, screaming child at arm's-length by each hand; she dealt each of her young relatives a sharp, impartial smack, and told Drusilla to look after them until she returned. Then she followed the maid out to the landing.

"What does my aunt want, Becky? Do you know?"

Becky looked rather frightened. "No, miss, I don't, but I've never seen her so angry, and that's a fact! Mr. Firkin's with her, but it can't be anything to do with him, because it was only after Mr. George come in that she started screaming for you."

Caroline looked sharply at her. "George has come back?"

"Not ten minutes ago, miss, and maybe it's that as set the missus off."

"Maybe," Caroline agreed rather wearily, "though I cannot imagine what George's escapades have to do with me. Surely even my aunt cannot hold *me* responsible for them!"

She went slowly down the stairs, with a reluctance increased by the knowledge that she would find Mr. Firkin below. She knew now that she could never bring herself to marry him, even if she lived in poverty to the end of her days. It was this matter, rather than the cause of her aunt's displeasure, which was engaging her mind as she opened the drawing-room door, and she was totally unprepared for the torrent of abuse which greeted her.

"So there you are, you bold-faced, lying jade!" Mrs.

Cresswell's voice was strident with fury. "No doubt you thought you'd been very clever, imposing on us all with your mealy-mouthed innocence, but you've done it for the last time, my girl, you can be sure of that! Come here and tell me what you've got to say for yourself, before I turn you out of the house for good!"

Caroline had halted just inside the door and now stood leaning against it, shaken out of her usual self-possession by that unlooked-for blast of invective. Her aunt was standing in the middle of the room, her stout figure quivering with rage, her rather coarse features alarmingly suffused. Behind her, Sophy crouched on a low stool, apparently half frightened and half excited, while Mr. Firkin occupied a chair close to the fire, his commonplace and wrinkled countenance wearing an expression of shocked disapproval. George was standing by the window, fidgeting uneasily with one of the curtains and looking as though he regretted having come home.

"I do not understand," Caroline said in a low voice. "You have no right, ma'am, to speak to me in this fashion."

"No right?" Mrs. Cresswell shrieked. "We'll see about that, my girl! So Captain Wilde was to take you to his father's house, was he? You were staying there, were you, the four days you were away? Why, you deceitful hussy, George has come straight from Brightstone Park, and they've not seen you there for a twelvemonth!"

Caroline had turned pale, and lifted a hand involuntarily to her cheek. She said in a shaken voice: "Why should George go to Brightstone Park?"

"Never mind why he went, miss! That's neither here nor there! What *is* to the point is what you've been up to these four days past. Not that there's any need to ask! When a young woman goes off with one gentleman, and comes back days later with another, and dressed up as fine as fivepence, there's no doubt how she's been occupying herself in the meantime!"

Caroline remained leaning against the door, too dismayed and confused even to defend herself.

"Well, have you nothing to say?" her aunt's shrill voice blared out again. "That's no wonder, I'm sure, when you know you've been found out!" She swung round to face Mr. Firkin. "Just as well for you, Horace, that it's happened as it has! I told you all along you were a fool to think of marrying her, and now see how right I was. She'd have made a cuckold of you before the month was out." The old man made no reply, and Lizzie turned again upon Miss Cresswell. "As for you, my lady, you can pack your things and get out, back to your fine Captain, or to Sir Nicholas What's-his-name, or to the devil, for all I care. I'm not housing a lightskirt under my roof, and that's certain!"

Caroline drew a deep breath and stood erect. She was very white, but perfectly composed. "Certainly I shall go, Aunt Lizzie," she said quietly. "You are quite mistaken, but you will never believe that, and I have no wish to remain in a house where I am thought of so badly."

She turned, and opened the door, and went out. George took a step forward, then halted again and stood biting his nails in obvious indecision.

In the hall, Becky, who had been unashamedly listening at the keyhole, put her hand on Miss Cresswell's arm, but Caroline paid no heed and went blindly past her towards the stairs. Becky followed her in silence, but when Caroline's bedroom was reached she could contain herself no longer, and said desperately: "Oh, miss, what will you do? Where can you go?"

"I shall go to my friend, Mrs. Fenton, Becky. She will let me stay with her, I know, until I can find an eligible post in some respectable household." Caroline spoke quite calmly, although she was still white and trembling with the shock of what had happened. "You must not worry your head about me."

As she spoke she was pulling open drawers and cupboards, lifting her belongings out. Becky, watching her, said indignantly: "You'll be better off anywhere than you were here, that's certain. Her and her wicked, lying tongue! 'Twas all I could do not to come in and tell her so to her face."

"I am almost glad that it has happened," Caroline remarked reflectively, "for I do not think I could have borne to stay here much longer." She folded a rather shabby shawl, laid it on the bed and added with a faint smile: "I am glad that you, at least, do not believe the worst of me."

"Oh, Miss Caroline, as if I could!" Becky was almost weeping with earnestness. "Wherever you've been these past few days, you must have had good reason for it, and *I* don't have to be told there was nothing improper about it!" She paused, thinking this over, and then added naïvely: "Not that I could've blamed you, anyway. Such a fine-looking man as he was, and that lovely carriage and horses!"

"Oh, Becky!" Caroline started to laugh, and found that tears were running down her cheeks. She sat down on the edge of the bed and indulged in a bout of weeping which greatly relieved her feelings, while the little maidservant put her arms round her and patted her shoulder in a motherly way which would have done credit to a woman twice her age.

Presently, when Caroline had recovered her composure, and done what she could to remove the traces of her tears, she allowed Becky to help her to pack, and then changed from her shabby gown into the green dress and velvet pelisse.

"I cannot take these things with me now," she said, looking at the battered trunk and the valise, "for I have no money for a hackney, and shall be obliged to walk to Brook Street. Tell my aunt, if she inquires, that I will send for them at the earliest opportunity. I shall write to my uncle from Mrs. Fenton's house, for he, at least, has never been unkind, but it is from you, Becky, and you alone, that I am truly sorry to part."

She put her arms round the girl and kissed her, and Becky, much affected, clung tightly to her, and wept a little, and declared that she would never forget her. Then they went downstairs together, and a few minutes later Caroline heard the door of her uncle's house close behind her for the last time.

She had plenty to occupy her thoughts during the walk, but by the time she reached Brook Street her ankle had begun to ache again, and it was with profound relief that she knocked on Mrs. Fenton's front door. It seemed a long time before the summons brought forth any response, and when at length the door opened, the butler looked at her with an expression of considerable astonishment.

"Mr. and Mrs. Fenton have gone into the country, miss," he informed her. "They left for Brightstone Park three days ago, and I do not know when they expect to return."

Caroline stood staring blankly at him, while a feeling of sick dismay laid hold upon her. It had never occurred to her that Mark and Letty would have left London, but now she realized that it was the obvious and natural thing for them to do. When the news of the abduction of the supposed Jennifer Linley reached them, they would have wasted no time in setting off for Brightstone to take counsel with Mr. and Mrs. Wilde.

The butler was looking at her with some concern. "Is anything wrong, miss?" he asked anxiously. "Can I be of any assistance?"

"No," Caroline said slowly. "No, thank you, it was not important. I—I will write to Mrs. Fenton."

She turned away and began to walk slowly and rather aimlessly along the street, trying to ward off a growing feeling of panic, for her situation was now exceedingly awkward. The April afternoon was drawing towards twilight, and with no money in her purse she could neither seek lodging at an inn nor buy a seat on a stage-coach bound for Hertfordshire. She had no other acquaintances in London except the Linleys, and for obvious reasons she could not ask help of them. What, then, was she to do?

The memory of a strong, black-browed face which for the past few days had never been far from her thoughts, rose temptingly in her mind, but she thrust it resolutely aside. Mr. Ravenshaw would undoubtedly deal with this crisis as promptly and efficiently as she had seen him deal with others, but she had no right to ask his help, nor could she present herself at his house without creating a situation fraught with embarrassment, and giving colour to her aunt's unworthy suspicions.

By this time her heedless footsteps had carried her into Bond Street, where the window of a milliner's shop offered a welcome excuse to pause. She stood staring, without actually seeing any of them, at the elegant hats and bonnets displayed therein, and leaned all her weight on her right foot in an unobtrusive effort to ease the throbbing pain in her left ankle. When at length she turned away from the shop she found that a fashionably-dressed gentleman was studying her with insolent familiarity through his quizzing-glass; her cheeks burned, and she bestowed upon him a glance so fierce that in some disorder he let the glass drop and walked away, but the incident served to show Miss Cresswell the impossibility of her present situation. Only one class of woman, young and stylishly dressed, was likely to be found walking unescorted through the heart of fashionable London.

There was only one course open to her, and that was to humble her pride and return to her uncle's house. Perhaps, if she were lucky enough to find him at home, he could be prevailed upon to let her remain for the night, and advance her the money to pay her coach-fare to Brightstone Park. With the utmost reluctance she turned her steps once again towards the house which she thought she had left for ever.

By the time she reached the corner of the familiar street, she was tired out and limping badly, and it was with mixed feelings that she saw her cousin George standing on the pavement outside his father's house. He was engaged in earnest and apparently acrimonious conversation with his friend, Mr. Trench, and did not observe Caroline's approach. It was his companion who first caught sight of her, and he immediately gripped George's arm and said something in a low voice which brought the younger man swinging round to stare at her. Then Trench said something else, and they both moved forward to meet her.

Bartholomew Trench bowed profoundly, sweeping off his hat from glossy, well-oiled chestnut locks and displaying excellent teeth in an ingratiating smile. He was a rather overpowering gentleman in his late thirties, good-looking in a florid, fleshy way and smugly conscious of the fact.

"My dear Miss Cresswell," was his fulsome greeting, "what happy chance has brought you back to us? Here is

George fretting himself into a fever on your account. Desolate at having caused you so much inconvenience and distress."

"Bart's right, Caroline," George assented eagerly. "It was a mutton-headed thing to do, though I meant no harm. If I had known you were home again I'd have said nothing to Mama." He looked puzzled. "But why have you come back?"

Caroline hesitated. She had no wish to discuss her present unhappy situation in front of Mr. Trench, though if he had been to the house he had no doubt already heard her aunt's version of the affair.

"The truth is," she said reluctantly, "that I find myself in a little difficulty. Mrs. Fenton, with whom I had hoped to stay, is out of town, and I have not the means to go farther afield. I came back in the hope of finding my uncle at home, and obtaining assistance from him."

George shook his head. "He's gone to the Cock-pit, cousin. You know what that means!"

Caroline did know. When Henry Cresswell sought recreation with his cronies at the Cock-pit Royal, he rarely returned home until the early hours of the morning, and then in a condition which precluded him from being of assistance to anyone, even to himself. Her heart sank, and panic began to take possession of her again.

"George," she said desperately, "can *you* not help me? I am sure you did not intend to make mischief, but it *is* largely your fault that I find myself in this plight. If you will lend me my coach-fare to Brightstone, I will pay you back as soon as I reach Cousin Esther's house."

He coloured up to the eyes and began to stammer incoherent excuses. Mr. Trench came to his rescue.

"I'm sure George would be delighted to oblige you, ma'am, but the fact is, the poor fellow is badly dipped. Pockets very much to let. However, no need to despair. Allow me the privilege of assisting you with a small loan. Very happy to oblige."

This was not at all to Caroline's taste, for she had no wish to find herself under an obligation to Bartholomew

Trench. That forceful gentleman, however, brushed her protests aside.

"My dear lady, think nothing of it. It is a pleasure as well as a privilege to assist beauty in distress. But you cannot travel by the night-stage, you know. Shocking conditions, not at all the thing. Permit me to make a suggestion. I lodge with my cousin, Mrs. Pomfret. Respectable widow, very genteel household. I am sure she will be delighted to offer you hospitality for the night."

"Oh no, indeed!" Caroline exclaimed. "It is excessively kind of you, Mr. Trench, but I could not impose upon your cousin in that fashion. I do not mind travelling by the night-stage, if—if you will be so obliging as to lend me the fare."

Mr. Trench regarded her with a knowing eye. "I see what it is," he said reproachfully. "You do not trust me, ma'am. In that case, George shall speak for me, and for my cousin. He is well acquainted with us both, are you not, George?"

"Oh, yes," George agreed unhappily. "There's no cause for uneasiness, cousin. You will do very well with Mrs. Pomfret. Bart is quite right, you know, about the night-coach. You cannot travel so, particularly on your own."

"Then that is quite settled!" Mr. Trench beckoned in a lordly way to a passing hackney, and, producing some money from his pocket, handed it to George. "Tell you what we'll do, ma'am. You look to me to be tired out, so I'll take you at once to Mrs. Pomfret. Meanwhile, George will buy you a ticket on the morning stage, and then come back here to collect your things and bring them to you. No need for you to enter the house at all. Feel certain you do not wish to do so."

This was quite true. It was equally true that Miss Cresswell had no desire to drive off alone with Mr. Trench, but unfortunately no third alternative offered itself. She was certainly very tired, and the chilly April dusk which had now settled over the streets reminded her very forcibly that if she declined this invitation the night would find her with no roof over her head.

The hackney-coach had by now halted beside them; George repeated his assurances that all was well, and that he would rejoin her as soon as he had carried out his errand. Caroline cast one more glance at the blank and unfriendly portals of her uncle's house, and with a certain measure of relief, but an even stronger feeling of misgiving, allowed Bartholomew Trench to hand her into the coach.

11

Mr. Ravenshaw Is Perturbed

FOR a considerable time after Caroline's retreat from the drawing-room, Mrs. Cresswell continued to hold forth on the subject of her niece's misdemeanours. After a while Mr. Firkin took his leave, and George contrived to slip out of the house at the same time.

The fact that her audience was now reduced to one did nothing to halt Lizzie Cresswell's flow of oratory. When Sophy spoke enviously of the elegant clothes in which Caroline had come home, and the splendid carriage in which she had arrived, to say nothing of the fine appearance of her escort, her fond Mama promptly boxed her ears. Caroline, Mrs. Cresswell prophesied, would come to a bad end, and it was clear that she had been turned out of the house not one moment too soon. Already, it seemed, she had begun to corrupt her innocent young cousin.

A little more than half an hour after Caroline had left

the house, an imperative summons fell upon the front door, and Sophy, running to the window, reported in awe-stricken tones that a curricle drawn by four splendid horses and attended by a liveried groom, was standing in front of the house. The visitor himself was hidden from her view by the pillars flanking the front door, but after a minute or two Silas came into the drawing-room with a card in his hand. The gentleman, he said, had asked for Miss Caroline, but on being told that she was not at home, requested that Mrs. Cresswell would receive him instead. Lizzie took the card and looked suspiciously at the legend it bore.

" 'Mr. Guy Ravenshaw'," she read aloud. "Why, that's the gentleman who's to marry Miss Linley! What can he want here? You'd best show him in, Silas."

Silas announced Mr. Ravenshaw, and Lizzie turned to greet him with a smile which immediately froze on her lips. Whatever his name might be, she had no difficulty in recognizing this tall, black-haired, extremely well-dressed gentleman as the stranger who had escorted Caroline home the previous day.

Amazement at what she conceived to be his impudence deprived her of speech, and while she was still seeking vainly for words, Sophy said blankly: "But your name is not Ravenshaw! Caroline told us you were Sir Nicholas Renfrew."

"Sophy, hold your tongue!" her mother commanded sharply, and turned a belligerent gaze upon her visitor. "Well, Mr. Ravenshaw, or Renfrew, or whatever your name is, what do you want with me?"

Guy had come prepared to be civil, but the tone of that greeting slew the intention at one stroke. The black brows drew together over his cold grey eyes, and he said with a bite in his voice: "I desire, ma'am, to see your niece, Miss Caroline. Your servant tried to fob me off with some rig-marole about her having left this house, but I am not so easily discouraged. Perhaps you will be good enough to tell me the truth."

"The truth, is it?" Mrs. Cresswell repeated. "Let me tell you there's been a deal too much truth uncovered this day for Miss Caroline's liking—or for yours either, I dare say, when you know the whole!"

"Nevertheless, ma'am, I desire to know it, and that as soon as may be, but first, let me assure you my name *is* Ravenshaw. I have never heard of Sir Nicholas Renfrew."

"Then if you're the gentleman that's engaged to Miss Linley, you ought to be ashamed of yourself," Lizzie told him roundly, "and so should that wicked, deceitful niece of mine! Pretending to be the poor girl's friend, and then carrying on with you behind her back—upon my word, I never heard the like of it! And you! Bringing her home in your carriage-and-four, as bold as brass, and then coming back here and demanding to see her. I should like to know what manner of house you think this is!"

"I thought, ma'am," Guy retorted blightingly, "that it was a house in which Miss Cresswell was treated, if not with consideration, at least with common civility. I see that I was mistaken. Since whatever explanation she chose to give you of recent events was obviously not believed, I shall not attempt to offer one, but this I will say. The suspicions which you so plainly entertain dishonour you far more than they dishonour her!"

"So it is just suspicion on my part, is it?" Mrs. Cresswell said stridently. "I suppose I only suspect that she has told me nothing but lies ever since she came back and that she was dressed in a fashion no decent young woman in her position ever could be. A present from her cousin, indeed! *I* know the kind of cousin who gives presents like that!"

With a strong effort Mr. Ravenshaw controlled his temper, and Sophy, who since the reception of her first remark had maintained a wary silence, gave a little shiver of fright as she looked at him. She was well used to quarrels, but in her experience they always involved flushed faces, raised voices, perhaps even physical violence. This man's white-lipped, cold-eyed anger, his deadly quiet, was something quite new to her.

"I did not come here to quarrel with you, ma'am," Guy said after a brief pause, and Sophy shivered again at the quality of his voice. "If you will be good enough to tell me where I may find your niece, I will put an end to a conversation which must be as disagreeable to you as it is to me."

Mrs. Cresswell, unabashed, gave one of her eloquent sniffs. "As to where she may be now, I should suppose *you* to have more notion than I have," she retorted. "Unless, of course, the sly hussy has some other gentlemen at her beck and call besides you and Captain Wilde. All I know is that I turned her out of this house, bag and baggage, as soon as I found out the tricks she's been playing. I have the morals of my own girls to think of!"

"You turned her out?" Guy repeated incredulously. "But where has she gone? Has she any money, any friends with whom she can seek shelter?"

"She'll find both soon enough, I've no doubt," Mrs. Cresswell said sharply. "Her kind always do, though what any of you can see in that skinny, white-faced, red-headed minx is more than I can tell. One thing's sure, though! She's not setting foot in this house again."

"Most certainly she is not! Do you think I would permit —" he broke off as though afraid of saying too much, and after a moment in which he appeared to be struggling to maintain his self-control, he added curtly: "Good-day to you, ma'am. You have told me more than enough."

He swung round and strode out of the room, considerably startling Silas, who was loitering in an aimless way suspiciously close to the drawing-room door. Mr. Ravenshaw looked sardonically at him, but as the man hastened to throw open the front door for him, suddenly thought of something, and paused.

"If Miss Caroline should return here, or send any message," he said briefly, "be good enough to inform me at once." He took one of his cards from his pocket, scribbled something on its back, and handed it, with some money, to the servant. "That is my direction, and there will be a reward for you if your news is prompt and dependable."

Silas, finding himself the recipient of the largest gratuity which had ever come his way, assured Mr. Ravenshaw that he would do his best, and bowed this open-handed visitor reverently out of the house. Then, slipping both card and money into his pocket, he went off to the kitchen to inform Becky and the cook that he would be the last man alive to blame Miss Caroline because she preferred the protection of that well-breeched swell to a respectable but menial position in her uncle's house.

Mr. Ravenshaw's anger, profound though it was, had dulled neither his wits nor his memory, and casting his mind back over the conversations he had had with Miss Cresswell, he recollected that she had spoken several times of a sister of Captain Wilde. He could only hope that, having been cast out by her aunt, she had sought refuge with this lady and that he would find her there.

His temper was not soothed by the delays occasioned by the heavy traffic in the narrow streets of the City, but at last he reached the more fashionable part of the town, and drew up before the door of his sister-in-law's house in Park Street. As soon as they were alone he said imperatively: "Jane, do you know Mrs. Fenton? Have you her direction?"

Jane Ravenshaw regarded him with some surprise. She was a handsome, fair-haired young woman of three-and-twenty, and between her and her formidable brother-in-law there existed, rather surprisingly to some people, a strong bond of sympathy and affection. This was his second visit to her house that day. During the first he had recounted to her the surprising events of the past few days, and she, divining several other things of which he said nothing, had been both intrigued and delighted.

"Mrs. Fenton?" she repeated in answer to his question. "Yes, I am slightly acquainted with her. She lives in Brook Street, I believe, but why in the world should you want to know that?"

He told her, and added a brief description of his interview with Mrs. Cresswell. Jane was profoundly shocked.

"What a dreadful woman she must be! I know you feared that Miss Cresswell might find her situation a trifle awkward, but this, surely, is worse than anything you imagined. Do go at once to Mrs. Fenton's, Guy, for I know you will not be easy until you are certain that all is well.

Oh, and ask Miss Cresswell if I may have the pleasure of calling upon her tomorrow. I do so much want to make her acquaintance."

He promised to do so and went away, leaving Jane to think over what he had said, and to try to picture to herself the sort of life which Caroline Cresswell must have led. She was still doing this, in a very ill-informed way, when Mr. Ravenshaw returned, far sooner than she had expected. One look at his face was enough to tell her that something was very wrong indeed.

"The Fentons are out of Town," Guy said curtly in reply to her anxious question. "Caroline called there more than an hour ago, but she left no message and that fool of a butler does not even know which way she went."

Jane gave a gasp of dismay, but rallied after a moment and said with determined cheerfulness: "There must be someone else, some other friends to whom she can turn."

Guy shook his head. "I do not think so. After what has happened she can hardly go to the Linleys, and I fancy there is none among her uncle's acquaintance with whom she is upon sufficiently intimate terms."

"There is yourself, Guy," Jane offered, after an instant's hesitation.

"Yes," he said quickly, "that is my hope. I will go home at once, and pray that I find her there. If I do not—Jane, can you imagine what it would mean to be alone and friendless in London, with no roof over your head and perhaps no money in your purse?" He broke off, looking at her with a faint, rueful smile. "No, of course you cannot, and I am glad of it, but believe me, it is imperative that I find Caroline without delay."

"Of course you will find her," Jane agreed firmly, "and when you do, you must bring her here. I shall wait for you."

"Have you no engagements this evening?"

"Nothing of any importance. I could not enjoy myself, in any event, not knowing what has become of Miss Cresswell. I am sure that she and I are going to be friends."

"You're a good little soul, Jane," he said gratefully, bestowing a brotherly embrace upon her, "and I wish to

Heaven I had brought Caroline to you yesterday. Had I foreseen this situation I would have done so, but at the time it seemed preferable to dispose of certain other matters first."

When he arrived back at his own house, a disappointment awaited Mr. Ravenshaw, for neither Miss Cresswell nor any message from her had come there during his absence. He went slowly into the library and stood frowning abstractedly at the fire, undecided for once in his life. He had not the smallest idea where to begin his search, and his efforts to concentrate on the problem were repeatedly distracted by disquieting thoughts of the various disagreeable situations in which Caroline might already have found herself. Finally, failing any better idea, he resolved to call first upon Lady Linley. Her ladyship might be able to furnish him with some clue, however slight, on which to base his search.

He went out into the hall again, and found one of his footmen engaged in an altercation with some unseen person who was apparently trying to gain admission to the house. Mr. Ravenshaw heard him say in an exasperated tone: "For the last time, young woman, you can't come in here. Now be off with you, or you'll find yourself in trouble."

With a swift lifting of his hopes Guy went quickly forward, saying imperatively: "What is this? Does someone wish to see me?"

The footman was given no chance to reply. At the sound of that commanding voice he stiffened instinctively and half turned from the door, and the importunate visitor, ducking quickly past him, scuttled into the hall and slid to a breathless halt in front of Mr. Ravenshaw. She was a freckle-faced young girl in a shabby gown, with a threadbare shawl clutched round her thin shoulders, and Guy felt quite sure that he had never seen her before in his life.

"Please, sir, I *must* speak to you," she gasped desperately. " 'Tis about Miss Caroline."

The footman, advancing with an air of outraged apology upon the intruder, found himself checked by an imperatively lifted finger. Before his shocked and astounded eyes Mr. Ravenshaw turned, beckoned the shabby visitor to follow him into the library, and closed the door behind them.

"Now," Guy said curtly, "tell me who you are. Have you a message from Miss Caroline?"

"If you please, sir, I'm Becky, maid at Mrs. Cresswell's, but I haven't got a message or nothing," the girl said breathlessly. "It's just that I'm that worried about Miss Caroline, and I don't trust that Mr. Trench, nor Mr. George neither, for that matter, and why she should go off with them I don't know, for she told me it was her friend Mrs. Fenton she was going to."

She broke off and stood twisting the ends of her shawl, and Guy saw that there were tears in her eyes. He saw also that she was much younger than he had at first supposed, and obviously frightened as well as agitated. Curbing his own impatience, and the misgivings aroused by Becky's disjointed remarks, he said in a much kinder tone: "I happen to know that Mrs. Fenton is out of Town, so that is one part of the mystery solved. Now come and sit down by the fire, and tell me all you can about Miss Caroline and where you think she may be at this moment. We are both worried about her, it seems, but between us we may be able to help her."

Considerably reassured, Becky ventured to take another and closer look at him. Only concern for her beloved Miss Caroline could have urged her to force her way into this imposing house and accost its owner. Now she saw that the fine gentleman who had seemed so fierce and haughty at first was regarding her in a quite kindly fashion, so that she felt sufficiently emboldened to do as he told her, and went forward and perched herself nervously on the edge of the chair he had indicated. Mr. Ravenshaw sat down facing her, and said with a smile: "That is much better. You have not the least need to be afraid of me, and if you can tell me where to find Miss Caroline I shall be exceedingly grateful to you."

Becky smiled uncertainly in return, and wiped her eyes

on the corner of her shawl before starting the story she had to tell. Guy let her recount it in her own way, refraining from comments which he felt sure would fluster her, and so learned in detail what had happened in the Cresswell household that afternoon. It was an account which brought the frown back to his brow, and a decidedly grim expression to his whole countenance, but Becky was shrewd enough to realize that his anger was not directed at her, and did not allow herself to be alarmed by it. She explained that she had been at an upper window of the house when she saw Miss Cresswell talking to her cousin and Mr. Trench in the street below.

"I was going to run downstairs, sir, and tell her as how you'd come looking for her, but before I could as much as call out to her she got into a hackney with Mr. Trench, and Mr. George walked away by himself." She seemed to fear that this might give Mr. Ravenshaw a false impression, and added anxiously: "You mustn't think any the worse of her, sir, for going with Mr. Trench. I could tell she didn't like it above half from the way she looked about her."

Guy's frown deepened. "Do you mean that he forced her to accompany him?"

"No," Becky said slowly, "she went of her own free will, sir, but it seemed to me she'd rather not have gone at all, only didn't know what else to do." She looked at Guy in a troubled way, and added, with an air of wisdom oddly at variance with her lack of years: "But he's not a proper person for her to be going with, sir, and that's a fact! He's not a gentleman, though he tries to make out he is, and I wouldn't trust him—no, not an inch, I wouldn't't!"

In spite of his anxiety he could not help smiling a little at this.

"I am happy to see, Becky, that you regard me more favourably that you regard Mr. Trench." He saw that she was looking puzzled, and added in explanation: "You cannot be afraid to trust me, or you would not be here."

"Miss Caroline trusts you, sir," Becky replied shrewdly, "and that's good enough for me. She said as how you'd been very kind to her. Silas told me what you said to him to-day and where you lived, so as soon as I saw her drive off like that, I came here just as fast as I could."

"You acted very properly," Guy assured her. "Now tell me, do you know where this man, Trench, lives?"

Becky shook her head regretfully. "No, sir, I don't. Mr. George'd know, of course, and maybe the missus, too, though I couldn't swear to that."

"Very well!" Guy rose to his feet and pulled the bell-rope. "It is obvious that I shall have to begin my search at Mr. Cresswell's house, so I will take you back with me." He paused, looking reflectively down at her. "I told Silas that I would pay well for the information I wanted."

Becky's chin came up, and she flushed. "I don't want no reward," she said indignantly. "What I done was for Miss Caroline, that's all, and don't you forget it."

Mr. Ravenshaw took no exception to this impertinence. He said quietly: "You are very fond of her, are you not?"

"That I am, sir! Always treated me kindly, Miss Caroline did, and it fair made my blood boil sometimes to see the way she was put upon in that house. I don't know what I shall do without her, and that's a fact!" She seemed to be on the point of tears again, but managed to control them. "And thank you all the same, sir, but I'd as soon go back on my own. If the missus finds out I been here, like as not she'll lay a stick across my back."

The footman came quietly into the room, and Guy said over his shoulder: "Ask the housekeeper if she will be good enough to come here immediately." He waited until the man had gone, and then asked quietly: "How old are you, Becky?"

She looked surprised. "Fifteen, sir."

"And are you happy at Mrs. Cresswell's?"

"Oh no, sir," she replied simply, "but there's nowhere else for me to go. I'm a foundling, you see."

He nodded, but said no more until the housekeeper came into the room. Becky, who had occupied the interval in looking about her with awed eyes at the most magnifi-

cent apartment she had even seen in her life, eyed the
newcomer rather warily.

"Ah, Mrs. Devon," Guy said pleasantly, "I desire you
to do something for me. This young woman," he nodded
towards Becky, "has been of very great help to me and I
wish you to find a place for her among the female servants. The exact nature of the post I leave to you." He
turned to Becky, who was regarding him with incredulous
amazement, and added kindly: "Go with Mrs. Devon, my
child. I do not wish you to suffer for what you have done,
and I think it will be better if you remain in my household.
There is no need for you to speak to anyone of the matter
which brought you here, but do not worry your head over
Miss Caroline. I promise you that you will see her again
very soon."

Becky started to stammer out her bewildered thanks,
but was cut short by a smile and a quick shake of the head
as Mr. Ravenshaw went out of the room. He had changed
his mind about using one of his own carriages to go in
search of Miss Cresswell, for it had occurred to him that
the less his own servants knew about the matter, the better
it would be. He summoned a hackney to carry him to the
City, hoping that by this time George Cresswell would be
at home, since Mr. Ravenshaw was in no mood for any
further delay. He felt that Caroline had already been in
Mr. Trench's company for far too long.

When he alighted in the street where Henry Cresswell
lived, he discovered that another hackney was drawn up
outside the house, while the manservant and a fair-haired
youth who from Becky's description he recognized as
"Mr. George" were engaged in placing in it a trunk and a
valise. Mr. Ravenshaw paid off his own jarvey and strolled
forward.

George Cresswell's nerves were already in a highly agitated condition, and when a light but imperative tap fell
upon his shoulder he swung round with a gasp of alarm.
The light from the open door of the house revealed a
strong dark-complexioned face with sardonic lips and very
hard grey eyes.

"Mr. George Cresswell, I believe?" the gentleman said quietly. "What a fortunate chance that I arrived when I did. My name is Ravenshaw, and I require some information from you."

12

Further Consequences of Deceit

THE deep misgivings with which Caroline had accepted
Bartholomew Trench's invitation were presently soothed a
little, for during their journey he behaved with perfect
propriety, and conversed upon various harmless topics
with so much good sense that she began to wonder whether she had misjudged him. She still could not like the situation, but comforted herself with the reflection that it was
for a short time only, and that the morrow would see her
on her way to Brightstone Park.

When they reached their destination, however, her earlier doubts revived. The street in which Mrs. Pomfret lived
had seen better days, and about those houses which were
not frankly slatternly hung a depressing air of decayed
gentility. Mrs. Pomfret's residence gave the impression of
being somewhere between the two, for though the windows were hung with limp and rather grubby curtains, and

both the brass door-knocker and the step below would have been the better for cleaning, no dirty children clamoured about its threshold, as they did outside several neighbouring houses, and those who drew near to stare at the occupants of the hackney fled in disorder at a single sharp command from Mr. Trench.

He unlocked the front door with a key which he took from his pocket, and ushered Miss Cresswell through a dark and narrow hall redolent of stale cooking into a parlour overlooking the street. The room was empty, and after poking without much effect at the fire which was smouldering dully in the grate, Mr. Trench excused himself and went in search of his cousin.

Left alone, Caroline took uneasy stock of her surroundings. The room was furnished with a kind of shoddy elegance, but a film of dust lay over everything, the upholstery of chairs and sofa was soiled by much use, and the atmosphere generally depressing. Caroline, looking about her fastidiously, reminded herself that she should be grateful for shelter of any sort, and that but for Mr. Trench she would have found herself without a roof over her head at all.

When he came back into the room she was standing by the fireplace, trying to warm her chilled fingers at the one small flame which flickered among the coals. He came across to join her, saying genially: "Mrs. Pomfret will be with us directly. She was not in the expectation of receiving company, and has gone upstairs to change her gown. Pray sit down, Miss Cresswell."

He pulled a chair closer to the fire, adding as he did so that the room was not very warm, and once more wielded the poker. The small flame flickered and went out.

"Dashed inconvenient," Mr. Trench remarked, eyeing the black, smoking mass resentfully. "Bella never could make a good fire. No notion of it at all. Make you my apologies, ma'am."

"It is of no consequence, sir," Caroline replied politely. "I am quite comfortable, I assure you. My hands were a trifle cold, that is all."

"Not a bit surprised, ma'am. Very chilly evenings at this

time of year. Ought to carry a muff." He calmly possessed himself of one of her hands, holding it between his own large and not altogether cleanly fingers, and shook his head disapprovingly. "No, no, this will not do at all! Must certainly have a muff. Allow me to make you a little present of one."

"Certainly not, sir!" Caroline said sharply, freeing herself from his grasp. "You were good enough to assist me out of a difficult situation, but pray do not make it impossible for me to be grateful."

"No offence, dear lady, no offence," he replied equably. "Like to see a pretty woman comfortable, that's all. No harm in accepting a small gift from a friend, no harm at all."

"Thank you, sir, but I already possess a perfectly good muff," Caroline said coldly. "I have at present loaned it to a friend, but I have no doubt that she will shortly return it to me."

As she spoke there arose in her memory a picture of the chintz-hung bedchamber at the Cap and Bells, and Agnes picking up the muff from the floor where Jenny, in her haste and excitement, had left it lying. Was that really no more than five days ago? It seemed that a whole lifetime had passed since then.

To her relief Mr. Trench did not pursue the subject, but instead resumed his attack upon the fire, which after some minutes rewarded his efforts with a few spurts of flame. Caroline, acutely uneasy now, sat as far away from him as possible and wished fervently that her hostess would put in an appearance.

Some fifteen minutes passed before this wish was granted, and even then it did not bring the reassurance for which Miss Cresswell had hoped. Mrs. Pomfret was a tall, angular woman of about fifty, attired in a startlingly youthful style which would have better become a lady thirty years younger. Her crimped locks were an improbably dense black, her face lavishly painted, and a faint but unmistakable odour of gin clung about her. She greeted Caroline with overpowering friendliness, calling her "dear child," expressing horror at her predicament, and assuring her that she was welcome to stay in her house for as long as she liked.

Caroline thanked her civilly, but assured her that she would be going into the country the next day, and would not impose upon Mrs. Pomfret's hospitality any longer than was strictly necessary. Secretly she was wishing that she had never accepted it; she had felt safer and more at ease during her imprisonment at the Meakes' lonely cottage than she did now.

It was now past six o'clock, and Mrs. Pomfret, who apparently did not keep fashionable hours, declared that the dinner was spoiling and must be served at once. They sat down to table in the parlour, waited on by a grubby little maidservant with a depressing sniff, but though Caroline had eaten very little since breakfast-time she found it impossible to summon up any appetite, for her uneasiness was increasing with every passing minute.

When the meal was over, her hostess disappeared in the wake of the servant, and Miss Cresswell waited in vain for her to return. She had moved from the table to sit on the sofa by the fire, but Mr. Trench was still in his place, with a bottle of port before him and the apparent intention of remaining where he was until it was finished. The wine did not seem to be having the least effect upon him except to make him more voluble than ever. He kept up a constant flow of conversation which was obviously meant to impress her, interspersed as it was with well-known names, but Miss Cresswell, having some acquaintance with the Polite World, remained unimpressed.

"I cannot think where George can have got to," she said at last, taking advantage of a momentary pause in Mr. Trench's flow of anecdote. "Surely he should have been here by now?"

"No need to worry about George, dear lady," Trench assured her blandly. "Stopped to eat his dinner somewhere, I dare say. Wouldn't want to eat it at home, y'know. Not in favour with his mother, or his grandpa either, as I expect you are aware. Don't seem to realize they can't keep a young man in leading-strings for ever. High-spirited lad, George! Old enough to want a little amusement from time to time."

"He is also old enough to realize how much he stands to lose if he quarrels with his grandfather," Caroline said sharply. "You are serving him an ill turn, Mr. Trench, in encouraging his wildness."

She broke off, listening to footsteps in the hall which terminated in the unmistakable sound of the front door closing, and in sudden suspicion jumped up and hurried to the window. Pulling aside the curtain, she was just in time to catch a glimpse of her hostess walking away along the street. Caroline swung round again to face the room.

"Mrs. Pomfret has gone out!"

"Quite right, ma'am," Mr. Trench agreed affably. "Gone to visit friends. Very discreet woman, Bella! Knew we wouldn't want to be disturbed."

Caroline stared at him, all her vague suspicions crystallized now into very real alarm. Controlling with difficulty an instinctive impulse to make a dash for the door, she said coldly: "It seems that both you and Mrs. Pomfret have greatly mistaken the matter. I cannot possibly remain here alone with you for the rest of the evening, and you had no right to suppose that I would."

Mr. Trench pushed back his chair and rose to his feet, still smiling with utmost affability. He came round the table and took Caroline persuasively by the arm.

"Come now, my dear, no need to affect these innocent airs with me, no need at all. I'll own you deceived me in the past with your mock prudishness, but not any more. I know your little secret now, you know." He chuckled, and began to draw her towards the sofa again. "Well, well, no more about that! I'm a broad-minded man, I hope."

"How dare you, sir!" Caroline jerked her arm free, speaking with breathless indignation. "I will not stay here to be insulted in this fashion! Pray let me pass!"

Trench shook his head. He was still smiling, but there was something behind the smile which made her heart turn cold. There was more here, she realized with sudden intuition, than a mere amorous design upon her virtue;

just for an instant she had glimpsed in this man a vicious ruthlessness which terrified her. A moment later it was gone, leaving nothing but the odious familiarity of words and look.

"Very prettily done, ma'am, but wasted upon me. I am not such a simpleton as to believe the tale you tried to fob off on your aunt. Visit to relatives in the country!" He laughed, and slid an arm about her waist. "No, no, that will not do! I have been about the world a little, and I know that that gown you are wearing never came from a country dressmaker. Sly little puss!"

Goaded by fright and anger, Miss Cresswell was betrayed into a reckless show of temper. Her left arm was pinioned to her side by Mr. Trench's tightening embrace, but she swung the right with all her strength and dealt him a resounding slap across the face that made him gasp. Involuntarily he released her and she made a dive for the door, but he was nearer to it than she was and caught her before she reached it.

"Show your claws, would you?" he said viciously, foiling a second blow by catching her about the wrist. "Foolish thing to do, my dear. Very foolish indeed. Must have been spoiled by your rich gallant, but if he bore with your tantrums, I will not. Soon teach you how to behave."

There was the sound of a carriage drawing up in front of the house, and a moment later a distinctive double knock fell upon the front door. Caroline increased her struggles, but Trench merely laughed and thrust her farther into the room.

"Only George, my dear," he told her mockingly, "and he won't interfere. No, by God! Knows better than that. Does what he's told. You'd best do the same, if you don't want to get hurt. Come now, kiss and be friends!"

He was pulling her closer to him, his heated countenance very near her own, and in sudden overwhelming panic Caroline raised her voice in a cry for help. She had heard the servant come from the kitchen to open the door, and felt that even George's feeble support would be better than none.

"Let me go, you beast," she panted. "Let me go! George! George!"

A swift footstep sounded in the hall and the parlour door was thrown open, but it was not George Cresswell who stood upon the threshold. Caroline stared for one incredulous moment, and then with a sob of relief wrenched herself from Mr. Trench's suddenly slackened hold and stumbled forward with outstretched hands. Mr. Ravenshaw took them in a hard, reassuring grip, but said with calm formality: "I am happy to have found you at last, Miss Cresswell, for I have been following you about London for most of the afternoon. I bring you an invitation from my sister-in-law, which I believe you may care to accept. She desires you to give her the pleasure of your company for a few days."

Caroline nodded, only half comprehending what he said, caring for nothing except that he had come as though by a miracle to bring her nightmare to a merciful conclusion. She said in a shaken whisper: "Thank God you have come! Please, please take me away from here!"

"With the greatest pleasure in the world," he replied calmly. "I have a hackney waiting, and your baggage is already in it. You cousin had been kind enough to attend to that." He moved aside from the doorway and added over his shoulder: "Come in, Mr. Cresswell. Your friend, I believe, is expecting you."

George came reluctantly past him into the room, looking in a helpless, frightened way at Bartholomew Trench, who still stood as though petrified, staring at Mr. Ravenshaw with dropped jaw and starting eyes. Guy paid no heed to him, but, discovering Miss Cresswell's pelisse on a nearby chair, picked it up and held it for her to put on, and then handed her her bonnet, reticule and gloves.

"Let us go, ma'am," he said quietly. "Jane will be anxious for you to join her. I do not think you need trouble yourself to take leave of Mr. Trench."

These last words were spoken with a cool, challenging glance at the other man, but Mr. Trench uttered neither reply nor protest. The faintest expression of regret came into Guy's grey eyes, but he said nothing as he turned to escort Miss Cresswell out of the house.

They were in the carriage and driving away before Caroline was sufficiently in command of herself to speak. Guy had made no attempt to break the silence, and at last she said in a low, diffident voice: "I do not know how you happened to come to that house, but I have never been so thankful to see anyone in all my life." This brought no response, and after a brief pause she went on, more diffidently than before: "You must think it very odd in me to have gone there as I did, but, you see, Mrs. Fenton was away, and I had no money, and nowhere else to go——" the words faded into silence, and she sat twisting her hands nervously about the strings of the bonnet which lay in her lap.

"I am fully acquainted with all the circumstances, ma'am," he replied in a hard voice, "and I appreciate the difficulty in which you found yourself. The only thing which sticks in my throat is the fact that you apparently found this man Trench more worthy of your trust than myself."

She uttered a faint denial, but he went on harshly: "Why, in the name of Heaven, did you not come to me? You cannot have supposed that I would refuse to help you?"

"No! Oh no, but how could I come to you? I had no right, and I have caused you so much trouble already." She tried to speak composedly, but failed most lamentably, for this quarrel, coming as it did after the shocks and strain of the day, was more than she could bear. Her voice broke, and for the second time that day the usually composed Miss Cresswell gave way to tears.

The effect was immediate. Mr. Ravenshaw, whose anger had been a purely natural reaction from the anxiety he had suffered on her behalf, was instantly stricken with remorse. It had always been his custom to regard tears as a feminine weapon of a particularly despicable kind, but now that cynical dictum was wholly forgotten. He simply gathered the woe-begone figure into a close and comforting embrace, and said urgently: "My poor child, there is no need to cry! I am the greatest brute in nature to treat you so, after all that you have been through to-day."

Miss Cresswell's denial of this was vehement but indistinct, since her face was buried in the many capes of his greatcoat, but after a minute or two she became aware of the indecorous nature of this position. With the utmost reluctance she raised her head from his shoulder and groped for her handkerchief, saying unsteadily: "I am truly sorry to behave so foolishly, and I do not know why you should be so good to me. I am sure I do not deserve it."

At her first movement to free herself he had let her go, and she sat up and dried her eyes, trying hard to recover her composure. This was not easy. She was very much afraid that she had betrayed herself, for her heart was beating breathlessly fast, in a way which had nothing to do with her recent alarming experiences, and she could only be glad of the darkness that hid her face from him.

"If I treated you as you deserve," Guy said reflectively, in a tone of some amusement, "I should probably beat you. I would not go through this day again for a fortune."

There seemed to be no suitable reply to this. Caroline resolutely blew her nose, tucked her handkerchief away and pulled on her bonnet, tying the strings firmly beneath her chin. It was easier, she felt, to be dignified in a bonnet than with one's hair uncovered and considerably ruffled by a gentleman's embrace.

"Where are you taking me, sir?" she asked meekly after a little while.

"To my sister-in-law, as I told you." The amusement in his voice was more pronounced than ever. "You cannot have been attending, Miss Cresswell. Or did you imagine that that was merely a polite untruth to cover some less respectable intention?" He paused expectantly, but there was no response. Guy laughed softly. "Very well, I will tease you no more tonight. You shall go to Jane for the present, but I will take you to your cousin's house whenever you wish. In the circumstances, though, it would probably be as well to write to her first. She must be exceedingly anxious about you."

"She must, indeed!" Caroline agreed in a stricken voice,

for she had forgotten that as far as the Wilde family were concerned she had not been heard of since her abduction five days before. "So much has happened to me lately that I scarcely know whether I am on my head or my heels. I do not even know how you contrived to find me this evening."

He told her, describing the events which had taken place since his arrival at her uncle's house that afternoon. For the most part she listened without interrupting, but when he mentioned in passing the provision he had made for Becky, she found it impossible to refrain from comment.

"Oh, how good you are!" she exclaimed impulsively, laying a hand on his arm. "Who else would have concerned themselves so for the poor child?"

There was a tiny pause before he replied, and then he said with a very sardonic intonation: "Rid yourself of the notion, ma'am, that I make a practice of indulging in philanthropic gestures. I merely like to pay my debts. The girl had rendered me a great service, and it would have been the rankest ingratitude to send her back to face the consequences of what she had done."

Caroline smiled to herself in the darkness, but said no more. It was plain that he desired no thanks for what he had done, and that he saw nothing out of the way in providing for an ill-treated little servant girl. It was strange, she thought, that a nature capable of such spontaneous kindness should present so very different a picture of itself to the world at large.

"After that, everything was quite simple," Guy concluded briefly. "I was fortunate enough to find your cousin leaving his father's house, and the rest you know."

"Yes, indeed, and can never thank you enough for coming to look for me; I was dreadfully frightened. But there is one thing, sir, which I do not quite understand. Why did you go to my uncle's house in the first instance?"

"To see you, Miss Cresswell," he replied calmly. "I hoped to persuade you to come driving with me. I had a notion that you might wish to know the outcome of our adventures. Have you no curiosity at all?"

"Of course I have," Caroline said promptly, firmly subduing her elation at this proof that he had wished to see her again, "but I imagined that I would be obliged to wait until I could hear the rest of the story from Jennifer or Mrs. Fenton."

"Not at all. As the originator of the whole scheme, it is only just that you should be informed immediately of the results of it." He sounded again as though he were amused. "When I left you yesterday I went straight back to my own house, where, as you can imagine, I found that my servants had been considerably mystified by my disappearance, and even more so by the letter which I sent from Colonel Morecambe's house. However, my butler informed me that late on the evening of my departure, my cousin Pelham had visited the house again." Caroline uttered an exclamation of surprised indignation, and Guy laughed. "Precisely, ma'am! He has never lacked impudence. He must have driven straight back to London, left his man to dispose of the curricle and horses, and gone immediately to my house. He told the butler that I had requested him to meet me there, and expressed surprise that I had not already returned."

"Well," Caroline said indignantly, "that is really the outside of enough! What was his purpose in going there? To avoid suspicion of being involved in your disappearance?"

"Partly that, I believe, though he had another motive as well. He told the butler that he would wait until I returned, as the matter which we were to discuss was of some importance, but after remaining long enough to lend colour to his story he affected annoyance, said that he would leave a note for me, and was duly conducted to the library. I have a writing desk there, where I usually deal with my correspondence." He paused, and then added in his driest tone: "As Pelham was well aware, it is also my habit to keep in it a considerable sum of money."

"Oh, good God!" Caroline exclaimed in shocked tones. "Do you mean that he had the effrontery to rifle your desk, and then walk calmly out of the house?"

"I mean exactly that, Miss Cresswell. He certainly left a

letter for me, a characteristic document explaining that in view of recent events he felt that his health would benefit from a holiday abroad, and telling me the direction of the livery-stable where I would find my curricle and horses. He added that he regretted the necessity of returning these to me, but that they were a trifle too well known for him to sell. He then handed the letter to my butler, and walked off with a large roll of bills and as many small articles of value as he could comfortably conceal in his pockets. I do not know how much he was obliged to pay his valet and the others, but bearing in mind the fact that he had once more possessed himself of Miss Linley's diamond ring, I fancy that he must have come out of the affair richer by some fifteen hundred pounds."

"He is the most wicked, unprincipled young man I have ever heard of!" Caroline said indignantly. "Do you know, sir, he was ready to murder you that night at the cottage, after his man had struck you down?"

"I can well believe it," Guy replied coolly. "In fact, I feel that I have escaped very lightly, for it will be a long time before he ventures to show his face in England again. Moreover, the price he demanded for the safe return of his prisoner was twenty thousand pounds."

"Twenty thousand!" she repeated faintly. "Would you have paid it, sir?"

"Certainly, if it had been impossible to rescue her by any other means, but fortunately the necessity did not arise. I can well imagine the glee with which Pelham would have discovered her identity, if the money had been safely in his pocket. To have ransomed my future wife for such a sum, only to find that she was already on her way to Gretna Green with another man, would have made me look so very ridiculous."

Caroline shuddered. "Thank heaven it did not come to that, though the present situation is quite bad enough."

"I fancy it is not quite as desperate as you suppose. Having informed myself of Pelham's past activities and future intentions, I then paid a call on Lady Linley." He chuckled. "A somewhat trying interview, to say the least of it."

"I believe you, sir, and to tell the truth, I was very glad that you refused my offer to go with you. I dare say her ladyship holds me to blame for the whole affair."

"Yes, her comments on your character and conduct were not at all flattering," Guy said thoughtfully, "though I believe I eventually convinced her that you had acted from the most praiseworthy motives, and that her own conduct in the matter was not above reproach. I was obliged, of course, to tell her the whole story, and since Miss Linley's disappearance has made such a noise in the world, it will be impossible to deny that it happened. However, it has been decided to say that the supposed kidnapping was merely a ruse to cover her elopement, since that will shortly have to be made known also. In that way your name can be kept out of the affair, which is the point that matters most to me."

"You persuaded Lady Linley to agree to that?" Caroline asked in amazement.

"It was not easy, I admit, but in the end her ladyship was brought to see that after the shabby way in which her daughter has treated me, my wishes are entitled to some consideration. I will have you know, Miss Cresswell, that it is no small thing to be jilted almost on the eve of one's wedding."

She could not help laughing at this. "You know very well, sir, that you do not care a rap for what the world may say to that. As for losing Jenny, you told me yourself that since she is so deeply in love with Roland, you accounted it a fortunate escape."

"True, but we cannot expect Lady Linley to see it in quite the same way. The important point, however, is that she agreed, and though a certain number of people will have to be told the truth, I think we can depend upon them to respect the confidence." He broke off as the hackney came to a halt, and leaned forward to open the door. "Journey's end, Miss Cresswell! You will find Jane very eager to welcome you."

In some trepidation Caroline allowed herself to be escorted into the house, for she could not help feeling that Mr. Ravenshaw had painted too glowing a picture of his sister-in-law's readiness to accept a total stranger as her guest. From the moment they entered the drawing-room, however, her doubts were set at rest, for Jane jumped up out of her chair and came forward with outstretched hands.

"My dear Miss Cresswell, I am so very glad to see you! Guy has been gone for such an age that I began to fear some accident had befallen you, but now you are here, and all is well. I will just take you upstairs to put off your bonnet and pelisse, and then we will go in to dinner. Guy, you will stay to dine with us, will you not?"

"With very great pleasure, Jane," he replied with a smile. "In fact, I have been depending on it."

Jane laughed, and led Caroline away to a bedchamber where her own maid was in attendance, and Miss Cresswell's trunk and valise had just been set down.

"I have instructed Alice to wait upon you, as you were unable to bring your own abigail with you," Jane informed Caroline smoothly. "You will find her very able, I assure you." She watched the other girl take off her bonnet, and added enviously: "What beautiful hair you have! I have always wished that I could be a red-head or a brunette, instead of an insipid blonde."

Miss Cresswell could not help smiling a little at this, for she had always regarded her colouring as a drawback rather than an asset, but it was impossible to suspect Jane Ravenshaw of being anything but sincere. Caroline thought her exceedingly pretty, with her fair curls and deep blue eyes, and said so, matching frankness with frankness. Jane smiled and shook her head.

"Oh, I am nothing out of the ordinary," she said ruefully, "but you, my dear Miss Cresswell, must always take the eye." She laughed. "You will be thinking me excessively ill-bred, I am sure, to be talking to you in such fashion upon such short acquaintance, but indeed, I feel that I know you quite well already. May I call you Caroline?"

"Indeed you may," Caroline said warmly, "and I cannot tell you how grateful I am for all your kindness. I was afraid—" she broke off, for the maid, who had just lifted the lid of the trunk preparatory to unpacking it, had uttered a shocked and startled exclamation which drew the attention of both ladies upon her.

"What is it, Alice?" Jane asked in surprise.

"Well, madam, I don't rightly know, but I'd like you and Miss to witness that I've but this moment opened the trunk. I'd not want Miss Cresswell to think her things got into that state in this house, and they can't, surely, have been packed like that!"

Jane and Caroline went to look into the open trunk, and then exchanged a startled glance. The contents were in wild confusion, as though they had been flung in pell-mell by someone in frantic haste. Alice, unfastening the valise silently held it out for their inspection, revealing a similar state of chaos inside.

"No," Caroline said slowly after a moment, "they were certainly not packed like that. It is obvious that someone has been through them since."

13

The Matchmakers

"But why?" Jane said insistently, by no means for the first time. "Why should anyone wish to search Caroline's baggage?"

Dinner was over, and the two ladies and Mr. Ravenshaw were gathered about the fire in Jane's charming drawing-room. There had been barely time before the meal to acquaint Guy with the startling discovery they had made, and during it the presence of the servants had made any discussion impossible, but as soon as they found themselves alone Jane had returned to a subject which she seemed inclined to regard with much more alarm and dismay than did Caroline herself.

"Has Miss Cresswell no theory to put forward?" Guy asked with a smile. "Come, ma'am, surely you can throw some light upon the mystery."

Caroline shook her head. She could think of no reason why anyone should be interested in her few personal belongings, and at that moment, being possessed by a sense of complete well-being, was not particularly concerned to find one. Jane's warm welcome, followed by an excellent dinner, had done much to restore her to her customary spirits; she was tired, but pleasantly so; her chair was very comfortable, and her left foot reposed on a footstool placed for her without comment by Mr. Ravenshaw when he observed that she was limping; Guy himself was smiling at her from the opposite side of the fireplace. This could, she knew, be no more than a brief, delightful interlude, but while it lasted she was as near perfect contentment as she had ever been in her life.

"I cannot imagine who could have done it," she said lazily. "It must have occurred at my uncle's house, yet everyone there knew better than to expect anything of value to be concealed amongst *my* property. Unless, of course, Aunt Lizzie suspected me of making off with her best silver teaspoons."

"I wish you will be serious," Jane said, with an indignation only partly assumed. "If such a thing had happened to me, I should have been thrown into the strongest agitation, but you seem to treat it as a mere jest."

"Oh, you are not yet very well acquainted with Miss Cresswell, Jane," Guy assured her solemnly. "When you know her better, you will realize that it takes a great deal to overset *her* nerves."

"To tell you the truth," Caroline replied confidentially, "so many hair-raising things have happened to me during the past few days that the mere fact of having my boxes searched seems very trivial. A week ago, Jane, I should have felt just as you do. Now I find that I can accept it as a matter of course."

Jane looked from one to the other, and shook her head in mock rebuke. "I can see that neither of you intend to treat the matter with proper seriousness," she said with a smile. "Guy, I have something to tell you which you may regard as less amusing. Lady Dinsmore came to see me today."

He looked up sharply. "Aunt Augusta? What brought her here?"

"Curiosity, I am afraid," Jane replied. "She had come straight from Lady Linley, and what she learned there brought her at once to me."

He shrugged. "It does not matter. There was never any hope of keeping the affair from her, thanks to Pelham's part in it, for though the world may be allowed to believe that he went abroad to avoid his creditors, it is only right that his immediate relatives should be told the truth. Fortunately, their number is not large. Did you tell her the whole story?"

"Yes, for I thought that was what you would wish me to do. She was a little put out that you had not been to see her, but I explained that you had not as yet had time to do so, but had formed the intention of calling upon her tomorrow."

He smiled, but shook his head. "Diplomatic, Jane, but quite mistaken. I have no intention of calling upon Aunt Augusta tomorrow. I am going to take Miss Cresswell driving." Caroline looked up quickly, encountered a quizzical glance that made her heart beat faster, and in some confusion lowered her eyes again. "If she will give me the pleasure of her company," Mr. Ravenshaw added softly.

"Well, as it happens, that does not matter in the least," Jane replied, apparently unaware of this piece of by-play between her guests, "since Lady Dinsmore said that she would be calling upon me instead. She also said that we were well rid of Pelham, and that you need not fear that either she or Sir Arthur will breathe a word to anyone, and you know, Guy, I feel sure that that is true."

"I am quite certain that it is," he agreed indifferently. "Aunt Augusta may pride herself upon her frankness, but where any matter private to the family is concerned, she may be trusted to hold her tongue. I am grateful to you, Jane! You have spared me the necessity of explaining it all to her."

Jane smiled and shook her head. She did not feel it necessary to disclose to him the fact that Lady Dinsmore had shown only the most perfunctory interest in the iniquity of her younger nephew, all her attention being centered upon the lady who figured so largely in the affair. Lady Linley, it seemed had painted an extremely unflattering picture of Miss Cresswell, and Jane had felt herself in duty bound to correct what she felt sure must be a false impression. Lady Dinsmore had listened with deep interest, and finally given it as her opinion that there was a good deal more in the matter than met the eye.

"Guy dancing attendance upon a female?" she had said in her forthright way. "That is something which I never thought to see, for even Miss Linley received from him no more attention than was demanded by courtesy. Cresswell, you say? I remember Richard Cresswell thirty years ago—a graceless scamp, if ever there was one! No looks to speak of, but more charm than was good for any man. He married Marianne Kelshall, who was as poor as he was himself, but she died when the child was born. That must be all of twenty-five years ago. So Guy is to bring the girl to visit you, is he? What does that portend, I wonder? I will call upon you tomorrow, Jane, and you may tell me what you think of her."

No, Jane reflected now, stealing a glance at her brother-in-law's strong profile, it would certainly not do to let him know about that. He had never taken kindly to intrusion upon his personal affairs, and even she, who was upon better terms with him than anyone else, would not venture any attempt to force his confidence. Having had an opportunity to observe Guy and Caroline together, any doubts of the accuracy of her suspicions were now at an end, but she was content to await patiently the outcome of the affair.

Aloud she said: "Lady Dinsmore told me that she found Lady Linley on the point of setting out for Westbridge. It seems that she has decided to make the best of things, since nothing can now be done to alter them, and has gone to assure Captain Wilde's parents that she is ready to accept the match."

"I am heartily glad to hear it," Caroline said emphatically, "for though I felt sure that her ladyship would come about in the end, I feared that it might take a little time.

She is really very fond of Roland, you know, and was quite happy about the match until *you,* sir," with a mock-reproachful glance at Mr. Ravenshaw, "put more grandiose ideas into her head. After that, of course, she could not be persuaded to relinquish them, even though it meant breaking Jenny's heart, and Roland's, too."

"Not, that is, until the ingenious Miss Cresswell took a hand in the affair," Guy retorted teasingly. "No doubt you are feeling very pleased with yourself, now that everything has fallen out as you supposed."

"Certainly I am," she replied saucily. "It is always heartening to discover that one is right. In fact, there is only one thing which does *not* please me. If Lady Linley has gone to Westbridge, she no doubt intends to remain there until Jenny and Roland return from Scotland, so I shall see her at Brightstone Park, and cannot hope to escape the scolding which I am sure she is longing to give me."

"Then do not go to Brightstone, ma'am," Guy said promptly. "Stay here with Jane."

"Yes, Caroline, do!" Jane agreed eagerly, laying her hand on the other girl's arm. "I shall be so very happy to keep you with me."

Caroline looked from one to the other, her eyes unusually bright. "You are both so kind," she said unsteadily, "but indeed, indeed I must not stay! I shall go to Cousin Esther for a time, though she does not really need me, you know, for she has an unmarried sister who lives with her. I must look about me for a post as governess in some respectable household. I can claim considerable experience in that direction, and it should not be very difficult to find a place."

"Surely you need not be in any haste to seek employment?" Jane protested. "I think you ought to stay with me for a while, Caroline."

Miss Cresswell smiled and shook her head. "If I did so, Jane, I should very soon acquire a taste for idleness, and then where should I be? Do not look so distressed! I realized many years ago that I should be obliged to support myself, and I resolved then never to be a charge upon anyone." She gave a rueful little laugh. "The thing is that I inherited from my Papa an incurable love of luxury, which I have to keep very firmly in its place if it is not to get the better of me. So you see, you will be doing me an ill turn if you persuade me to indulge it."

"I would not want to do that, of course," Jane said doubtfully, "though I wish I could be sure how much of what you say is true, and how much mere excuses. Guy, why do you say nothing? Perhaps your advice would carry greater weight than mine."

"I say nothing, Jane, because I am quite certain that Miss Cresswell will follow whatever course seems best to her, no matter what advice she may be given, and regardless of the consequences. Although I hope very much that she will stay with you, I shall not try to persuade her to do so against her will."

Jane was disappointed, but after a little consideration fancied she had discovered the reason for Mr. Ravenshaw's attitude. With no money in her purse, and none of her other friends in Town, Caroline was for the present completely dependent upon him, and Jane knew that he would not seek to take advantage of the fact. So she let the subject drop, but later, when Guy had taken his leave, and the two ladies were enjoying a friendly gossip before retiring, she referred to it again. Chivalry might prevent Guy from trying to persuade Miss Cresswell to remain in London, but his sister-in-law did not feel herself to be similarly handicapped. Moreover, during the course of the evening a brilliant idea had occurred to her.

"Caroline," she said impulsively, "I wish you will reconsider your decision to leave London. No, listen to me for a moment," for the elder girl had shaken her head warningly, "I am not offering you charity. The thing is that my Mama is forever plaguing me to have some respectable female to live with me, and saying that it is not right for me to be quite alone. I know that if I do not soon engage a companion, Mama will do so for me, and that would be beyond bearing. Do say that you will stay! I am sure that we should deal extremely well together."

For a moment or two Miss Cresswell was sorely tempted. She had taken an instant liking to Jane, and this offer would mean the end of her present difficulties, but neither of these considerations was foremost in her mind. To remain permanently in this house, where Guy Ravenshaw was a frequent visitor, seemed at first sight the answer to an unspoken prayer, but even as she opened her lips to say that she would stay, the utter folly of such a course dawned upon her. However considerately Jane treated her, she would still be a paid dependent, ranking only a very little way above the upper servants; she would be no more a part of Guy's world than if she had remained in her uncle's house. The only sane course would be to place as great a distance as possible between them, so instead of agreeing with Jane's suggestion, she shook her head and said gently:

"I am sure we should, my dear, and it is exceedingly kind in you to think of it, but I do not believe that it would serve. For one thing, I feel sure that your Mama intends you to engage someone a good deal older than I am, and for another it would be extremely difficult for you to explain to her how you came to offer the post to me. If she ever found out about my adventures during the past week, she would probably decide that I have no claim to respectability whatsoever."

"As to that, I could tell her that Mrs. Fenton sent you to me," Jane replied promptly, "but I shall not say any more to you on this head at present. Just promise me that you will think about it, and I shall not despair of you agreeing, for there is no need to make up your mind immediately. You will not be going to Hertfordshire for a few days, now will you?"

"I ought to go tomorrow," Caroline said in a troubled voice, "for it will not do for people to know that I am staying with you. Mr. Ravenshaw has taken great pains to make it appear that Jenny's kidnapping was merely part of a plan to enable her to elope with Roland, and we must not do anything to betray the truth."

"How, pray, can your staying with me do that? By this time, Pelham will be out of the country, and everyone else who knows the truth can be trusted to remain silent. I suppose that I may have a friend to visit me if I choose?" She observed that Miss Cresswell was about to speak again, and added severely: "And do not say anything nonsensical about not going driving with Guy tomorrow. There is not the smallest reason in the world why you should not do so."

Caroline remained unconvinced, but since she had been firm on the larger issue, she felt that it would do no harm to take what pleasure she could from the present.

She was more tired than she realized, and slept late next morning, Jane having given orders that she was not to be disturbed. When she had risen and breakfasted she was prevailed upon, somewhat reluctantly, to accompany her hostess on a shopping expedition to Bond Street. There were a good many other fashionable people patronizing the famous thoroughfare, and several times Jane was greeted by acquaintances, to each of whom she calmly presented her friend, Miss Cresswell, while Caroline, still in the reckless mood of the previous evening, turned a deaf ear to the inner voice which spoke warningly of the unwisdom of her present behaviour.

Midway through the afternoon, Lady Dinsmore arrived in Park Street on her promised visit, and was both surprised and gratified to find Miss Cresswell there. She swept into the drawing-room where the two young ladies were sitting, a tall, commanding woman of sixty, dressed in a style which indicated both excellent taste and a large fortune, and with a cast of countenance which marked her unmistakably as a Ravenshaw. Caroline made her curtsy, and found herself being studied by a pair of shrewd but not unkindly grey eyes.

"So this is Richard Cresswell's daughter!" her ladyship remarked by way of greeting. "Yes, no need to tell me that! You are very like him, Miss Cresswell. The same colouring and the same smile. Jane, you did not tell me that Miss Cresswell was to stay with you."

"It was not then decided, ma'am," Jane replied calmly. "She is shortly going to her cousin, Mrs. Wilde, in Hertfordshire, but has agreed to spend a few days with me first."

"Mrs. Wilde, I presume, is the mother of this young man who has carried off Miss Linley from under Guy's nose?" Lady Dinsmore said cheerfully. "I am told, Miss Cresswell, that you are largely responsible for that."

"I merely showed them how it might be done, ma'am," Caroline replied. "The match between them was made long ago, by mutual trust and affection."

Her ladyship nodded, but appeared to have no further interest in Captain Wilde and his bride, and instead began to question Miss Cresswell closely regarding her childhood and girlhood. Jane was very much afraid that Caroline would be offended by this blatant curiosity, or that Lady Dinsmore's notorious frankness would prompt her to say something embarrassing, but neither of these things occurred. Caroline answered promptly and candidly, with no hint of resentment, and only began to falter in her replies when the events of the previous day were reached. Jane was just wondering how to come to her rescue when a welcome diversion was created by the arrival of Mr. Ravenshaw.

"I thought," said Lady Dinsmore pointedly as he bowed over her hand, "that you meant to call upon me to-day. But perhaps you are here as a result of the message I left for you with my butler?"

"Not at all," he replied coolly. "I have come to take Miss Cresswell driving." He turned from her to greet Caroline, taking her hand and looking down at her with a smile which caused his aunt's eyebrows to lift a fraction. "Well, ma'am, has Jane yet succeeded in persuading you to prolong your visit?"

"For a few days, sir," she replied. "I feel that I am imposing upon her kindness, but she will not have it so."

"Of course she will not!" Lady Dinsmore announced unexpectedly. "It is a very good thing for her to have a companion of her own age staying in the house. Yes, Jane, I know you have a great many friends, but that is not at all the same thing."

Caroline was suddenly stricken by the fear that Lady Dinsmore was about to make the same suggestion as Jane had done the previous evening, and was thankful when her hostess remarked that if she intended to drive out with Guy she had better go and put on her hat, as he would not wish to keep his horses standing. So eager was she to escape from her ladyship's presence that she quite forgot the protests she had intended to make on the score of propriety, and went upstairs at once to make ready for the outing.

"I like that girl!" Lady Dinsmore remarked when the door had closed behind her. "She has a great deal of commonsense, and does not put herself forward in any way. Well, Guy, this is a sad tangle your affairs are in! As I told Jane yesterday, the one good thing which has come out of it is the fact that we are rid of Pelham at last."

He raised his brows. "I cannot entirely agree with you, ma'am. A good thing certainly, but neither the only one nor yet the best."

"Oh?" She regarded him expectantly. "What, then, is the best?"

"What do you suppose?" There was a slightly malicious mockery in his voice. "Surely I must account myself fortunate in escaping marriage with a lady as unwilling as Miss Linley? What could such a union have brought to either of us but great unhappiness?"

She looked faintly disappointed, but rallied after a moment and said forcibly: "That is very true, and in that respect I am sure it has all happened for the best, but the fact remains that it is your duty to marry. You will have to choose another bride."

"I intend to do so. Let us hope that I choose more happily next time."

More than that he would not say, but turned the conversation to matters of general interest, and kept it there until Miss Cresswell came into the room again. When she had taken leave of the other ladies, and Guy had escorted her out of the house, Jane looked across at Lady Dinsmore with mischief in her eyes. "Well, ma'am? Are you satisfied?"

Her ladyship pursed her lips. "Partially, Jane. If it were any other man than Guy, I should have no doubt that he is in love with her."

"Why, pray, should you suppose Guy to be more immune from the tender passion than any other man?" Jane retorted with some heat. "I have always believed him to be capable of very deep feeling, and that the right woman would have no difficulty in capturing his heart. That is why I never liked his engagement to Miss Linley."

"You think, then, that Miss Cresswell is the right woman?"

"I am sure of it, and what is more, I believe that Guy is sure of it also. It is true that they have been acquainted only a very few days, but when one considers the circumstances—"

"Oh, Guy was never slow to make up his mind, no matter how important the issue involved! Well, well, I suppose it would serve! To be sure, she is no beauty, but her style is very striking, and I fancy she has a great deal of her father's charm. It is a pity, however, that she has no fortune."

"Dear ma'am, what can that signify? Guy has no need of a rich wife, and her birth, at least, is as good as his."

"Oh, better, my dear, no doubt of that! The Cresswells are a very old family indeed. I have no quarrel with the match on that score, I assure you."

"And I have no quarrel with it on any score, for I am convinced that they were meant for each other. I have never seen so great a change in anyone as in Guy during these past two days." She began to laugh. "And you know, ma'am, that even if we both viewed the possibility of such a marriage with the strongest disapproval, it would make not the least difference! Guy will not ask either of us to advise him in the matter."

14

Conversation in the Park

WHILE this conversation was taking place, Mr. Ravenshaw and Miss Cresswell, unaware that their future was being decided by Lady Dinsmore, were driving in the direction of Hyde Park. They were alone, for after handing his companion up into the curricle and taking his place beside her, Guy had curtly ordered his groom to wait for him in Park Street. Caroline made no comment, but after the curricle had moved away from the house, she said dubiously: "Was it wise, sir, to leave your man behind? Should he not have come with us?"

He flashed her a quick, laughing glance. "Can it be, Miss Cresswell, that you are nervous of being alone in my company?"

"Hardly that, sir," she replied drily. "I am concerned merely to keep within the strictest bounds of propriety."

"You amaze me, ma'am," he murmured. "However, I

understand from Jane that she has already presented you to several of her friends, and it will not be thought wonderful that I should be driving a guest of hers."

"Will it not?" she retorted. "I was under the impression, Mr. Ravenshaw, that you are not much in the habit of gallanting females."

He smiled, but made no reply, and for a minute or two they drove on in silence. There was a good deal of traffic about, and Miss Cresswell watched with admiration her companion's handling of his mettlesome team. After a little while she asked curiously: "Are these the horses, sir, with which your cousin made off that night?"

"They are, ma'am, and you may imagine how glad I was to have them restored to me. Fortunately Pelham is a tolerable whip, and they had come to no harm at his hands."

"They are magnificent animals," she said warmly. "My father taught me to appreciate the finer points of a horse, and of driving, too, but unfortunately he was never, during my recollection, in a position to maintain a stable. It has always been my ambition to handle the ribbons."

"One day, Miss Cresswell, I will teach you," he said calmly, "though not with this team. They are by far too strong for a lady."

Caroline was at a loss to know how to answer this. He spoke as though the present state of affairs could continue indefinitely, as though they would be seeing each other repeatedly upon equal terms, and she knew that it would be fatally easy to fall into the same way of thinking. To remind herself of the great gulf which must always yawn between them, she said after a moment: "I was so very thankful, sir, that you came when you did. Lady Dinsmore had just asked me how I happened to be visiting with Jane, and I was cast into great confusion. Not for the world would I have told her the truth."

"I am happy, then, that I arrived in time to rescue you. I believe that you are right, and that it would be best to keep the episode of Mr. Trench to ourselves."

"I am sure *I* do not wish to speak of it. Do you know,

the more I think about it, the more convinced I become that he had some purpose in enticing me to that house?"

Mr. Ravenshaw's lips twitched, and there was a suspicious tremor in his voice as he replied gravely: "I should think that it is highly probable."

Miss Cresswell cast him a darkling glance. "Now you are laughing at me," she said indignantly. "Of course he tried to make love to me, but I do not mean that. There was just one moment when it seemed as though a mask had dropped from his face, and all his vanity and geniality, even his odious gallantry, showed as no more than an empty shell with something indescribably cruel and evil within it. I have never been so frightened in all my life! Now tell me that you think this no more than a disordered fancy."

"I think," Guy said quietly, "that last night you were tired and overwrought by all that had happened, and by the position in which you found yourself. Certainly Trench is an unpleasant character, and probably even a downright scoundrel, but he will not be permitted to alarm you again."

They were into the Park by now, joining the throng of carriages which was passing to and fro, for this was the fashionable hour of the promenade, and Society was taking the air in carriages, on horseback and afoot. Miss Cresswell was aware of numerous curious and startled glances turned upon her, and not even the knowledge that she was as stylishly dressed as any lady in the Park could set her entirely at her ease, though she contrived to dissemble the embarrassment she felt. A large number of people acknowledged Mr. Ravenshaw, but to all greetings he replied with no more than a smile or a bow, so that when at length he was hailed by a young man dressed in the extreme of fashion Caroline was startled and dismayed to find him drawing rein. The exquisite gentleman strolled up to them and bowed.

"Servant, Ravenshaw," he drawled, but then, as his glance shifted to Miss Cresswell, mild curiosity gave way to astonishment, and both eyes and voice sharpened considerably. "Good God! Caro!"

Caroline found herself looking down into the handsome but slightly dissipated countenance of Sir Reginald Linley, and bowed with as much composure as she could muster. "Good afternoon, Reginald. It is a long time since we met."

"So it is, by Jove! I didn't recognize you at first. But how is this? I did not know that you were acquainted with Ravenshaw."

"It is just possible, Linley, that you do *not* know everything about me," Guy said gently, "or even about Miss Cresswell. She is at present staying with my sister-in-law, and has done me the honour of driving out with me."

The satirical tone was not lost upon Sir Reginald, who hurriedly begged pardon and said that it was none of his business anyway. Mr. Ravenshaw agreed, and asked blandly if there was any way in which he might be of service to him. Reginald looked vaguely embarrassed.

"No, no! Just wished to say, devilish business this, Ravenshaw! Had the whole story from m'mother. Felt I owed you an apology."

Guy's brows lifted. "Indeed? Am I to understand, then, that you were aware of your sister's intention?"

"Lord, no!" Reginald replied hastily. "I knew, of course, that she was kicking up the devil of a fuss about being compelled to marry you after Roland came home, but there was nothing *I* could do about it. Ask Caro, if you don't believe me! As for knowing of the plot, do you suppose I would have gone chasing off to Whetstone, and spent two devilish days there, arguing with constables and magistrates and Lord knows what besides, if I'd known all the time that Jenny was safely on her way to Gretna Green?" He sighed deeply, and added that he didn't know what had come over his family during the past week.

"Bad enough Jenny making a bolt for it, without having a robbery and murder at my uncle's house. You heard about that, I suppose?"

Guy nodded. "Yes, a very shocking affair. Have the culprits yet been found?"

"One of them has, in a manner of speaking. The Runners caught up with him somewhere down by the river, and the fellow tried to swim for it and was drowned. No doubt he *was* concerned in the robbery, for a large part of the loot was found in his lodging, but the Runners think the actual murderer is still at large. They hoped his confederate would give evidence against him, but now they find themselves at a standstill. Seems they have a suspicion who he is, but can't arrest him for lack of evidence."

Caroline shivered. "It is a charming thought, is it not," she observed, "that a murderer may be walking freely among us at this very moment."

"He is hardly likely to be walking here, Miss Cresswell," Guy pointed out with a smile, "even though there are a number of exceedingly eccentric characters in the Polite World."

"Lord, no!" Reginald agreed heartily. "Depend upon it, the rogue, whoever he is, will be lying low in some thieves' den or other with Jenny's ruby pendant burning a hole in his pocket. Daren't try to sell it, you see, because it's the one thing now that could hang him."

"The pendant was not recovered then?" Caroline asked in some surprise.

"No, and my uncle's as mad as fire. Seems he's had that stone for years, waiting for some occasion important enough to warrant having it set, and he thought he'd found it in Jenny's wedding. Thinks the world of the chit, y'know. Always has! Says he'd still give the ruby to her, if it could be found, though what use such a gaud would be to her now I can't imagine. Worth a small fortune, of course, but if she ever sold it, the old gentleman would never forgive her."

"It would, of course, be no use to her while she follows the drum," Caroline agreed fairmindedly, "but the war will not last for ever, and Jenny and Roland will come back to London one day. She could wear it then."

"It seems to me," Mr. Ravenshaw interposed coolly, "that the immediate importance of the pendant is whether or not it will be the means of bringing a murderer to justice. Frankly, I doubt it! So small an object would not be difficult to smuggle out of the country."

"That's what the Bow Street fellows say," Reginald replied gloomily. "Threw my uncle into a fine rage, as you can imagine. Thought he was going to have an apoplexy, myself!" He seemed about to take his leave when another thought occurred to him, and he added triumphantly: "Knew there was something else I wanted to say to you, Ravenshaw! Do you know what's become of Pel? He was supposed to dine with me yesterday, but he never came, and now I find that he's left Duke Street altogether."

There was a moment's silence, while Caroline steadfastly regarded a passing carriage, and Mr. Ravenshaw looked down inscrutably at Reginald's upraised face. Then he said quietly: "That is quite true. I am afraid, Linley, that you will not see Pelham in England again for an appreciable time."

"So that's it!" The change in Reginald's voice brought Caroline's gaze sharply back to him, and she was dismayed to see the sneer twisting his lips, and the contempt in his eyes. "Pel was right, then! He told me it was useless to turn to you for help in any kind of trouble. By God, Ravenshaw, I'm damned glad Jenny did serve you that trick! I've no wish for any closer acquaintance with you."

He nodded curtly to Caroline, clapped his hat on his head, and strode away with none of the languor he usually affected. Guy said nothing as he put his horses in motion again, and when Caroline stole a glance at him there was only a slightly grim expression about his mouth to indicate that Sir Reginald's words had annoyed him. He appeared, in fact, to be far less angry than she felt herself.

"Oh, why do you let people think so badly of you?" she said impulsively. "Reginald obviously believes that your cousin was obliged to fly the country because you refused to pay his debts, and he will spread that story all over Town."

The set of his lips relaxed, and he cast her a humorous, sidelong glance. "What if he does? It is no more than the truth."

"No, but it is far less!" she retorted hotly. "People will say that you refused to help him from malice, or callousness. They do not know how badly he has behaved, and they lay all the blame on you. Why do you not expose him?"

Guy shrugged. "Because the opinion of the world in general has never held the smallest interest for me," he replied indifferently. "The few people whose opinion I do value know me well enough, I believe, to regard Pelham's accusations at their true worth. The rest may believe what they choose."

"But it is so unjust!" she said indignantly. "What is more, there is not the smallest reason for it. To allow yourself to be regarded so unfavourably simply because you cannot be bothered to correct a false impression, is ridiculous. No, worse than that! It is sheer arrogance!"

"So I have often been told," he agreed cordially. "Miss Cresswell, are you trying to pick a quarrel with me?"

Colour blazed into her cheeks and she caught her lower lip between her teeth, overcome with confusion at having allowed her feelings to get the better of her. After a moment, however, she said with as much dignity as she could command: "Certainly not, sir. It would be most unseemly."

"I suppose it would!" This time the laughter in his voice was unmistakable. "And Miss Cresswell, of course, will never exceed the bounds of strict propriety. I stand corrected, ma'am!"

"No," she replied seriously, "I think I do. I had no right to speak to you in that fashion, and I ask your pardon for it. My only excuse is that having been given an opportunity to discover the true worth of both you and your cousin, it grieves me to see you so misjudged."

"My dear ma'am, you had every right!" he said quickly. "I know that my behaviour in this must seem absurd, but it is not all empty arrogance, you know. I realised years ago that to disprove Pelham's allegations against me would mean disclosing his own peculiar standards of conduct, which in its turn meant bringing considerable discredit upon the name we both bear. I did not choose to do that." He laughed gently. "Do not suppose, however, that I have martyred myself upon the altar of family pride. I really care very little for what people may think of me.

Now let us speak of something more agreeable. Jane tells me that she is going to the play tonight. Do you accompany her?"

Caroline shook her head. "No," she said firmly, though with a trace of regret. "Jane was kind enough to invite me, but it will not do for me to be going about with her, and meeting her friends. Only conceive how awkward it would be if I applied for a post as governess, and found that my prospective employer was someone I had met while staying under her roof. Besides, I have nothing suitable to wear." She gave a little chuckle. "Jane wished to lend me one of her dresses, but you may imagine how impracticable *that* suggestion proved to be."

Since Jane was tall, and built on queenly lines in contrast to Caroline's reed-slim grace, Guy had no difficulty in believing this. He would have liked very much to provide her with an evening gown, but since he was certain that she would refuse it, even if it came in the guise of a gift from Jane, he was obliged regretfully to abandon the idea.

So that evening, when Jane, exquisitely gowned and curled, had left for the theatre, Miss Cresswell settled herself by the fire in the small saloon with a recently published novel. Rather more than an hour had passed, and she was deeply absorbed in the book, when the butler came in to inform her that Mr. George Cresswell desired to see her. He added apologetically that as the young gentleman had described himself as Miss Cresswell's cousin, and insisted that his business was urgent, he had not ventured to say that she was not at home.

Caroline received the news with mingled surprise and dismay. After the events of the previous day she would have been very glad to sever all connection with her uncle's family, and with George in particular, but she felt that only some matter of vital importance could have brought him in search of her, and so she consented reluctantly to see him.

When he entered the room she was shocked by the change in his appearance, for the boy looked positively hag-ridden. His normally high colour was quite lacking, there were dark circles beneath his eyes as though he had not slept, and his hands trembled continually. Caroline was aware of an unexpected impulse of pity.

"Come in, George, and sit down," she said pleasantly, laying aside her book. "This is unexpected, indeed. How did you know where to find me?"

"Mr. Ravenshaw told me last night that he meant to bring you here," George replied. "He said the fact that he was placing you in his sister-in-law's care should be sufficient to correct any false impression I might be harbouring. I suppose he meant that it proved there had been nothing improper between you."

"Did you believe that there had?" Caroline asked curiously.

He shrugged. "I hadn't thought about it at all. None of my business, anyway, though I was sorry to have set the cat among the pigeons by telling Mama that you hadn't been to Brightstone Park. Where *did* you go, cousin? How does Ravenshaw come into it?"

She smiled and shook her head. "If I told you, George, you would probably not believe me. What *I* would like to know is why you went to Brightstone, or, for that matter, why you have come here."

The words seemed to recall him to his errand, which curiosity had momentarily enabled him to forget. He gave a groan, and dropped his head upon his hands.

"I had to come," he said wretchedly. "I tried all night and all day to think of some other way, where I wouldn't have to tell you the truth, but it was no use. Now time's running out, and I'm getting desperate!" With a swift, unexpected movement he left his chair and flung himself on his knees beside her, clutching frantically at her hands. "Cousin, you must help me, for your own sake as much as for mine! If it's found out there's no knowing where it may end."

"My dear boy, of course I will help you if I can! There is no need to distress yourself so." Caroline spoke with deliberate calm, clasping the trembling fingers firmly in her own, though her heart sank at the prospect of further complications in an already tangled situation. "Just tell me quietly what you wish me to do."

She thought that her words and manner had reassured him slightly, but his next remark seemed as unintelligible as the last. Without moving from his position beside her, he said urgently: "It's your muff, the fur muff your cousin gave you! For God's sake, Caroline, tell me where it is! You weren't carrying it yesterday, and it wasn't in your boxes, and Bart says you told him you had lent it to a friend. Which friend? How soon can you get it back?"

Miss Cresswell freed one hand from his and pressed it to her forehead, for this conversation seemed to be bordering upon lunacy.

"Am I going mad, or are you?" she asked plaintively. "Do you mean to tell me that it was you who searched my trunk and valise, and that you were looking for my muff?"

"Yes, yes! I'm sorry about prying into your things, but I had to try to find it. You don't understand!"

"I most certainly do not, and you are doing nothing to make the situation plainer," she retorted tartly. "What in the world has the whereabouts of my muff to do with you?"

George bit his lip and his eyes fell before hers, while a dark tide of colour flooded into his white face.

"I hid something in it," he said in a low voice. "On the day you went away. You left it lying on the table in the hall while you went upstairs for something you had forgotten, and I saw that the lining was torn, and it seemed a first-rate hiding-place. That's why we must get it back, before anyone else finds it! If they do, the pair of us may land in prison."

The most profound misgiving clutched at Miss Cresswell's heart, for the mention of prison cast a far more serious light upon the affair than she had expected. In a voice which was not quite steady she said anxiously: "George, what sort of scrape are you in? *What* did you hide in my muff?"

He lifted his face again towards hers. He was as pale now as he had been flushed a moment ago, and there was panic and despair in his eyes.

"A pendant," he said in a low voice. "The ruby pendant stolen from old Linley's house a week ago."

15

Miss Cresswell Makes a Decision

FOR an instant the room seemed to spin wildly around her, and George's white, desperate face receded to a great distance, while disjointed fragments of Sir Reginald's remarks floated through her mind. Dimly she was aware that her cousin had risen and was gripping her by the shoulders and speaking urgently, in a voice which seemed to come from very far away.

"Caroline, don't look at me like that! I'm not a thief! It was Bart who stole the confounded thing—yes, and killed the servant as well. I had nothing to do with it! I swear it!"

With a tremendous effort she conquered the faintness which had threatened to overcome her, and put up a groping hand to clutch the front of his coat.

"Wait," she said faintly. "Wait a moment! Give me time to collect my wits. You say it was Bartholomew

Trench who committed robbery and murder at Mr. Linley's house?"

"Yes, he and another man. A servant stumbled on them and gave the alarm, and Bart killed him so that they could make their escape. I only learned of it afterwards. Caroline, we must get that damned pendant back!"

"Yes, that is the most important thing. I do not properly understand yet how you came to have it, or why you hid it in my muff, but that can wait for the present. I will send for the muff at once."

She got up and went rather unsteadily to the escritoire which stood against the wall. She was still trembling violently and a hundred questions were hammering in her mind, but she knew that her cousin was right. The need to regain possession of the muff and its incriminating contents must take precedence over everything else.

George followed her across the room and stood beside her as she sought pen and paper. He said uneasily: "Who has it now, cousin? Will they not wonder why you want it back so urgently?"

She shook her head. "I do not think so. I was going to lend it to Miss Linley, but she went away without it, and I asked her maid to look after it for me. I have only to send a note round to Mount Street, and she will return it. I will tell her that I am going away, and wish to carry it."

She wrote a few hasty lines, sealed and directed the note, and dispatched a footman with it to Mount Street, with instructions to give it to Miss Linley's woman. Then she returned to the sofa by the fire and sat down, motioning to George to sit beside her. He obeyed without protest.

"Now," she said quietly, "tell me the whole story. How did the pendant come into your possession?"

"Bart gave it to me to look after," George replied miserably. "I didn't know what it was, of course. It was just a small, sealed packet, and he told me it was something of value that he didn't want to carry about with him, and was afraid to leave in his lodging because he suspected Mrs. Pomfret of prying into his room when he wasn't there. I thought nothing of it at first, but when I reached home, and went to put the packet away, I started wondering what was in it." He hesitated, looking a trifle shamefaced, and then added defiantly: "In the end curiosity got the better of me, and I opened it."

"Did you realize whence it came?"

He shook his head. "Not immediately. I could see, of course, that it was worth a great deal, and I thought that perhaps Bart had taken it as security for a debt, or some such thing. He is a great gamester, you know, and he usually wins."

"Dishonestly, no doubt!" Caroline said scornfully, and then, as George made no reply, but appeared to have sunk into melancholy thought, she added sharply: "Well, go on! How did you discover the truth?"

"There was an account of the robbery in the newspaper. Papa pointed it out to me, because he knew that the Linleys were friends of yours. There was a description of the pendant, which was said to be the most valuable item stolen. You may imagine my feelings when I read that! My first thought was to rid myself of the thing, and I took it straight back to Bart's lodging. He wasn't there, and Mrs. Pomfret said he had gone out of Town for a few days. I didn't know whether that was true, or whether he was lying low somewhere, but it made me fear that the Runners were already on his track and that was why he had given the pendant to me. Then I thought that if he were arrested and the pendant not found, they might start questioning his friends. I suppose I panicked then, for the only thing that seemed to matter was to get rid of the jewel. I was going to throw it into the river, but then I realized that if Bart were *not* arrested he would want it back, and if I had disposed of it, there was no knowing what he might do. I mean, he had killed once for it already."

"Yes, I can understand you being afraid," Caroline agreed, "but what fiend prompted you to hide the hateful thing in my muff?"

"Oh, that was mere chance! When I reached home again you were just coming downstairs, and you told me that you were going away for a few days. Then I saw the muff lying there, with a tear in the lining, and it seemed a capital idea to put the pendant inside it, much better than hiding it somewhere in the house, as I had intended to do. So I unwrapped it and pushed it through the hole and down between the fur and the lining. I thought it would be simple enough to take it out again when you came home, and give it back to Bart."

"But, George, what a crazy thing to do!" she exclaimed in dismay. "Why, when you realized where the jewel had come from, did you not take it at once to Bow Street?"

"That was my first thought," he admitted, "but I was afraid they would not believe me. Even if they had done so at first, Bart would have been bound to implicate me when they arrested him, out of sheer malice. You do not know him, cousin! That genial manner is all a sham. He is the cruellest, most vindictive man I have ever met."

Caroline had no difficulty in believing this, for it merely confirmed her own estimate of Mr. Trench. What was more difficult to understand was why George had continued on terms of friendship with him after discovering his real nature, and she asked him to explain this. He uttered a groan, and once more buried his head in his hands.

"Because he has his claws into me so deep I cannot get away," he said miserably. "That is his way, you see! He makes himself as agreeable as can be, and takes a fellow about, and introduces him to this place and that, until he gets a hold on him that can't be broken. Then he changes his tune, and you have to dance to it, like it or not."

"What is his hold on you, George?" Caroline asked imperatively. "Come now, tell me! As well make a clean breast of the whole ugly business."

"I would have to tell you, anyway, to make you understand all the rest." He paused, running his fingers through his hair until the fair curls stood up in wild disarray. "I've been gambling; plunging far deeper than I could afford, and Bart holds vowels of mine to the tune of nearly a thousand pounds."

Caroline received this intelligence with more dismay than surprise, for she had suspected something of the kind. George had inherited his father's weakness for all forms of gambling as well as his mother's desire to emulate those above him in the social scale, and these failings had already produced much ill-feeling between him and his maternal grandfather.

"I see!" she said slowly. "This is a sad tangle, to be sure! What happened next?"

"Bart came back, sooner than I had bargained for. He asked for the packet he had given me, and I had to tell him the truth." He shuddered. "I thought he was going to kill me, and perhaps he would have done if he could have seen any way of getting his hands on the ruby again without my help. In the end, when he had calmed down a trifle, he told me to go after you and get it back."

"So that is why you went to Brightstone!"

"Yes, and you can imagine my dismay when the butler told me you weren't there, and weren't expected. I didn't know what to think. It didn't seem likely that you had eloped with Captain Wilde, for if you wanted to marry him no one could prevent you, yet it seemed the only explanation. Not that it mattered to me! I rode straight back to London to see if there was any word from you at home, for I'd not been near the place for a couple of days. I suppose I was a fool to blurt out the whole, but by then I scarcely knew what I was doing. I didn't mean to make trouble for you."

"Yes, you have told me so several times already," Caroline said impatiently, "but nevertheless, as soon as you had seen me turned out of doors, you ran straight to Trench with the story."

"Well, I didn't know what else to do. We went back home together, and I found out from Becky that you had gone to Mrs. Fenton, but just as we were discussing what to do next, you came walking down the street. That pleased Bart more than you can guess. He'd never forgiven you for that set-down you gave him, and he'd been hoping for a chance to make you regret it."

Caroline shivered, seeing again the squalid parlour of Mrs. Pomfret's house, and Bartholomew Trench's wine-flushed face with its smiling lips and merciless eyes. The danger, then, had been very real, as real as the evil she had sensed in the man, and but for Becky's quick wits, and Guy's concern for her safety, there would have been no escape from it.

"Afterwards, when Ravenshaw had taken you away," George went on, "Bart told me he would give me forty-eight hours to get the pendant back, and that if I didn't do so in that time, he would go to Grandfather Perkins and demand payment of my debts. You know what that would mean!"

"Yes, I do, but it would also mean that he had thrown away his best chance of recovering the pendant."

"Oh, he would get it back sooner or later, depend upon it, even if it meant watching you until he saw you carrying the muff, and then knocking you on the head and making off with it. You don't know him as well as I do. No one can get the better of him."

"Nonsense!" she replied forcibly. "You have been so completely under his thumb that you believe that to be true, but it is no such thing. A great deal can be accomplished by firmness and resolution, and we are not going to submit tamely to his demands. Setting aside all question of self-interest, it is our plain duty to see that he is brought to justice."

It was obvious from the manner in which George received this determination that such nobility of purpose found no echo in his heart. He looked very frightened, and said uneasily that the best thing would be to give Bart the pendant and then forget about it.

"Certainly not!" Caroline said indignantly. "We shall give it back to him by all means, but as soon as it is in his possession again, an information must be laid against him at Bow Street. They suspect him already, but since his confederate was drowned they have no evidence against him. Sir Reginald Linley himself told me that only this afternoon."

"Suppose Bart guesses what we mean to do? He is no fool, you know."

"You must make him believe that we are both so frightened of being involved that all we desire is to be rid of the pendant and to hear no more about it. It will not be necessary to deceive him for long, for once the Runners know that he has the jewel in his possession they will soon place him under arrest."

"Am I to tell him, then, that I have confided in you?"

"I think you will be obliged to do so," she replied with a frown, "for I cannot think of any other way in which you could have recovered the pendant. You may tell him also that I am exceedingly fearful that the Linleys will suspect me of giving information regarding the contents of Mr. Linley's house, and that on that account I may be trusted to keep silent about the whole affair." She paused, regarding her cousin's scared face with growing exasperation. "Good gracious, George! have you no ingenuity at all? Tell him what you please, so long as it satisfies him."

"I wish I were as certain as you seem to be that all will come out right," George said gloomily. "Would to God I had never opened that confounded package! Then I would have given it back to Bart when he asked for it, and none the wiser."

"But he would still have your debts to hold as a threat over your head," Caroline pointed out. "Be resolute, and we shall come about very well, I assure you! Once we have the pendant back, it will be only a matter of hours before Mr. Bartholomew Trench is safely behind bars."

It soon transpired, however, that the recovery of the stolen jewel was to be less easy than they had anticipated. The footman certainly performed his errand with the utmost dispatch, but when he came into the saloon again his hands were empty, and he brought the unwelcome information that Miss Linley's abigail was no longer to be found in Mount Street. She had been dismissed from her ladyship's service, and had returned to her parents in the country.

Caroline thanked the man and dismissed him before returning to her cousin, who was staring at her in white-faced despair. "Do not look so haggard, George," she said reassuringly. "This means only a trifle of delay. Agnes is entirely trustworthy, and may be depended upon to look after the muff until an opportunity occurs to return it to me."

"But do you know where to find her? Have you her direction?"

"Oh yes! Her father is a tenant of Mr. Wilde's. I have only to go to Brightstone, and then send for her. You will have to explain the matter to Mr. Trench, and beg a few hours' grace before he goes to your grandfather. Have you the means to travel into the country again?"

"Yes, I can hire a hack for the journey, but what about you, cousin? If you still have no money, I may be able to raise the wind for you somehow."

"No, there is no need for that," Caroline moved from the sofa and carefully replaced a glowing coal which had fallen from the grate on to the hearth; her face was hidden, but her voice was perfectly steady. "Mr. Ravenshaw was kind enough to say that he would take me to Brightstone whenever I wish to go. I had intended to remain in London for a few days, but it—it does not matter. I will tell him, and his sister-in-law also, that I feel it will be better to go into the country without delay."

George nodded, and sat for a moment lost in gloomy meditation before saying diffidently: "Cousin, could you not tell Ravenshaw the whole? He seems to have a decided partiality for you, and I dare say that a man of his wealth and influence could have Bart arrested on mere suspicion, and held until the pendant was recovered."

"No!" Caroline's rejection of this suggestion was uttered with a force which made her cousin jump. "Do you think I want *him* to know that I am concerned in this dreadful affair? I cannot—I *will* not ask him to come to my rescue again!"

She jumped to her feet and walked across the room to the escritoire where she stood drumming her fingers on its polished surface in such evident agitation that George realized that he had committed an unpardonable blunder, but after a minute or two she appeared to recover her composure, for she returned to her seat beside the fire and said quite calmly: "I will arrange to go to Brightstone, and you must do the same. As soon as I arrive I will send a message to Agnes and ask her to bring the muff to me at once. Then, later in the evening, I will contrive to slip out

and give you the pendant. It should not be difficult. Mr.
Wilde dislikes the fashion of dining late, and dinner at
Brightstone is always served at half-past five. I will pretend
to have the headache, or some such thing, and go up to
bed early."

George nodded. "That's right, and then I will rack up at
an inn for the night, and come on to London in the morning. Better not risk crossing Finchley Common after dark
with that ruby in my pocket. Where do you want me to
meet you?"

Caroline gave this question some consideration. The
rendezvous must be a place which George, a stranger to
Brightstone, could find without difficulty, and yet not so
far from the house that it would necessitate a long absence
on her part, since it was quite likely that one of the other
ladies might visit her room.

"When you went to Brightstone the other day," she said
at length, "I take it that you approached the house by way
of the main avenue?" George nodded, and she went on: "I
dare say you did not notice it, but between the village and
the lodge-gates, just after you cross the bridge, there is a
lane leading off to the right. If you follow that for about a
quarter of a mile, you will see on your left a gate which
opens on to a path through a small wood. Leave your
horse there, and walk along the path until it brings you
through another gate into the gardens, at the north end of
the lake. There is a folly there, built like a classical temple.
I will meet you there at eight o'clock tomorrow evening."

His cousin's competent planning served to overcome at
least a part of George's apprehension, but Caroline knew
him well enough not to depend upon his courage surviving
until the following day and she could not be easy concerning the outcome.

"Remember, George," she said finally, as he prepared
to take his leave, "if you stay at an inn anywhere in the
neighbourhood of Brightstone, do not disclose your name.
Above all, make Trench believe that fear alone is enough
to make us keep silent about this wretched affair, for if
you do not, there is no knowing what may happen. Do not
forget, too, that the responsibility of laying information at

Bow Street will also rest upon you, for I shall be too far away to be of any help in that." She paused, clasping his hands in her own, scanning the weak and rather scared young face with anxious eyes. "George, be resolute, I beg of you! In this way you can free yourself from Trench once and for all, but you must make a push to help yourself. The success or failure of the whole plan depends on you!"

16

Moonlight on the Lake

WHEN Jane Ravenshaw discovered, at breakfast the following morning, that her guest had formed the resolution of leaving London that same day, she used every argument she could think of to dissuade her, but in vain. Caroline had had time, in the sleepless watches of the night, to envisage every one of them and to find a reasonable and definite answer to them all, so that in the end Jane had no choice but to send a note round to Grosvenor Square, informing Guy of Miss Cresswell's decision and asking him to fulfil his promise to convey her to Brightstone Park.

An answer to this was promptly forthcoming, announcing that he was entirely at Miss Cresswell's service, and would take her up in Park Street at noon. When he arrived, Jane received him in her dressing-room, for she wished to have a word or two with him in private before Caroline joined them. This desire was apparently shared by Mr. Ravenshaw, for as soon as they were alone he said abruptly: "What is the cause of this start? She told me yesterday that she was fixed in London for the next few days."

"I wish I knew," Jane replied worriedly. "All she will say is that she has come to realize how wrong she was to agree to that, and that to be staying in this house, yet not going with me into company, can only arouse curiosity which will cause embarrassment."

He frowned. "Something must have occurred to prompt this change of mind. Did Aunt Augusta say anything yesterday to make Caroline feel that her situation here was awkward?"

"No, upon my honour she did not! I was with them the whole time." She hesitated, and then added rather diffidently: "There is one thing, Guy, which may account for it. Her cousin, Mr. George Cresswell, called upon her yesterday evening."

"The devil he did!" Guy said quickly. "For what purpose, I wonder?"

"That I do not know. He stayed here for an hour or so, and during that time Caroline sent a message round to Lady Linley's house in Mount Street. My woman mentioned it to me while I was preparing for bed. I think she did not quite approve of a gentleman calling upon a young lady at such an hour, even if they are related. Caroline herself said nothing to me, and so I cannot speak of the matter to her. I would not like her to think that my servants are spying on her."

"Naturally not! Do you know what the message was about?"

"Oh, something to do with a package which Miss Linley's abigail was to have sent to her. I dare say it is not of the least significance. I have been wondering whether Mr. Cresswell brought some message from that odious mother of his, and Caroline is afraid that she may next descend upon her in person."

"Possible, but not very probable! I should think he would be more likely to bring a message from that rogue Trench. Perhaps it *will* be just as well for Caroline to go out of Town." He paused, and for a few moments there was silence, while both followed their own train of thought, until Mr. Ravenshaw considerably startled and alarmed his companion by remarking in a musing tone: "How long, I wonder, would it take to make the journey to Gretna Green?"

"Gretna Green!" Jane exclaimed in horror. "Guy, you would not!"

"What?" He looked at her with a frown, but an instant later his brow cleared and he laughed. "Did I speak that thought aloud? I did not mean to. Do not look so scandalized, my dear Jane! I am not proposing to bear Caroline off to the Border. I was merely wondering how soon we may look for the return of Captain Wilde and his bride, so that an announcement of their marriage in the newspaper may inform the world that I am free of that entanglement. My position at present is too damnably equivocal."

Jane, considerably relieved, agreed that this was true. During the previous evening a lady noted more for her malice than her good manners had in her hearing expressed surprise at seeing Mr. Ravenshaw driving in the Park that afternoon with a strange young woman, when all the world knew that his betrothed had been missing for nearly a week. Such conduct, she had hinted, displayed a degree of callousness unlooked for even in a man so notoriously hard-hearted as Guy Ravenshaw. Certainly, Jane thought, the sooner the facts were made known, the better it would be.

Before she could pursue the subject any farther, the door opened and Caroline came into the room. She had been informed of Mr. Ravenshaw's arrival, and was already wearing her outdoor clothes.

"Jane tells me, Miss Cresswell," Guy said as he shook hands with her, "that in spite of all she can say, you are adamant in your resolve to leave us. I am exceedingly sorry. I hoped to have the pleasure of your company for several days to come."

This was far harder to resist than all Jane's reasoned arguments. Caroline flushed, and said unhappily that he was very kind, but she had come to realize how difficult a situation was created for everybody by her presence in London. She hoped that she had not put him to any inconvenience by desiring to be taken to Brightstone Park that day.

"My dear ma'am, I am entirely at your service. Since the weather is so fine and warm I have taken the liberty of coming here in my curricle, but if you would prefer to make the journey by chaise I beg that you will tell me so. It need delay our departure by no more than a quarter of an hour."

"Oh no, indeed!" she replied promptly. "I would much rather go in the curricle than be cooped up in a closed carriage." She turned to Jane, holding out both her hands. "I do not know how to thank you for all your kindness, and I am truly sorry to treat you in what must seem to be a very off-handed fashion. Believe me, I would like nothing better than to stay with you if it were possible, but in spite of all that you may say, dear Jane, it is not."

"I have allowed myself to be persuaded that you are right," Jane replied, taking the outstretched hands, "but I cannot agree that it must always be so, and I shall look forward eagerly to another and longer visit from you." She leaned forward and kissed the other girl's cheek. "Goodbye, Caroline. I hope that we may meet again very soon."

Caroline thanked her, though she could not feel that there was any likelihood of that hope ever being fulfilled, and allowed Mr. Ravenshaw to escort her out of the house. Jane went into a saloon on the first floor which overlooked the street, and stood at the window to watch their departure. She observed that the groom was not accompanying them, and supposed Guy to be hoping that, unhampered by the presence of a servant, Miss Cresswell might confide in him the real reason for her sudden change of plan.

This supposition was correct, but Mr. Ravenshaw was doomed to disappointment, for Caroline's immediate resolve to keep her new problem from him at all costs had been strengthened by subsequent reflection. This was no such madcap scheme as aiding Jenny to elope; this time she was involved in a very serious and ugly crime, and she was practical enough to know that both she and George stood in very real danger, not only from Bartholomew Trench but also from the Law. If Trench, arrested, sought to implicate them in his guilt, they would be hard put to it to prove their innocence. Even her long-standing friendship with the Linleys would add weight to the charge. No, it was unthinkable that she should embroil Guy in anything so discreditable.

So although he found her willing to converse with vivacity and humour upon any impersonal subject, not a word did she say regarding her sudden desire to leave London, or the visit she had received from George Cresswell. Once or twice he tried, with the utmost delicacy, to approach these topics, but found himself firmly turned aside, and short of a direct question, which he felt he had no right to ask, there seemed to be no way of discovering the truth.

Midway through the afternoon, Letitia Fenton, sitting with her mother and aunt in the drawing-room at Brightstone Park, heard the sound of a vehicle approaching the house, and at once hurried to a window overlooking the carriage-drive. They had sustained a visit from Lady Linley the previous day, and Letty, being the first person concerned in the elopement to come in her ladyship's way, had received the full force of her condemnation. It was not an experience she desired to repeat.

To her astonishment, she beheld not her ladyship's chaise, but a curricle-and-four bowling in through the gateway on to the broad sweep of gravel fronting the house. There was no mistaking that dashing turn-out. Letty had seen it too often in the Park not to recognize it now, but it needed a second glance, and then a third, to identify the elegant female figure seated beside its driver. She uttered a gasp, and swung round to face the room again.

"Mama, Guy Ravenshaw has just driven up to the door, and what do you think? Caroline is sitting beside him, so elegantly dressed that for a moment I did not recognize her."

Mrs. Wilde, a plump and placid lady, received this startling piece of information with maddening calm.

"Well, my dear, if Caroline has decided to come to me at last, I am truly thankful, for I could never feel easy about her while she resided in her uncle's house. No doubt that disagreeable aunt of hers has picked a quarrel with her about her supposed visit to me. It was exceedingly unfortunate that her cousin should have been told she was not here."

"Very likely, Mama, but why should Mr. Ravenshaw bring her?"

"Why should he not, my love?" We know from Lady Linley how they came to be acquainted, and I expect he feels he owes her something after the shocking experience his cousin made her suffer."

"More probably he has seized on it as an excuse to come here and make himself unpleasant to us all," Letty retorted pessimistically. "To be sure, Pelham Ravenshaw has proved himself to be shockingly unprincipled, but that does not alter the fact that his cousin is the most disagreeable man alive. My heart positively bleeds for poor Caroline when I think of the way she has been thrust into his company."

When Miss Cresswell came into the drawing-room a few minutes later, however, she did not appear to stand in any need of sympathy. She entered briskly, smiled in a general way upon the three ladies, and bent to kiss Mrs. Wilde's cheek, saying cheerfully: "Cousin Esther, I have taken you at your word at last, and come to impose myself upon you for a while. I must ask you to forgive me for not having informed you of my intention, but the opportunity did not arise. May I make known to you Mr. Ravenshaw, who has been kind enough to drive me from London?"

Mrs. Wilde, assuring Caroline that she was always welcome at Brightstone, and then turning to greet her companion, became aware suddenly of the awkwardness of receiving the gentleman with whose promised wife her own son had just eloped, and of whom, from her daughter's unflattering description, she had formed no very favourable opinion. Even her habitual serenity was unequal to such a situation, and she floundered in a morass of greeting, introduction and apology, until Caroline, taking pity on her, interposed to ask whether they had yet seen Lady Linley.

"Yes, she called upon us yesterday, and told us the whole story," Mrs. Wilde admitted. "We were *so* relieved, my love, to learn that all was well with you. To be sure, it was very wrong of you to abet Roland and Jenny in that fashion, but you did not deserve—that is, we must all be grateful to Mr. Ravenshaw. I mean—" she broke off, totally at a loss, and this time it was Guy himself who came to her rescue, saying, with a humorous glance at Caroline:

"Miss Cresswell's action was certainly ill-judged, ma'am, but I am persuaded that it sprang from the most selfless motives, and it brought upon her consequences far more severe than anyone could have foreseen. I think you must agree that she has been sufficiently punished."

Caroline chuckled. "The hardship, sir, has not been all upon my side," she said frankly. "To tell truth, Cousin Esther, I have been extremely tiresome, and Mr. Ravenshaw has treated me with greater forbearance than I deserve. For the rest, I have explained to him exactly how it happened that Jenny and Roland found it necessary to elope, and we are agreed that no one is to be blamed for it."

Mrs. Wilde looked rather dubiously at Mr. Ravenshaw, and found that in spite of his somewhat forbidding cast of countenance, there was a good deal of comprehension in the cool grey eyes. He said quietly: "That is perfectly true, ma'am. I can only regret the distress which I must, quite unintentionally, have caused, and I assure you that I bear your son no grudge for what has happened. I trust that he and Miss Linley will find happiness together."

There was no mistaking the sincerity of these words, and Mrs. Wilde's first opinion of him underwent a drastic change. Casting an eloquent and reproachful glance at Letty, she could only thank Guy for his forbearance, and express again and again her sense of obligation.

Letitia, for her part, was totally bewildered, for this was not at all in tune with Mr. Ravenshaw's character as the world knew it. Caroline, too, appeared not to stand in awe of him in the least, but instead to be upon the friendliest of terms with him, and that, too, was quite inexplicable. She was all impatience to get to the root of the matter, and when after a few minutes Caroline said that she would go upstairs to put off her bonnet and pelisse, seized eagerly on the opportunity to carry her off to her own bedchamber. She would have plunged into the subject as soon as the drawing-room door closed behind them, but before she could do so Caroline said urgently: "Letty, do you know where Jenny's abigail lives? Her father is one of Mr. Wilde's tenants." Mrs. Fenton merely stared, and she added impatiently: "Agnes, you know! Lady Linley dismissed her, and she came home to her parents."

"Yes, I know," Letty said blankly, "but why in the world do you want her?"

Caroline explained briefly about the muff, but instead of dispelling her friend's perplexity, the explanation served only to increase it.

"She will have kept it quite safely, I dare say," she remarked, "but I cannot see why you wish to send for it as soon as you set foot inside the house. You cannot possibly need it just at present."

"I want it back!" Caroline said flatly. "Oh, Letty, for pity's sake stop asking questions, and let me send someone with a message to Agnes!"

Mrs. Fenton eyed her with some dismay, almost ready to believe that Miss Cresswell's recent adventures had deranged her wits, but seeing that her own curiosity would not be satisfied until Caroline's extraordinary request had been complied with, she led her to her own room, waited while she scribbled a note, and then sent a servant off with it to Agnes's home, which fortunately was situated barely a mile from the Park itself. That done, she turned to the matter foremost in her mind, and came straight to the point.

"Caro, do tell me, for I am positively agog to know! Why should Guy Ravenshaw, of all people, escort you to Brightstone?"

Caroline, having laid aside her bonnet, was engaged in rearranging her hair, and her eyes met Letitia's eagerly-inquiring glance in the mirror.

"Because, my dear, with you out of Town he was the only friend I had in London. Indeed, I do not know how I would have gone on without his help."

Letitia digested this information in silence for a moment or two, while Miss Cresswell dealt with an unruly curl. At length Mrs. Fenton said: "Well, I can scarcely credit it! I am sure it is not in the least like him to wish to help anyone."

"Is it not, indeed?" Caroline swung round from the mirror to face her. Her cheeks were faintly flushed and her eyes sparkling with anger. "Let me tell you, Letty, that Guy Ravenshaw is the kindest, most chivalrous man I have ever met. You may believe what I say! I have spent enough time in his company this past week to form a sound opinion of his character." She paused, obviously controlling her feelings with a strong effort, and then added more calmly: "I must not quarrel with you! We had better go downstairs again before I lose my temper altogether."

Letitia agreed in a stunned way, and followed Caroline down to the drawing-room with her thoughts in a turmoil. They found that Mr. Wilde and Mark Fenton had come in during their absence, and that everyone was conversing with apparent amiability. When greetings had been exchanged the conversation became general once more, but it was not long before Mr. Ravenshaw rose to take his leave. Declining an invitation to stay and dine, he took a courteous leave of his hostess, her sister and Letitia, but when he turned to Caroline she said breathlessly, reckless of what the others might think: "I will step out to the door with you, Mr. Ravenshaw. There is something I wish to say to you."

He knew a moment's hope that she was going to confide in him at last, but when they reached the steps leading down from the front door to the carriage-sweep she was silent for so long that at length he prompted her quietly.

"There was something you wished to tell me, Miss Cresswell?"

She made a little, helpless gesture. "I am trying to find the right words," she said in a low voice. "I wanted to thank you, to tell you how grateful I am for your kindness, your care of me through all our adventures and misadventures, but I do not know how to do it."

"It has been my very great pleasure," he replied gravely, "just as it will be my pleasure to continue to serve you if the opportunity occurs." He paused, but she made no response, and he realized that whatever problem now troubled her, if problem there were, she would not share it with him. "You have only to tell me how," he added gently.

She shook her head. Her throat ached with the effort of holding back her tears, and when she spoke her voice was stiff and strained.

"Thank you, but there is nothing," she said, and held out her hand. "Believe me, I shall always remember, and be grateful."

He took the hand and stood holding it for a moment, looking down at her averted face. Perplexity and concern were in his eyes, but he merely said, with the faintest trace of humour: "We *shall* meet again, you know!"

He lifted her hand to his lips, and then released it and went quickly down the steps to the waiting curricle. Caroline stood motionless, her head bent to hide the tears that now filled her eyes, and heard his brisk command to the groom to stand aside, and then the trampling of the greys' hooves and the sound of wheels as the light, swift carriage swept away. She dared not believe his parting words; there must not be another meeting.

She had little need to feign a headache as an excuse to retire immediately after dinner, for with Guy's departure a mood of deep depression settled upon her, and not even the arrival of Agnes a short while afterwards, with the precious muff carefully wrapped in paper, afforded her much relief. She forced herself to answer the maid's eager questions and to commend her quick-wittedness at the time of the abduction, but she was thankful when she went away. As soon as she was alone, she carried the muff up to her room and, having locked the door, thrust a trembling hand through the rent in the silk lining. For a few sickening sec-

onds she groped in vain, and then her shaking fingers encountered a small, hard object and drew it out.

It lay in her palm, a delicate, intricate design in gold
and diamonds, with the great ruby blazing at its heart, and
for a few moments she stared in silence at this beautiful,
deadly thing which had already cost one man's life and
could bring another to the gallows. Then she wrapped it
carefully in a handkerchief, bestowed it in the bosom of
her gown, and went downstairs to dinner.

The meal seemed endless, and Mrs. Wilde, observing
her cousin's languid air and indifferent appetite, said that
she must be tired after her journey. Caroline admitted it,
confessed to a headache, and when the ladies rose from
the table said she thought that she would go to bed.

Darkness had fallen by the time she slipped out of the
house, and the moon was rising above the trees at the edge
of the park. The gardens, familiar to her since childhood,
seemed curiously unfriendly in the cold, still half-light,
and she shivered in spite of the thick cloak she had
wrapped about her. The ornamental lake shimmered faintly like polished steel as she hurried along its bank, and on
a knoll at its northern end stood the miniature temple, its
white pillars dimly reflected in the chill waters. In the cold
silence of the spring night it was an alien place, ghostly
and sinister. Her heart was thumping apprehensively as
she mounted the shallow steps, the ruby pendant clutched
in one hand, and it was in vain that she reminded herself
that it was only George she had come to meet, George
who was younger and weaker and more frightened than
herself.

She halted between the slender columns and stood staring into the shadows beyond, straining eyes and ears for
some indication of his presence. She saw nothing but the
faint, luminous reflection of the moonlight on the lake,
heard only the sigh of the breeze and the lap of water at
the foot of the steps.

"George," she whispered. "George!"

A shadow moving among the shadows, a footfall on the

marble floor, and the sense of another human presence to bring reassurance for an instant before a voice spoke softly to fill the night with horror. A familiar voice, with a cold and deadly purpose echoing through its hollow geniality.

"Regret to disappoint you, ma'am, but George is lying bound and gagged in my gig on the other side of the wood. Foolish to have placed any dependence upon him. Silly fellow blurted out the whole plot to me after only the smallest persuasion."

Frozen terror melted and she turned to fly, but the dim-seen figure moved more quickly than she. An arm encircled her, jerking her back against him, holding her helpless there; a hand covered her mouth, stifling the scream which was her only hope of rescue.

"Not so fast, my dear," said Bartholomew Trench's voice in her ear. "I'll take the pretty trinket first. Great pity George told you about it. Never liked the thought of killing a woman, but can't let you live to tell that tale!"

17

Mr. Ravenshaw Takes Command

GUY RAVENSHAW drove away from Brightstone Park in a very thoughtful frame of mind, for he could not rid himself of the conviction that in spite of her denials Caroline was deeply troubled. So great was his preoccupation that he would probably not have noticed the young woman walking towards him had she not been so obviously anxious to avoid recognition. After one startled glance at the approaching curricle, she first looked wildly about her as though for a way of escape, and then hurriedly pulled up the hood of her cloak, so that his attention was drawn to her in spite of himself. He had an excellent memory for faces, and recognized Jennifer Linley's abigail without difficulty. He brought his team to a halt.

"You are Miss Linley's maid, are you not?" he said sharply. "What are you doing here?"

"Please, sir, I live here," Agnes stammered, staring apprehensively up at him. "My Pa's head groom to Mr. Wilde, up at the Park."

Mr. Ravenshaw's eyes narrowed. "I see," he remarked thoughtfully. "And now you are awaiting your mistress's return from Scotland?"

Agnes nodded, not yet certain whither these questions were leading. She had been horrified to see Mr. Ravenshaw driving towards her, and fully expected a shattering rebuke for the deception she had practised, but, as much to her surprise as to her relief, it did not come. Mr. Ravenshaw's cool grey eyes rested thoughtfully on the parcel which she was clutching to her bosom, and he asked where she was going.

"Up to the Park, sir," she replied. "Miss Cresswell sent for me, not half an hour since, to take her muff up to the house at once."

He frowned. "Her muff?"

Agnes explained how it came to be in her possession, and for a moment or two longer he continued to regard her, the frown still lingering on his brow. Then he said briefly: "You will find Miss Cresswell at the Park, but do not tell her of this meeting. We do not wish her to think that we have been gossiping over her private concerns."

"No, sir," Agnes agreed doubtfully, and curtsied as the greys moved forward again. She was completely out of her depth, but too relieved at having escaped so lightly to think of disobeying his command.

Guy continued on his way more puzzled than before, for though Caroline's urgent desire to come to Hertfordshire was now explained, the explanation deepened rather than lessened the mystery. Clearly there was some peculiar virtue attached to the muff, since the recovery of it was of such vital importance that she had barely arrived at her cousin's house before sending for it, but he could not imagine what it could be. The only certainty was that George Cresswell, too, had some interest in it; and if George were concerned, why not Bartholomew Trench?

Guy could easily have driven back to London without a halt, and that, in fact, had been his intention, but when he reached Barnet a sudden impulse made him stop at the

Green Man, in the centre of the town, and bespeak dinner there. He was not a fanciful man, but he was aware of an odd reluctance to leave Hertfordshire, and of a growing certainty that something was very much amiss. It was not long before he was able to give his vague misgivings a more definite form.

He was standing at the window of his private parlour, idly watching the busy scene in the street below while behind him in the room a waiter prepared the table for his meal. Barnet was a busy town, for through it passed the traffic of both the Great North Road and the Holyhead road, but Guy was occupied more with his own thoughts than with the animated scene before his eyes. Suddenly his casual gaze sharpened, and he leaned forward to stare at a gig which had just come into sight, travelling towards the north. It was some distance away, but Guy's sight was keen and he had no difficulty in recognizing its driver as Bartholomew Trench. Beside him, huddled into his greatcoat and looking the picture of abject misery, sat young George Cresswell.

Mr. Ravenshaw sat down to his dinner with graver forebodings than before, for it could be no mere coincidence which brought those two of all men driving north into Hertfordshire that evening, and before the meal was done his decision had been made. He would go straight back to Brightstone Park, tell Caroline what he had seen, and ask her to explain these mysterious comings and goings. That she might consider this an unwarranted intrusion upon her private affairs no longer mattered. The reappearance on the scene of Bartholomew Trench had thrust such considerations aside.

He did not hurry unduly over the meal, for he knew that even if Trench and his companion did not also halt somewhere to dine, his four fleet horses would make nothing of the delay. At length, having paid his shot, he strolled out into the yard, and while he stood there waiting for the greys to be harnessed, a chance snatch of conversation reached his ears.

"No sir, I don't remember no gig like you mention, nor likely to. Lord love us, do you think I can call to mind

every carriage as stops here during the course of the day?
Besides, it might not have stopped here at all. Plenty of
other inns in the town, and anyway, the Red Lion takes
most o' the north-going traffic."

Guy turned to look at the speaker. It was one of the ostlers, and the man he had addressed was a sturdy individual, respectably but soberly dressed, with a calm, square
face and an imperturbable manner. Catching Mr. Ravenshaw's eye as the ostler hurried away, he shrugged and
shook his head.

"Suppose the fellow's right, sir," he remarked, "but it
don't make my task no easier. I feared this'd happen if I
wasn't close upon 'em when they reached the town, but
that dratted horse of mine went lame." He paused, rubbing his chin thoughtfully with one hand, and then added
hopefully: "Don't suppose you've seen such a turn-out,
sir? Shabby-looking gig, high-stepping chestnut horse, two
men?"

"I may have done," Guy replied indifferently. "One
may see a dozen such in as many miles. Can you not be
more particular?"

"Well now, let's see!" the stranger said thoughtfully.
"The driver's a big fellow, not as tall as you, sir, but
stouter. Reddish-brown hair, and a smile as comes too
easy and means too little. The other's no more than a lad.
Fair hair, blue eyes, something of a dandy in his dress."

Mr. Ravenshaw continued to regard him with apparent
lack of interest, but in fact he was now very much on the
alert. That brief but graphic description brought to mind a
very clear picture of Bartholomew Trench and George
Cresswell as he had seen them drive past the Green Man
barely an hour before, but he had no intention of commit-
ting himself until he had learned more concerning his
questioner. That bland, unruffled air, he thought, was mis-
leading at first glance. The stranger's eyes were exceedingly shrewd, and missed very little of what went on around
him, while there was a certain latent authority in his deliberate voice.

"I believe I have a faint recollection of seeing the men you describe," he said after a moment. "Is your business with them urgent?"

"I'd be grateful, sir, if you could tell me when and where," the other man replied. "It'd save me a deal of time, and give me a better chance of coming up with 'em."

Mr. Ravenshaw's eyes narrowed a trifle, and his lips tightened. "I asked you a question, my friend, and until it is answered I have no intention of placing any strain upon my memory," he said unpleasantly. "I may be able to set you on the track of your friends, or I may not, but unless I am given some hint of your purpose in following them, I shall not make the attempt." He paused, watching the approach of his curricle, with two ostlers clinging to the greys' heads. "Allow me to advise you to make haste. I see that my carriage is ready, and I do not mean to delay on your account."

The other man continued to regard him for a moment or two, and then turned his head to study the curricle-and-four. Guy shrugged slightly and moved away, but was detained by a compelling hand on his arm.

"Very well, your Honour," the stranger said in a low voice. "Reckon I don't have no choice. I'm Benjamin Crane, sir, o' Bow Street, and I should like very much to know what brings them two gentlemen into the country this evening."

This information was anything but pleasing to Mr. Ravenshaw, since it cast a far more serious light on the affair than he liked, but he merely raised his brows a trifle and said coolly: "Bow Street, eh? Well, in that event I suppose I must do my best to help you. I fancy that the men you are seeking drove northwards past this inn a little more than an hour ago."

"That far ahead, are they?" Mr. Crane remarked gloomily. "My thanks to you, sir. I'll see about getting a fresh horse right away."

"One moment!" Guy said imperatively. "I am travelling towards the north. Allow me to offer you a seat in my curricle." Crane hesitated, and he added sardonically: "I will undertake to convey you over the next few miles at a better pace than you can hope to achieve on your own."

"I can believe that, your Honour," Mr. Crane assured him, eyeing the greys with considerable respect. "It's very civil of you to offer, very civil indeed."

"Surely it is the duty of every honest citizen to assist the officers of the Law?" Guy replied ironically. "However, I shall be obliged if you will tell me whether or not you mean to accept the invitation. I am in some haste myself."

Mr. Crane appeared to come to a sudden decision. "I'll accept, sir, and grateful," he announced. "I'm no great rider, and that's a fact!"

Mr. Ravenshaw made no reply to this, but mounted to the box-seat of the curricle and waited for the officer to take his place beside him. While they emerged from the inn-yard and threaded the busy streets of the town, neither man spoke, but once these had fallen behind them Guy allowed his horses to lengthen their stride, and asked casually: "What is your business with these two men? Of what crime do you suspect them?"

Mr. Crane was leaning back in his seat with folded arms, his gaze apparently fixed on the road ahead, but as he answered the question his shrewd, bright eyes slid round towards his companion.

"Robbery, your Honour," he said deliberately, "and murder!"

The curricle plunged forward as the greys broke into a gallop, but were steadied again in an instant. Mr. Ravenshaw's expression had not changed, and his voice was level and unemotional when he spoke again.

"A serious affair! Are you at liberty to tell me more?"

"I don't see why not, sir. The crime was committed just over a week ago at the house of a Mr. John Linley. A servant murdered and a quantity of valuables stolen."

"Most of which have since been recovered, with the exception of a very valuable ruby pendant." Guy glanced at his companion. "I am acquainted with Dr. Reginald Linley, Mr. Crane, and had the story from him."

"Then you'll know, sir, as one of the men concerned was drowned while evading arrest, and that the other is still free for lack of evidence against him. It's him as is driving that gig I've been following all afternoon."

Guy's thoughts moved like lightning, assembling a coherent whole from fragments of information gleaned here and there during the past few days. A single jewel, immensely valuable but fatally incriminating, the only remaining fruit of that night of robbery and violence; a woman's muff, the perfect hiding-place for it; a series of chance happenings which had left the muff in the care of Jennifer Linley's waiting-woman, and so totally beyond the reach of those who had hidden the jewel in it. Now it was restored to its rightful owner, and the man who had done murder for the sake of what it contained was driving along the road to Brightstone Park.

"Bartholomew Trench!" Crane said reflectively. "That's his name, your Honour! We've had our eye on Mr. Trench for quite some time, but this is the nearest we've ever come to proving anything against him."

"And his companion?" Guy asked, and waited with only outward calm for the Runner to reply. So much depended upon the answer to that question.

Benjamin Crane shook his head. "He's no criminal, sir—yet," he replied indulgently. "Just a green youngster as is a sight less knowing than he thinks he is. Cresswell, his name is! Got a fancy to be a bang-up sporting and gambling man, and a grandad who's in a very prosperous way of business—fair game for such as Trench. The boy's been on the town in his company these three months past, so I dare say he's in pretty deep by now. He's one as would have cause to be grateful to me if I could put Trench where he deserves."

Guy made no immediate reply to this, but drove on in silence for a few minutes while he considered his next move. There was only one explanation of Trench's present journey—he was on his way to recover the pendant from Caroline—but Guy doubted very much whether she was expecting to see him. With his earlier vague misgivings hardened now into a very real alarm, and heedless of the rapidly fading light, Mr. Ravenshaw urged his horses to a faster pace.

"I wish I knew what's taking Trench out o' London," Mr. Crane remarked at length. "Towards the coast, now, I could have understood, and been very happy to follow him, since it's not likely he'd go without the jewel, but northwards—" he broke off, shaking his head in a very pessimistic fashion, but his words had given Guy the opening he desired.

"I take it, Mr. Crane," he remarked, "that your sole concern is with the man Trench, and not with young Cresswell at all?"

"Not unless he turns out to be mixed up in the Linley affair," the Runner replied cautiously. "I'm not saying he is, mark you, but him and Trench have been mighty close these past few days. But you're right sir, in saying that Trench is my real concern. To take him would be something indeed! A real feather in my cap, as you might say!"

"It may be," Guy said deliberately, "that I can help you to place that feather there, Mr. Crane, but it must be upon my own terms." A swift glance at his companion showed him that the other man was watching him with the utmost intentness. "There is a lady who has been drawn—quite innocently, I assure you—into the affair, and my first concern is to protect her."

"Ah!" said Mr. Crane obscurely, and groping in his pocket he produced a battered notebook. Thumbing through its pages until he found the one he sought, he held the book up, peering closely at it in the gathering dusk. "Two days ago," he went on, "Trench took a young woman to his lodging, and an hour or two later Cresswell arrived there with another gent, who took her away again. A bang-up Corinthian he was, by all accounts!" His glance flickered over Mr. Ravenshaw's immaculately-attired person, rested for a moment on the team he drove, and then returned to the strong, dark profile presented to him. "That'd be you, sir, I take it?"

"Myself, Mr. Crane," Guy agreed coolly. "The lady is George Cresswell's cousin, who is at present visiting other relatives at a house in this county. It is my belief that Trench is now bound for that house. If that is so, you will perceive that it is in my power to be of considerable assistance to you."

Mr. Crane admitted this, a trifle warily. His profession brought him into contact with all sorts and conditions of men, and he was a sufficiently good judge of character to realize that this particular man would not be easily bested. In fact, he was uneasily aware that command of the situation was rapidly passing out of his hands.

"I will strike a bargain with you," Mr. Ravenshaw continued. "If I make it possible for you to arrest Trench, with sufficient evidence to convict him, will you agree to forget whatever part is played in the affair by Miss Cresswell and her cousin? I give you my word that, to the best of my belief, they have both been drawn into it by Trench against their will."

Benjamin Crane was exceedingly anxious to make that arrest. On two previous occasions the man had slipped through his fingers for lack of evidence, although Mr. Crane knew beyond all doubt that he had committed the crimes of which he was suspected. There would be great personal satisfaction in laying him by the heels, and, when weighed against that, the guilt or innocence of George Cresswell and his unknown cousin was of very little account.

"I'll agree, sir," he said after only a moment's hesitation. "Give me Trench, with that ruby in his pocket, and we'll say no more about young Cresswell, or the lady."

So, as the miles sped by and the twilight deepened, Mr. Ravenshaw told Benjamin Crane all he knew or suspected of the whereabouts of the stolen pendant. At each village and toll-gate the Runner sought news of their quarry, and each time found that the distance between them had lessened. It was quite dark by the time they left the high-road for the lane which led to Brightstone, and Guy was obliged to check his team to a walk until the moon should have risen high enough to light their way, but he reassured his companion by telling him that they were now within a mile or two of their goal.

In the village street he drew rein before the inn, and Mr. Crane descended from the curricle and entered the tap-room in search of news. Here for the first time he drew a blank, but as he was turning to the door again a country-man in smock and leggings, who was sitting by the fire with a tankard in his hand and a dog at his feet, volunteered the information that he had seen two men in a gig only a short while before.

"Turned down the lane to Three Elms Farm, they did," he informed Mr. Crane. "I'd been taking a look at the lambs in the top pasture, and were coming down through Long Meadow when I saw 'em."

The Runner thanked him, and after a few more questions, put with a deceptively casual air, concerning the exact location of the lane, he placed some coins on the table, invited his informant to drink his health, and strolled out of the inn again. Swinging himself up into the curricle, he said briskly: "Seems you were right, sir! They're making for the house by a back way."

The lane was easy enough to find, and they had not gone many hundred yards along it before a horse whinnied loudly from the shadow of the trees on their left. Benjamin Crane, pistol in hand, was down from the curricle almost before it had come to a halt, and by the time that Guy had tethered his horses and gone across to the gig which could now be dimly discerned at the edge of the wood, the Runner was up into the vehicle and bending over what appeared to be a large bundle which lay half under the seat.

"Young Cresswell, your Honour, gagged and bound," he said in a hoarse whisper. "Bide still, lad! I've got a knife here. Soon have you out of this."

Guy swung himself up on to the step of the gig and said in a low but commanding voice: "Cresswell, attend to me! I am Guy Ravenshaw. Where is Trench?"

The incoherent sounds which were coming from the prostrate figure increased in volume, and then as the gag fell away, George gasped for breath and said in a cracked whisper: "Gone to meet Caroline. Stop him, for God's sake! He means to kill her."

Mr. Crane heard the hard, indrawn breath of the man

beside him, and hacked with increased energy at the cords binding George's arms. Guy said briefly: "Where?"

"Temple by the lake—other end of the path," George replied disjointedly as Crane heaved him into a sitting position and attacked the ropes about his legs. "She's expecting *me*—for the pendant. Bart found out."

Without another word Mr. Ravenshaw sprang to the ground and vanished into the shadows. Benjamin Crane thrust the knife into George's hand and followed as fast as he could, catching him up just within the wood for the simple reason that Guy had halted to wait for him.

"If you cannot make less noise, my friend," he said acidly, "you would do better to let me deal with Trench on my own. If Miss Cresswell reaches the temple before us, and he has warning of our approach, he will use her as a hostage while he makes his escape. I do not intend to have her danger increased by your blundering!"

Mr. Crane begged pardon, said that he would not offend again, and besought Mr. Ravenshaw to lead the way. He found some difficulty in keeping up with the younger man's swift stride, and was decidedly breathless by the time they reached the far side of the wood, and saw the little temple some fifty yards away, a black bulk against the silvery shimmer of the water beyond.

With a gesture enjoining caution, Guy pushed open the gate and stepped forward, keeping to the shadow of the trees which dotted the intervening stretch of grass, and so with Crane at his heels came up to the rear of the temple. As they moved cautiously along that side of the building which lay in shadow, they heard a man's voice speaking softly, and a moment later found themselves looking between slender columns at two figures which stood very close together in the moonlight at the top of the steps leading down to the lake.

"No use struggling, my dear," Trench was saying, and the words came clearly to the watchers by the wall. "Thought you'd be very clever, didn't you, and inform the Runners as soon as the pendant was in my possession again? But Bartholomew Trench wasn't born yesterday, you know! I'll have the ruby, right enough, but you'll tell no one of it. Be lying at the bottom of the lake yonder. Treacherous things, these marble steps. Very easy to stumble on 'em. Tragic accident, everyone will say. No one to know the bump on your head wasn't caused as you tumbled down."

Caroline made a desperate, futile movement, and Trench laughed.

"That will do no good," he said in a jeering tone. "You'll not get the better of me, my dear, and neither will George. Both go the same way. Only difference, George will be found on Finchley Common with a bullet in his brain. Have it all planned, you see. Now give me that jewel you are clutching so tightly. Must make sure of that, after all the trouble it's put me to."

Still keeping one hand across her mouth, he shifted the grip of the other to hers, forcing her fingers apart and wrenching the jewel away. She was still struggling desperately, and as he slackened his grip on her in order to thrust the pendant into his pocket, she broke from him. For an instant it seemed that she might escape, but then his clenched fist rose and fell, and she subsided in a crumpled heap at his feet.

Benjamin Crane was hardly aware of Mr. Ravenshaw leaving his side, for the swiftness of the movement took him completely by surprise, and before he could collect his wits the thing was done. At one moment Bartholomew Trench was stooping above the girl's huddled figure, and the next he was sprawling on the grassy slope before the temple, and even as Mr. Crane came out of his stupor of astonishment and started forward, Guy had followed, hauled Trench to his feet, and promptly knocked him down again.

What followed was not so much a fight as a massacre. Trench certainly made some attempt to defend himself, but between the sheer unexpectedness of the attack and the blows he had already received, it was utterly fruitless, and in little more than a minute all was over. Mr. Crane, bending over his prisoner's inanimate form, fumbled in his pockets and produced the ruby pendant; holding it up by its slender chain, he turned triumphantly to Mr. Ravenshaw, only to find that he was no longer beside him. Having assured himself that there was no immediate likelihood of Trench coming to his senses, the Runner turned back to the temple, where Guy was kneeling at Miss Cresswell's side.

"She's not hurt bad, sir, I hope?" he asked, and Guy shook his head.

"No, merely stunned, I believe. She will come round directly." He glanced up as Crane came to stand beside him. "Well, are you satisfied?"

"More than satisfied, sir, though how I'm to explain the state he's in"—a jerk of the head indicated his prisoner—"is more than I can say."

"Simple enough! He resisted arrest, and you were obliged to use force." Guy lifted Caroline in his arms and stood up. "You are welcome to take full credit for it, and it can only add to your consequence."

"Maybe, if I could get anyone to believe as I done it," Mr. Crane retorted gloomily. "From what I can see of it, your Honour, you've broke his jaw."

Mr. Ravenshaw was already turning away, having apparently lost interest in the discussion, but at that he paused and glanced over his shoulder. His brows lifted, and he said in a tone of faint surprise: "Does it matter?"

He did not wait for a reply, but bore Miss Cresswell down the steps and along the path in the direction of the house. Mr. Crane stood looking after him, rubbing one hand against his square chin.

"Aye, you're a cool one, and no mistake!" he said aloud. " 'Does it matter?' indeed!" A sudden chuckle shook him. "Oh well, I suppose it don't, at that!"

18

The Temple of Diana

CAROLINE came dizzily back to consciousness, and to the realization that she was being borne along in a pair of strong arms. She started to struggle wildly, but the arms merely tightened their hold a little, and a familiar voice said quietly: "Don't be afraid, my dear! The danger is over and done with."

Sheer astonishment made her open her eyes, and the bright moonlight showed her that she was neither mad nor dreaming. "You!" she whispered incredulously.

"Yes, it is I," Mr. Ravenshaw replied calmly. "You have had a very shocking experience, but it is all over now. Bartholomew Trench is under arrest, while you, my poor child, will soon be safe in your cousin's care. I am taking you back to her at once."

"My head aches so," she murmured, "and I do not understand at all what has happened."

"That does not matter just at present," he replied soothingly. "I will explain it all to you another time, but I give you my word that there is nothing more for you to worry about."

She sighed with mingled perplexity and relief, and closed her eyes, but after a moment or two opened them again to ask urgently: "What about George?"

"He has come to no harm. We found him bound and gagged in Trench's gig, and he told us where to find you."

She made no reply to this, but allowed her head to sink back again upon his shoulder. In spite of her throbbing headache she was dreamily content with her present situation, and would have been glad to prolong it indefinitely, but when he turned away from the lake towards the house, commonsense reasserted itself in spite of her. She sighed again, this time with regret, and said reluctantly: "I have recovered my senses now, sir, and am quite capable of walking the rest of the way."

"Very likely," he replied calmly, making no attempt to set her down. "There is, however, no necessity for it."

"Indeed, there is! You cannot march me up to the front door in this fashion. Only consider what the servants must think." He paid no heed to this, and she clutched at the collar of his coat, giving it a little shake. "Mr. Ravenshaw, please listen to me!"

"Well?" He halted and looked down at her, and in the moonlight she could see that he was smiling. "Do not agitate yourself, Miss Cresswell! You have sustained a severe shock, you know."

"No more severe than that which my cousins will suffer if we present ourselves at the door in this fashion," she retorted, "particularly since they believe that I am at this instant laid down upon my bed. Do, pray, set me down, and let us consider for a moment what we ought to do."

Mr. Ravenshaw glanced about him. A short distance away towered a great cedar tree with a seat built about its trunk, and after a moment's hesitation he carried Caroline across to it and lowered her gently on to the seat. Sitting down beside her, he said quietly: "I have no doubt at all what *I* ought to do, and that is to place you in Mrs. Wilde's care as soon as may be. Whatever you may say, I cannot believe that after such an experience as you have just undergone, you do not feel in need of it."

"I feel quite dreadful," Caroline said frankly, "and I do not understand in the least what has happened, but of one thing I *am* certain. The fewer people to know of what has just taken place, the better. No one is aware that I have left the house. If I slip quietly in again, and go straight to bed, no one need ever know. Admit, sir, that that would be by far the best."

"I will admit nothing of the kind. You need to be properly looked after."

"I am not so poor-spirited that I cannot make shift to look after myself," she replied, "and I would far rather do that than embark upon all the explanations which would be needful if we disclosed what has happened." She put out her hand towards him, and added pleadingly: "Do you not understand? This is such a very shocking affair that I cannot bear for anyone else to know of it!"

He took the hand and rose to his feet, drawing her up with him. "Yes," he said in a low voice, "I do understand, my dear, and I will plague you no longer on that score. I should have thought of that aspect of the matter for myself. Come now, how do you propose to enter the house without being seen? I will take you as far as the door."

Her fingers tightened gratefully upon his for a moment, but she merely said: "There is a door by the bowling-green which has been very little used of recent years. Letty and Roland and I used to go in and out by that way when we were children."

"Come, then!" Guy drew her hand through the crook of his arm and held it there. "You must show me the way, and when I have seen you safely within, I will go back and do what I can to ensure that no whisper of this affair leaks out by any other means."

Miss Cresswell found that in spite of her stout words she was very grateful for the support of his arm as they made their way through the gardens towards the older part of the house. When the door was reached she halted and turned to face him, lifting her eyes to meet his.

"This time I shall not even try to thank you," she in a low voice, "for you saved my life tonight, and there are no words which can properly express gratitude for that. Always, it seems, when my need is greatest, you come to my aid."

"If I may continue to do so," he replied gravely, "I shall be well content." He paused for a moment, his eyes searching her white face, and then added in a lighter tone: "Can you really reach your room undetected?"

She nodded. "Yes, but if by ill-luck I should see any-one, I shall say merely that I thought a walk in the fresh air would make me feel more the thing." She gave the ghost of a laugh, and gingerly touched her head just above the right ear. "On one score at least I need no longer be untruthful, for I now have in earnest the headache which I feigned earlier in the evening."

"Cold comfort, to be sure!" Guy's hand lifted to the same spot, his long fingers sliding gently through her hair. He said with a quiver of amusement in his voice: "There is a very large bump indeed, but it will be better directly."

"Wretch!" said Miss Cresswell feelingly. "How very un-handsome of you to cast my own words at me in that fash-ion, particularly when I do not feel equal to retaliating."

"Most unsporting," he agreed with a smile, and lifted her hand to his lips. "I will bid you good-night now, ma'am, but it will not be many days before I visit you again, to see how you go on and to explain to you what really occurred this evening."

He kept that parting promise three days later, and only he knew how great a degree of self-command had been needed to prevent him from keeping it even sooner. The fine weather continuing, he once more made the journey to Brightstone Park in his curricle, and as he emerged from the avenue on to the carriage-sweep his glance went involuntarily to a certain great cedar tree a short distance away. Then he drew rein, for a slim, red-headed figure was sitting on the seat beneath it with a book in her hand. Mr. Ravenshaw handed the reins to the groom who sat beside him, with a command to drive round to the stables, and,

...he curricle, went quickly towards

...as he approached, the colour deepening ..., and he saw with relief that she had ap- ...covered from her recent ordeal. Taking the ...put out to him, he said with a smile: "There is ...ma'am, to ask if you are feeling better. One has ...look at you."

...he laughed. "Indeed, Mr. Ravenshaw, I am feeling perfectly well. To be sure, I still have a bruise on the side of my head, but it is hidden by my hair and so does not matter in the least. I have been thinking how very fortunate it is that I was not struck upon the brow. A black eye would have been exceedingly difficult to explain away."

He looked rather amused. "You have an enviable talent, Miss Cresswell, for making the best of things. I have noticed it repeatedly."

"You will admit, I think," she replied cheerfully, "that at present I have a great deal to be thankful for."

"I, also," he agreed with a smile. "To find you alone was more than I dared to hope for."

The swift colour rose again in her cheeks, but she said lightly: "It is very fortunate, to be sure! You have come, have you not, to tell me how you contrived to arrive so opportunely on the scene the other night?"

"That is one reason for my presence here," he admitted. "May we talk freely, or are we likely to be interrupted?"

"Well, I should not think so, for there is a great deal of excitement going on indoors. I must tell you that Jenny and Roland arrived home last night, and half an hour ago Lady Linley descended upon us. Her ladyship has not yet forgiven me, and I thought I would give her an opportunity to become reconciled to her daughter and son-in-law before intruding *my* discordant presence upon the scene."

"In that event," said Mr. Ravenshaw firmly, "let us remove farther from the house. I wish Captain Wilde and his bride nothing but good, but there is bound to be some slight awkwardness attendant upon our first meeting, and I would prefer to postpone it for the present. Come, Miss

Cresswell, take a turn about the garden with me, and I will explain the matters which are perplexing you."

Caroline having no fault to find with this suggestion, they strolled away from the house in the direction of the lake. As they went, he described his meeting with Benjamin Crane, and how it had provided him with the clue he sought to the puzzle of her sudden decision to leave town, and the pursuit by Bartholomew Trench.

"I never imagined that the Runners would be coming after me," Caroline said when the whole story had been told. "How dreadfully shocked you must have been."

"I was," he replied. "The mere thought that you meant to try another fall with Trench, with no one to help you but young Cresswell, filled me with the gravest alarm. I did not, however, leap to the immediate conclusion that you had planned the robbery or even that you were concerned in it. Apart from my fear for you, the strongest emotion of which I was conscious was disappointment that you had not seen fit to confide in me."

"Oh, if you had known how much I wanted to!" she said fervently. "All the way from London, and again when you said goodbye, I was obliged to exercise the strongest self-control to resist pouring out the whole miserable story. George wanted me to do so."

"That," Guy remarked, "is the first evidence of good sense which I have known your cousin to display. Why did you not take his advice?"

"Oh, how could I? You had been so kind, helped me so much already, and this was such a dreadful affair. I could not involve you in a crime." She broke off, for their idle footsteps had brought them to the end of the lake, and the little temple was only a few yards away. Caroline stopped short. "Let us turn back! I cannot approach this spot without remembering that dreadful night, and I do not think I shall ever be able to bring myself to enter the temple again."

"Nonsense!" Mr. Ravenshaw replied firmly. "You had a shocking experience here, I know, but you must not allow it to prey upon your mind. Trench is safely behind bars twenty miles away, and there is nothing whatsoever to alarm you now."

He drew her arm firmly through his and made her walk with him up the steps and into the temple. It was no larger than a small room, with two graceful marble seats curving away from a central niche which held a statue of the goddess Diana, and a carved frieze around the walls depicting the legend of the hapless Actaeon. The sunshine laid the shadows of the pillars in straight lines upon the floor, the lake sparkled at the foot of the steps, and all around was the bright pageantry of spring.

"You see," Guy said softly, "there is nothing whatsoever to alarm you. This is merely a charming folly set in a very pleasant garden."

Caroline looked about her, and the ghosts of fear and horror which had haunted her dissolved and vanished. She gave a rather uncertain little laugh.

"Yes," she said, "you are quite right. I was being foolish beyond permission, and I am glad now that you made me come in here." She moved across to one of the seats and sat down, lifting her eyes in grave inquiry to his. "Are you quite sure, sir, that no word of this affair need ever leak out?"

"Quite sure," he replied reassuringly. "Crane has his prisoner and enough evidence to convict him, and your cousin has been shown the necessity of preserving a discreet silence. I drove him back to London in my curricle while Crane conveyed his prisoner in the gig, and I took the opportunity of reading him a homily on the folly of permitting such men as Trench to batten upon him. I do not know how long the effect will last, but he has promised to return to his grandfather's counting-house, and I think he has been sufficiently frightened to apply himself with diligence to his work, for a time at least."

"I am so glad," she said earnestly. "He is not a bad-natured boy, but he has no strength of character, and his mother indulges him beyond what is right." She paused, and then added more lightly: "So George has learned a lesson he will not soon forget. Mr. Linley will have his ruby restored to him, and may bestow it upon Jenny as he meant to do. Jenny herself, and Roland, are at this moment making their peace with Lady Linley. All, in fact, ends well."

He came to stand beside her, resting one foot on the edge of the seat and his elbow on his bent knee. "And Miss Cresswell?" he asked with a smile. "Has *she* made no plans for the future?"

"Indeed I have," she replied. "Letty—Mrs. Fenton, you know—has asked me to go to her as governess to her little boy. She has several younger children as well, so I am likely to be fully occupied for some years to come. I shall go with her when she returns to London."

"I see!" He continued to look down at her with an expression she could not read. "Are you determined, Miss Cresswell, to accept this post?"

Her eyes widened. "I should be very foolish not to! Theodore is a dear little boy, and I know that in Letty's house I shall be treated with far more consideration than is usually accorded to a mere governess. *I* think I am very fortunate."

"I have no doubt," he replied with some amusement, "that Mrs. Fenton would be in every way an admirable employer, but I, Miss Cresswell, have a somewhat different proposition to put to you."

"Oh," she exclaimed, "you are thinking of Jane's wish for me to go to her as a companion! I should like it very much, of course, but I do not really think that it would serve. I am sure that a companion should be an older and —and more sober person than I! And besides—"

"I am not thinking anything of the kind," he interrupted calmly. "When you stop talking long enough to afford me an opportunity, I am going to ask you to marry me."

She gasped, and her startled, incredulous glance flew up to his face again. After a stunned moment, she said faintly: "But you cannot marry *me!*"

His brows lifted, and the amusement in his voice became more pronounced. "May I ask why? You are not, by any chance, already married, or promised in marriage?"

"You know perfectly well that I am not!" She jumped up from the seat and began to walk about in the strongest agitation, clasping and unclasping her hands. "But it is all so unsuitable! For one thing, I have not a penny in the world!"

"That, of course, is a severe blow to me," he assured her gravely. "However, I dare say we may contrive tolerably well upon what I have."

"You know that I have any number of quite dreadful relations!"

"I do not think that fact need trouble us." He took his foot from the seat and stood upright, watching her with laughing eyes. "If they attempt to impose upon us, you may rely upon me to dampen their pretensions very thoroughly."

She halted in front of the statue and stood with her back to him, running her fingers to and fro along the edge of the pedestal. "After the events of the past week," she said in a small voice, "I have not a shred of reputation left."

"All the more reason to be married as soon as may be!" He went across and took her by the shoulders, turning her to face him. "Have you done, my love, or can you find any more reasons to advance against accepting my proposal?"

"I am sure there are a dozen," she replied uncertainly, "but I cannot seem to call them to mind."

"In that event," he said firmly, "I will give you one very good reason why you should accept it." He put his hand beneath her chin and made her look up at him, and now there was no hint of teasing in voice or eyes. "I have fallen very deeply in love with you, Caroline."

Her hands came up to cover his, but in spite of this she felt compelled to say protestingly: "In barely a week?"

"In barely an hour," he replied promptly, "and I am coxcomb enough to believe that it was so with you also."

"Oh, it was," she whispered, abandoning pretence along with the attempt to bring him to his senses, "though I tried so very hard to fight against it. I never dreamed there was the least likelihood of your wanting to marry anyone as unsuitable as I must be by all worldly standards."

"I have told you repeatedly," said Mr. Ravenshaw, taking her in his arms, "that I do not allow the opinion of the world to influence me in anything, and in a matter such as this I would regard it as the greatest impertinence. Do not let me hear you talking such nonsense again."

There was a considerable pause before Miss Cresswell had an opportunity of saying anything at all, and then she remarked softly, with a hint of mischief in her voice: "You told me once that you desired no more than a marriage of duty and convenience, with a quiet, sensible girl who had no nonsensical romantic fancies in her head. I am not in the least like that, you know."

He nodded, laughter leaping into his eyes again. "Yes, my love, I do know it! We have been acquainted for little more than a week, and during that time I have been obliged to rescue you from imprisonment, seduction and murder, to say nothing of a trifling matter concerning stolen property. It is fortunate, is it not, that I have long since abandoned all my conventional notions regarding marriage?"

"Yes, but I do not think it is fair to judge me by the events of the past week," she said indignantly. "It was not my fault that all those things happened to me—well, not entirely—and you must not think I make a practice of getting into such scrapes. I have really led a very uneventful life."

Guy began to laugh. "I cannot tell you how relieved I am to hear it," he assured her. "Much as I love you, I do not think we really wish to spend the rest of our lives at the pace you have set during the past week. It would, I believe, begin to pall in a very little while."

"I am sure it would," she agreed, laughing. "Adventures are all very well in their way, but I think I have had enough of them now to satisfy me for a long time to come." She lifted her hand rather shyly to touch his cheek, adding more seriously: "But, Guy, my dearest, are you really sure? I still have some shockingly romantic notions, you know, and I believe it is not at all the thing to be quite desperately in love with one's husband."

"Then in that respect," he replied, capturing the hand and bearing it to his lips, "we shall set a new fashion, not conform to the old, for I shall have not the smallest hesitation in showing the world how deeply I am in love with my wife. If, however, her disregard of the consequences prompts her to embark upon any more reckless adventures, I shall take it very much amiss if she does not allow me to share them. Is that understood?"

Miss Cresswell, enchanted by this uncompromising attitude, nodded meekly, and, clasping her arms about his neck, surrendered her lips again to his.